SOLDIER GIRL

BOOK TWO of THE TOUCHERS

Also by Susan Berliner

AFTER THE BUBBLES (BOOK ONE of THE TOUCHERS)

THE SEA CRYSTAL AND OTHER WEIRD TALES

CORSONIA

THE DISAPPEARANCE

PEACHWOOD LAKE

DUST

Praise for Susan Berliner's books:

After the Bubbles (Book One of The Touchers)

"I absolutely LOVED this book! I was sorry to get to the ending. Great ending, by the way. The story is so original. Lots of surprises. So suspenseful...Thankfully it's not a true story, but I kept thinking - what if." – Susan Zajicek

"I've been a fan of Ms. Berliner's novels since her first published one, *Dust*. Each one delivers satisfaction and includes superb characterization, description, and dialogue. In *After the Bubbles* she has woven a beautifully horrific concept with everyday natural people's situations and with everyday events."
– Linda Commodore

"*After the Bubbles* is a great suspenseful story that holds the reader's interest throughout. I couldn't wait to see what would happen next." – Regina Munroe

The Sea Crystal and Other Weird Tales

"Once you start reading anything written by Ms. Berliner, you had better clear your calendar. Her characters are haunting, memorable, and real. It takes a special talent to be able to create a scene in a few pages, from beginning to end, and this is where the author excels. As soon as the story begins, you are thrust into a little microcosm where things look ordinary...mundane even. But then...plants start talking, or someone disappears, or someone who is there turns out that they were never even there in the first place!" – K.W. Skultety, *Gimmethatbook*

"From chilling mirror images, to fairy tale lives, to a world of dark dreams that comes to life, there is so much to explore in Berliner's world...It was a lot of fun to try to figure out where the twist in each of these stories would be. Honestly, most of the time I was completely wrong about where I thought they were going. Which, of course, made it that much more fun!"
– J. Nottingham, *Hopelessly Devoted Bibliophile*

"Around New Year's, my local cable station runs a marathon of Twilight Zone episodes...and that is sort of what this book put me in mind of - a little touch of the weird, but not too dangerous - something you could let kids read out loud during a sleepover. These stories are fun, and super-quick." – Rik Ty

Corsonia

"Well written and well paced." – *Julie's Book Review*

"I won't say *Corsonia* gave me nightmares, but my dreams were a bit more disturbing than usual! It was a great read, and gives the reader pause and makes you start thinking...could this actually happen? Not sure I ever want to find out!"
– Judy Barnes

"Thoroughly enjoyable vacation read! The author has an innovative way of weaving factual incidents or occurrences into fast paced fiction." – Arlene Bender

The Disappearance

"I enjoy reading books with time travel - and this book took you back and forth constantly! It was done in such a way that had me almost believing it was really possible."
— Michele Bodenheimer, *Miki's Hope*

"There are many modes of time travel, but this one takes the cake - so different from others I've read!...This group of characters working together to bring down one culprit is so different, so eclectic; it's a wonder they ever met each other! But that's what makes it work! I love 'The Sting' all over again."
— Lila L. Pinord

"I just loved this book! This is one of those books that will call you to pick it back up if you have the self-control to set it down for a moment. I was pulled in throughout the entire story because I could not wait to see what would happen next."
— Dawn Fitzpatrick

Peachwood Lake

"It is a marvelous coming of age horror story."
— *Night Owl Reviews (Top Pick)*

"Where else are you going to find a fish horror story that brings a young girl's life into focus?...I have no trouble recommending this book for the pre-teen/YA horror lover. Five out of five fairy kisses for this reader."
— Dottie Taylor, *Tink's Place*

"Great read. Fun and suspenseful. Best fish story since *Jaws*!"
— Peggy Derevlany

Dust

"Susan Berliner gives us an amazing mysterious supernatural story in *Dust*. It intrigues and holds the readers' attention, while pulling them in and not letting them put it down."
— *Night Owl Reviews (Top Pick)*

"*Dust* picks you up and takes you on a whirlwind ride, pun intended, and doesn't let you go until the final climax...It's a great piece of escapist fiction and a book to easily get lost in."
— Patricia Lane

"Susan Berliner's first novel is filled with drama, laughter, and engaging characters...As a high school English teacher...I give *DUST* an A+!"
— Brittany Mott

SOLDIER GIRL

BOOK TWO of THE TOUCHERS

Susan Berliner

Published by SRB Books

ISBN: 978-0-9839401-8-0

Cover design by Cassy Roop of Pink Ink Designs
Layout by Rik of Wild Seas Formatting
Author's photo by Rachel Leib Photography

Published June, 2019

Printed in the United States of America

To Merri and Jerry—

Wishing both of you

A long and happy marriage

Never give up.

There is no such thing

as an ending.

Just a new beginning.

– Anonymous

CHAPTER 1 – Leaving Walnut Lane

I'd always imagined heading off to college—having a roommate, pledging a sorority, going to parties on campus, taking art classes. I never even considered joining the army. But that was before the bubbles fell from the sky and destroyed the world. It seemed like my dreams about college happened a lifetime ago, although it's only been a couple months.

And all the time I spent agonizing about whether or not to run off with my boyfriend, Blaine—that was a total waste. Now we're both going to be in the army, fighting the touchers together.

Touchers are what I call the people the bubbles landed on. They turned into yellow monsters that kill humans just by touching us. We know they don't like water and the army's come up with a formula that can destroy them. The formula killed Cyndy Louise, the girl toucher on my street. But it's not strong enough yet because it takes too much work to kill them.

It wasn't easy leaving Mom and my brother, Danny. My mother begged me to stay, practically throwing herself in front of the door. It was embarrassing because Blaine, Danny, and Major Figueroa were all there. But I didn't change my mind.

The major had explained how important it was for us to keep fighting the touchers. With so few people left, the army needed all the volunteers it could get.

While I quickly packed some clothes, Major Figueroa stood at the bathroom sink helping Mom rebandage Blaine's newly-opened wounds. He'd been badly cut by broken glass three days ago when touchers smashed a window of the car he was driving.

"I'm going with you!" Blaine called out.

"You're still hurt!" I shouted back as I stuffed underwear into a suitcase. "You can't fight anybody right now!"

"I heal fast!"

"Rest now and get better," I heard the major tell Blaine. "Then three days from now, we'll come back for you."

I walked into the bathroom as Blaine looked up from his seat on top of the toilet, a sad expression on his cute face. "You'll make sure you get me in three days?" His voice sounded weak and shaky, as if he'd used up all his strength arguing. "Erin...?"

Crouching down, I held both his hands and kissed him gently on the lips. "I'll be back then. I promise."

———

After I said goodbye to Mom and Danny, Major Figueroa carried my suitcase to the Jeep and I stepped into the front passenger seat. That's where the other guy—Captain Hitchcock—had been sitting when Cyndy Louise touched him. I purposely didn't look in the back because I figured that's where his body was.

I tried my best to be brave and not cry—after all, I was a soldier now. As Major Figueroa started the car, I heard a woman's voice call, "Good luck!" When I looked up, I saw my neighbor, Mrs. Perez, and Kyle, the little black kid we'd rescued during our search for food, waving from her second floor window.

I waved to them and then the Jeep turned out of Walnut Lane—away from my family, Blaine, my neighbors, my house, my dog, Muffles. The tears started pouring down my cheeks and although I wiped them, I couldn't stop crying. I tried not to make noise, but I guess I didn't do a good job.

"Don't be ashamed to cry," Major Figueroa, who was about my mom's age, said softly. "You're leaving the people you love and risking your life." He squeezed my left hand. "It's a very brave thing you're doing, joining the army to help kill the enemy."

"Thanks," I whispered. "I'm just a little scared."

The major scratched his lightly bearded face and chuckled. "If I was in your shoes, Erin, I'd be a lot scared. But it'll be better at the base. There are a number of soldiers your age. You'll make friends, I'm sure."

Friends. That was a wonderful word. *Maybe I'd see Marci and some other kids from school.*

Major Figueroa was still speaking and I'd missed some of what he said. "...about ten miles from here. We're using a corporate park as our headquarters."

"Great," I said, without enthusiasm. I didn't feel much like having a conversation.

The major must have understood because he stopped talking and concentrated on the road, which was tough driving with all the car wrecks and bodies. The streets had been like that since the bubbles.

As I stared out the window, I saw a toucher across the street, running towards our Jeep. Touchers were easy to spot—bright yellow blobs with eyes and ears, arms and legs, but no noses or mouths. All sizes and shapes. No clothes, except shoes. They don't look anything like people.

"Toucher on the right," I said, raising my water gun.

"Does it have a weapon?"

"I don't see one."

"Too bad there's no formula left," Major Figueroa said as he pressed his foot on the gas pedal and sped forward. "But the road ahead's pretty clear so I should be able to outrace it."

When I turned to check, the toucher had faded in the distance.

I heard a loud thump as something hard banged against the Jeep. "Two touchers on the left!" I yelled. "They're throwing rocks!"

The major made a right turn at the next street, moving slowly as he maneuvered around broken glass and busted cars. When I looked behind us, the touchers were closer. Although I opened the window and squirted, I didn't hit them because they still were too far away. Then the smaller girl-thing lifted another stone.

"Rock!" I shouted.

Major Figueroa swerved the Jeep and the rock bounced onto the roof of a parked black car. When he reached the corner, the major made a left and returned to the main road. "Are you okay?" he asked.

"I'm fine," I said, leaning back in the seat and checking the windows again. Unfortunately, this was a typical car ride.

―――

"Here we are." Major Figueroa smiled and pointed to a large concrete sign that read "Ridgeview Corporate Park" as he turned into a smaller road where the grass had grown long and huge weeds jutted out above the blades. It was good camouflage because you couldn't see anything in there.

"Are you using the tall grass to hide from touchers?" I asked.

The major shrugged. "Not really. They know we're here and we can't hide all our transportation activity. There aren't many other vehicles on the roads these days."

"Have they attacked you?"

"Many times, and like everyone else, we've lost people they've been able to touch. But now that they know about our new weapon, they've left the base pretty much alone."

The long driveway ended and we reached a cluster of office buildings that circled a big parking lot. I counted seven buildings, all concrete and glass—the kind you see everywhere. Each was two or three stories tall and had the word "Unit" plus a number taped to the entrance: "Unit 1," "Unit 2"...

In the parking lot—above the Jeeps, SUVs, and cars—a large handmade "United States Army" banner had been strung across two light poles. The major parked in the front of the lot and smiled at me. "Welcome to the new army," he said.

―――

Major Figueroa and I walked into the nearest building, marked Unit 1. In the front lobby, a young guy wearing a wrinkled army uniform sat behind a desk. "Good afternoon, sir," he said, not saluting or standing. I guess the new army didn't bother with formal stuff.

"Good afternoon, Cody," the major said, putting his arm around my shoulders. "This is Erin Fredericks and she's joining us. After one of those monsters touched Brian Hitchcock, she helped me kill it—a very brave girl."

"I'm so sorry to hear about the captain," Cody said. After a short pause, he held out his hand. "Hi, Erin."

I shook Cody's outstretched hand. He had a long pimply face and wasn't at all cute, but seemed very nice.

"What's the best unit for Erin?" Major Figueroa asked. "Maybe Four or Six?"

Cody opened a loose-leaf binder on his desk and quickly turned the pages. "We could use her in Unit Four," he said, staring at one of the sheets. "They're down a man."

I had a bad feeling about why they were a person short.

"They've got some soldiers her age in Four?" the major asked.

"Yes—Roxanne, Lourdes, Manny, and a couple others."

"Great." Major Figueroa tapped my shoulder. "We're assigning you to Unit Four."

I picked up my suitcase and followed him, wondering about Roxanne, Lourdes, Manny, and the rest of Unit 4. *Would I like them— and would they like me?*

———

Unit 4 was another office building a little further from the road. After entering the lobby, Major Figueroa and I approached the soldier behind a desk—a really pretty dark-haired girl about my age. Instead of a uniform, she wore jeans and a tank top that showed off her big boobs.

"Hi, sir," the girl said, smiling at the major.

"Hello, Lourdes. How's everything."

The girl shrugged. "Okay, I guess, after...you know..." She stopped talking and looked at me.

"It's all right," Major Figueroa said. "This is Erin and she's joining Unit Four."

"Oh." Lourdes stared at me for a long minute before she spoke. "That's good."

But she didn't sound as if she believed her words.

"Where's Captain Stallings?" the major asked.

"In the back with the platoon."

"Please get him."

Lourdes nodded.

"She doesn't like me," I murmured when Lourdes was out of sight.

"It's not you. This unit lost someone last week and it's still very painful for all of them."

"Who did they lose?"

"A girl named Michelle Rios."

"What happened to her?"

"She was on a mission with..."

Before he could explain, a very tall and dark black man rushed forward and pumped the major's hand. "Major Figueroa! Good to see you—and I hear we have a new recruit." He smiled at me. "Glad you're joining us. Erin, is it?"

"Yes."

"Come with me, Erin, and I'll introduce you to everyone." He pushed me forward so quickly that I barely had a chance to turn and wave goodbye to Major Figueroa. But I did catch a glimpse of Lourdes who was back at her post—and frowning at me.

———

The captain marched through the hall, taking such big steps that I had trouble keeping up with him. "I'm not sure I introduced myself," he said. "My name's Fred Stallings, head of Unit Four. We've got twenty-four soldiers now, including you."

I nodded, not saying anything. It took all my effort to stay next to him so my words would have come out in gasps. I was relieved when he stopped at a large room with a dozen cots in two rows. Next to each bed was one of those cheap plastic drawers—the see-through kind on wheels.

"Just drop your suitcase here," he said, tapping lightly on a middle cot.

Michelle's?

Then the captain moved quickly again and I hustled after him.

We reached the back of the building and he opened the door. "Right now, we're doing fitness training," he explained. "Keeping in shape so we can attack the enemy without them touching us."

"I call them touchers," I said, hoping my voice sounded normal. "That makes sense."

"Is it safe to be outside when it's not raining?" I asked.

Captain Stallings shrugged. "Nothing's guaranteed. But they haven't come after us in over a week and if they do, we're ready." He pointed to a pile of water pistols on the ground next to a group of people sitting in three uneven rows on a lawn that had been recently mowed.

I'm not sure what I'd expected, but Unit 4 was a mixed bag. I counted four teens, a bunch of men and women in their twenties or thirties, several others about my mom's age, and at least five old people who could have been my grandparents. None of the soldiers wore army uniforms. Everyone was dressed in regular clothes—jeans or shorts and tees.

The captain marched me to the front of the group and rested his hands on my shoulders. "This is Erin Fredericks," he announced. "She's just joined the army and has been assigned to Unit Four. Please make her feel welcome."

Most of the people smiled at me and some even clapped. "Welcome, Erin!" one young guy in the back row called out. He had curly blond hair and was pretty cute, but not as cute as Blaine. *Blaine*...I really missed him. None of the kids on the grass were from Adams High and I didn't know anyone.

A girl about my age in the first row stood and walked over to me, holding out her hand. She had light brown skin, long black hair, and was very tiny—not even five feet tall. "Hi," she said. "I'm Rayna Patel and I'm so glad you're going to be with us." Then she smiled, showing off a mouthful of perfect white teeth.

I smiled at Rayna and shook her hand, feeling a little better. Maybe at least I'd have one new friend.

———

A few other people told me their names. An older lady, Gwen, said my red hair reminded her of her daughter. Then she looked like she was going to cry and quickly rushed away. The cute guy who had yelled out the welcome also told me his name: Josh. He squeezed my hand tightly, saying he hoped we'd be good friends.

"Me too," I said, smiling. But talking to him made me miss Blaine even more.

Luckily, there wasn't much time to talk. For the next hour, we did jumping jacks, ran races, climbed over a fence, and even worked our way through an obstacle course, dashing around five tires. I could see that everyone took the training session seriously. We all knew how important it was to be able to move quickly; it could mean the difference between life and death.

I was really tired when Captain Stallings blew his whistle. "At ease, everyone, " he said. "You've got free time till dinner."

The people separated, forming small groups and talking to each other as they entered the building. I stood by myself, not knowing what I was supposed to do.

"Come with me," Rayna said, tugging at my arm. "I'll show you around."

―――

It had been so long since I'd been with a girl my own age that it felt strange at first. Although I didn't say much, Rayna kept a running commentary as she walked me through the Unit 4 building. "This is our dining room," she said, opening the door of a large windowless room that might have once been used for company meetings. Then she flicked on the lights and I jumped.

"What's wrong?"

"You have electricity?"

"Of course." Rayna smiled. "We eat breakfast and lunch here and then have dinner with all the units at Headquarters."

"Oh."

"It's good to get together with everyone," Rayna continued. "It gives you the feeling of working as a team."

"How many people are on this base?"

"About a hundred fifty, I think." She smiled at me. "But we keep adding new soldiers like you all the time."

"You lose soldiers too," I said. "I heard this unit just lost someone last week."

"Michelle," Rayna whispered. "That was very sad."

"What happened?"

"The usual." Rayna stared at the gray tiled hallway floor. "One of the enemy got her."

"Touchers," I said. "How'd they do it?"

Rayna lifted her head. "Michelle was with two members of our unit, Manny and Eric, hunting for food. They were attacked by six of the..." She looked at me. "...touchers as you call them. Our team had water guns, but not the new formula, and then Michelle ran out of water."

"Were the six touchers working together?"

"Manny and Eric didn't know. They were too busy trying to get away."

"From what I've seen, usually the touchers work alone or, at most, in twos or threes." I shook my head. "It's not good if they're now working in larger groups."

"You're right," Rayna agreed. "It's not good at all."

———

"How'd you manage to survive the bubbles?" I asked as Rayna continued the tour.

She sighed. "I had swimming last period, but took so long getting dressed I didn't have time to dry my hair so I walked home from school with dripping wet hair, carrying my damp towel."

"No bubble landed on you and you weren't touched."

Rayna shook her head. "I think I was too wet."

"You were very lucky."

"I know," Rayna said. "But I'm the only one in my family who made it home—not so lucky. How about you?"

"My mom and brother are alive, but my dad didn't make it," I said. "How'd you find the army?"

"I was living with my neighbor and we were walking in the rain when I saw a poster taped on a store window with the address of the base. I was lonely so I decided to join."

"Your neighbor?"

"Lucy wanted to stay in her house. I've been here since early June so I hope she's all right."

"I do too," I said.

———

The rest of the main floor consisted of a second large room with cots for the other half of the unit; an officers' room; a rec room with books, games, big-screen TV, and pool table; a storage room; and bathrooms.

I stared at the line of showers in the ladies' room. "An office building with showers?" I muttered.

Rayna chuckled. "Whoever designed Ridgeview Corporate Park didn't include showers because the insurance companies, lawyers, and dentists here didn't need them. The army added showers when they converted these buildings."

Glancing at the shower stalls again, I realized they were newer than the sinks and toilets. Then I turned the sink faucet to the left and ran my hand under the water. "It's hot," I whispered.

"Of course."

We took the stairs to the second floor. "There's not much to see up here," Rayna explained. "We don't use the upper floors so the army hasn't wasted time cleaning them."

We stepped in and out of a group of offices. Each had desks, computers, phones, partitions—the typical stuff you'd see in one of these buildings. The problem was that papers were scattered all over the floors and desks and chairs were knocked over—like everyone had panicked and tried to run out, which was probably exactly what happened.

There must have been dead bodies too that the army removed. "It's giving me the creeps being up here," I said, rubbing my arms, now covered with goose bumps.

"I know what you mean," Rayna agreed. "It's so quiet. People should be shouting on their phones, computer screens should be lit up, and then the mess...Let's go back down."

―――――

We returned to the room where I'd left my suitcase and I unpacked, putting my stuff into the plastic cart next to my cot.

"My bed's opposite yours," Rayna said, jumping on her cot. She crossed her legs and watched me.

"What's everyone else doing now?" I asked as I dumped socks into the top drawer.

"Mostly hanging out in the game room, I bet."

"You don't have to stay with me. I'll be fine." I smiled at her.

"It's okay." Rayna sat on top of the thin blanket and leaned her head on her elbows. "Sometimes I like to come here and relax."

I didn't know if she was telling the truth or not, but I was glad for the company.

"Hey! What's goin' on?"

I looked up as Josh, the cute guy who'd introduced himself to me at training, dashed into the room.

"Not much," I said. "Just unpacking my stuff."

"Glad you're going to be bunking here." Grinning, he jumped onto the cot to my left. "That's next to me. It's guys and girls together," he added, noticing my puzzled reaction.

"I have a boyfriend," I whispered.

"Not here, you don't," Josh said. After winking at me, he headed out.

"He likes you," Rayna said. "And Josh's a nice guy."

"But I've already got a boyfriend," I repeated.

"That's pretty amazing these days considering how few people are still alive."

"Blaine was a student at UMass and he drove into my street about a month ago." I left out that he'd been traveling with his friend, Zach, who died trying to kill Cyndy Louise. "Since then, we've kind of been together," I continued.

"Where is he now?"

"He got hurt fighting the touchers. Major Figueroa promised to go back for him in three days so Blaine can join the army too."

"You're a lucky girl," Rayna said, nodding her head.

———

Since I had just one suitcase to unpack, it didn't take very long. "What do we do now?" I asked Rayna.

She pointed to the clock on the wall. "It's almost six. That's dinnertime. We have to go to the mess hall in Headquarters so if you're ready, we should start walking."

As we strolled to the main building, a loud gong sound made my ears rattle. "Do they do that for all the meals?" I asked.

"Just for dinner."

"Good."

Other soldiers joined us—all sizes and ages—crowding the parking lot and sidewalk. By the time we reached the Unit 1 building, we must have numbered about fifty.

"Do we have assigned seats?" I asked Rayna.

She shook her head. "We just sit at one of our unit's tables. It's marked."

We moved through the hallway until we reached a large lunchroom with folding tables pushed together and chairs along each side. As Rayna said, the front of each section contained a sign so we headed to the area marked "Unit 4."

Nearly half the seats at our tables were already filled with people I'd seen in the afternoon, including Lourdes, who again scowled at me, and Josh, who waved and patted the chair next to him. "Saved you a seat!" he called.

I turned to Rayna. "That's fine," she said, pointing to a chair opposite. "I'll sit over there."

"Thanks," I said, slipping into the chair beside Josh.

"My pleasure." He smiled at me. "I've been wanting to spend some quality time together." Then he spread his hands and shrugged. "Of course I was hoping for a little more privacy."

Glancing at the crowded noisy lunchroom, I giggled.

———

Eating in the mess hall was a lot like lunch in the school cafeteria except we were called by our unit numbers and then stood on line to get served by two soldiers behind the counter.

I don't know what dinner in the old army had been like, but this mealtime was fun, filled with sounds of talk and laughter. I guess everyone figured they could relax here. Most soldiers were dressed in regular casual clothes except a group of officers, all in uniform, who sat together at a separate small round table.

"Do they always eat by themselves?" I asked Josh, pointing to the officers.

"Yeah. They have a dinner meeting every night...What do you think of the food?"

"It's good," I said, tearing off a piece of fresh bread and taking a bite. "I haven't had hot food since we lost our power."

I stared at the stew on my plate. In it were peas, rice, and brown flecks, which looked like some kind of meat. I tasted the meat, but didn't recognize it.

"What is this?" I asked, showing Josh the brown tidbit in my spoon.

"Don't ask," he said, shaking his head. "No one's admitted anything, but we think it might be an animal we'd rather not know we're eating."

"Like a rat?" I immediately tossed the spoon into the plastic plate.

"More like a deer or squirrel."

"But not dog or cat?" I remembered the poor scrawny animals that roamed the streets near my house.

"I don't think so."

Spooning another piece of meat, I lifted it above the bowl and studied it closely. It didn't taste bad and I was really hungry so I dropped the mystery meat into my mouth.

———

During dinner, Josh introduced me to a couple more people my age in Unit 4. Manny, whose name I'd already heard twice, was a short pudgy kid with long uncombed black hair—not exactly my idea of a dream date.

"I heard you killed some of them touchy things," he said as he shook my hand up and down.

"Just one, Cyndy Louise, the girl on my block." When Manny didn't let go of my hand, I smiled and squirmed out of his tight grip.

"Them things ain't girls no more."

I shrugged. "I know. But she used to be a sweet girl named Cyndy Louise."

"We gotta kill them all," Manny said, shoving a large spoonful of stew into his mouth. "It's either them or us."

"We'll get them, Manny," Josh said, reaching around me and squeezing the boy's shoulder. "But this is dinnertime so take it easy. Just relax and leave the planning to Fred and the other officers."

Fred? They called Captain Stallings by his first name?

Roxanne, who sat across from me, next to Rayna, was also my age. She was pretty, with curly dark brown shoulder-length hair, and seemed very quiet.

"Hi," I said, smiling at Roxanne.

She nodded, then lowered her head and continued to eat, really concentrating on her food. Since she didn't say anything, I thought she didn't like me. *A friend of Lourdes?*

But when we left the table and Roxanne stood up, I realized she was super overweight, with enormous thighs and hips. Maybe she did like me and was just shy because she'd been picked on for being so heavy.

———

After dinner, I walked back to the Unit 4 building with Rayna, Josh, Manny, and Roxanne. "What happens now?" I asked. "Do we have to do things after dinner?"

"Like assignments?" Josh asked.

"I don't know." I shrugged my shoulders. "I thought soldiers in the army were always given orders."

Manny chuckled. "Not in this army. We got lots of free time here, especially at night. Wanna see a movie?"

"That sounds great," I said. My decision to enlist was looking better and better.

We watched *Dumb and Dumber,* a goofy comedy I used to love because it was so stupid. But seeing it made me feel sad because it was about the way life used to be and there was nothing funny about life now.

I guess Josh realized I wasn't enjoying the movie. "Want to do something else?" he asked. "Maybe a game of pool?" He pointed to the table in the corner of the room where two men and two women in their twenties or thirties held cue sticks.

"Those people are still playing."

"When they're done. I'll tell them to let me know."

I shrugged and Josh went to talk to the pool players. I saw one of the men smile and nod. About ten minutes later, the man Josh had spoken to tapped him on the shoulder. "It's all yours," he said.

"Are you good at this?" I asked as I followed Josh to the pool table.

"Not especially. How about you?"

"I've only played once or twice so don't expect much."

"Then we won't play for money," Josh said, grinning. "Let me show you how to hold the stick." He placed the pole under my armpit and arranged my fingers on it. "Then you push it like this, " he explained, moving my arm back and forth.

I copied what Josh did.

"Okay, now try it," he said, placing the balls in the rack.

Pulling my stick back, I hit the balls as hard as I could. They clanged against the edges of the table and one ball even fell into a hole.

"Way to go!" Josh said, squeezing my arm.

I smiled at him, feeling a little better.

———

Josh and I played two games of pool and both times he beat me by a lot. After the second game, I yawned and realized it had to be way past my recent bedtime.

"Do you know the time?" I asked. I didn't like wearing a watch and hadn't packed one.

Josh checked his wrist. "Only quarter to ten."

"That's late for me," I said, yawning again. "I've been going to bed before dark and getting up at dawn."

15

"Then you need some sleep," Josh said, taking my hand and leading me to the door. "Our wake-up time is 6:30. I'll walk you back."

"Thanks." I really was grateful because I didn't remember where our room was.

In the hallway, we met several other members of the unit and I greeted them, trying to memorize each name as Josh mentioned it. Then we reached our dorm room, which was next to a supply closet.

"Good night," I said.

"And good night to you too. I'm glad you're here with us."

"Are you going in?" I asked as I opened the door.

"Not yet." He waved and raced away.

I entered the room, which was dimly lit and empty except for one person sitting in the other bed next to mine. It was Lourdes.

———

I felt trapped. I couldn't walk out of the room and pretend I didn't mean to be there because I'd just said "Good night" to Josh and I'm sure Lourdes heard me. If I was supposed to be some kind of brave hero, I sure didn't feel like one.

Taking a deep breath, I forced myself to smile at Lourdes, who was staring at me—not scowling, but not smiling either.

"Hi," I said. "I'm Erin. We met earlier today when I came into the building."

"I remember."

She continued to look at me, making me more and more uncomfortable. "Did I do something wrong?" I asked.

Lourdes shrugged. "I don't know. Do you think you did?"

What was that supposed to mean? "Not that I know of. Like everyone else here, I'm just trying to destroy the touchers so we can get back our lives..."

"That's all you're trying to do?" She smirked at me.

"Yes, that's all."

Without speaking again, Lourdes slipped under the covers of her cot, fluffed the pillow, and turned away from me.

"Good night," I whispered. Either she didn't hear what I said or she was ignoring me. In any case, there was no response.

CHAPTER 2 – On Assignment

I didn't hear Josh or any other soldiers come into the room that first night. Maybe they were really quiet, but I think it was more that I was so exhausted.

The next morning, some kind of trumpet noise jolted me out of a deep sleep. "It's so loud," I murmured, rubbing my eyes.

"This is the army," Josh said. "It's six-thirty and that was reveille, the wake-up call." He jumped out of bed and grabbed a toothbrush.

"It's annoying," I whined.

"You better move," Josh said as he rushed out of the room. "Breakfast's in fifteen minutes."

Then he—and just about everyone else in the room—was gone. The only other person left was Lourdes, still snuggled under the blanket.

"How'd you sleep?" she asked.

"Fine, thanks. And you?"

"I'm good." She gave me a little smile.

This was an improvement. Maybe she'd forgiven me for whatever I'd done to bother her. "I've got to get ready," I said, grabbing my toiletries, tee shirt, and jeans. "Talk to you later."

Lourdes watched me leave. Unlike everyone else, she didn't seem to be in any hurry.

———

The signal for breakfast was three loud clangs. But the noise wasn't from a bell. "What made that sound?" I asked Rayna, who stood next to me at the bathroom sink.

"It's just a piece of metal pipe banged against another pipe," she said, chuckling. "Not real musical, huh?"

"No."

"I guess the army couldn't find any more bells. But it does get the message across."

We walked to our unit's dining room, which Rayna had shown me yesterday, and got on line for food. Breakfast was a choice of hot or cold cereal, canned peaches, bread, and coffee or tea. To me, it seemed like a banquet. I must have gobbled my food because when I finished and lifted my head, Josh, Manny, and a couple others were staring at me.

"Hungry?" Josh asked.

"Yeah," I whispered, hoping my face wasn't turning red. "This stuff is really good."

"If you think this food is good, you must've been eating crap!" Manny said, smacking the table with his hand and letting out a loud laugh.

"She hasn't had any hot food," Rayna pointed out. "And the bread is fresh."

"But everything else is crap—and it's the same crap every day," Manny complained. "Breakfast's supposed to be eggs, bacon, sausages, omelets, pancakes, waffles..."

"Enough," Josh said. "We're lucky to have this."

———

After breakfast, we all remained at the tables. "What now?" I asked Josh.

"We get our assignments," he explained.

"I hope I'm sent on a mission today," Manny said. "Especially after what they done to Michelle last week."

Nobody said anything else as we watched Captain Stallings step to the front of the room, holding several sheets of paper. "Good morning, soldiers," he began. "I just got a report from Headquarters that the enemy seems to be forming alliances."

He shook his head. "Obviously, this isn't good news. We also think they're becoming telepathic, but have no real proof. Six have been seen working together not far from the base and we're sending a team to destroy them before they finish whatever they're trying to do."

The captain glanced at the paper. "We're using two tanks, with four soldiers in each. "Manny—I want you with Edith, Rayna, and Charlie."

Manny, Rayna, and an older man and woman stood and walked out of the lunchroom together.

"Okay," Captain Stallings said. "For the second tank, I need Josh, Roxanne, Darryl—and you too, Erin." He nodded at me. "We're testing the newest formula. Let's kill these damn things!"

———

I left the lunchroom with my tankmates. As we walked, Darryl, a black guy in his twenties who was built like a football player, took my hand and pumped it several times. "Glad to be working with you," he said, smiling. "I'm sure you'll do a great job."

"Thanks." I returned his smile, not sure what else to say.

We entered what looked like a classroom—three rows of school chairs with attached writing boards, facing a large desk. Each chair board held a spiral notebook and pen. I took a seat and smiled at Rayna, who waved.

A large local map was taped to the front wall and I squinted, trying to find Walnut Lane and our army base. But I couldn't make out street names from my second row seat.

In his briefing, Captain Stallings used a pointer to show where touchers had gathered and the route we'd use to reach them. Everyone took notes so I did too, although I wasn't sure anything I wrote would help.

After he finished explaining how we'd attack the touchers, the captain paused. "Any questions?" he asked.

I raised my hand. "Shouldn't we get ourselves wet before going?" I suggested, because that's what we'd been doing at home. "It'll keep them away from us."

Captain Stallings nodded. "That's a good idea, Erin. But with hoses and water guns, you should be well protected."

"Not really," I argued. "You've lost people."

"True," the captain agreed. "But we're doubling the number of soldiers on our teams and Headquarters hasn't authorized us to get soaked so..." He held out his arms, palms up, and then checked his watch. "Be ready to leave at zero nine hundred hours."

Army time? I gave Josh a perplexed look.

"Nine o'clock," he whispered.

———

The eight members of our team stood in the first-floor hallway of our building gathering weapons from a plastic bin. The weapons looked familiar—filled water pistols. "Are these loaded with the new formula?" I asked Josh.

He shook his head. "No. It doesn't work in the guns because you need a lot more water mixed with that chemical stuff to kill them so we just use regular water to slow them down in case we get trapped."

"It didn't help Michelle," I whispered.

"That won't happen again!" Manny shouted. "I won't let it happen!"

"But you can't be sure," Roxanne said, shoving a pistol into the pocket of her jeans.

"I'll make sure," Manny insisted.

No one said anything else as we marched outside to the parking lot where two Jeeps, each with a water tank attached to the roof and a pair of green hoses tied to the sides, were set for us.

Josh slid into the driver's seat and I sat next to him, with Darryl and Roxanne in the back. They couldn't have been too comfortable since they were both big people, but neither complained. Then Josh drove out of the army base with Manny's truck right behind us.

"Make a left," Darryl said, reading the instructions Captain Stallings had given us.

"Go about a mile and turn right on Warren Street," Roxanne added.

The roads were quiet and I didn't see any touchers, but there were still all those wrecked cars and rotting bodies, surrounded by millions of flies. I pulled my head away from the window.

"Don't look at them if it bothers you," Darryl said.

"She can't close her eyes," Josh argued. "Everybody has to look."

"At the street, but not at the corpses," Darryl continued.

I tried to do what Darryl suggested—just stare at the road, although it was hard.

"Turn here," Roxanne said. "The enemy is supposed to be on the next street."

"Guns ready, everyone!" Josh said. "We're going in!"

———

Josh drove slowly as we stared at the deserted-looking houses. This had been a nice block with big homes on both sides, but now many windows were broken and no one lived here anymore—at least no people did. Maybe touchers had moved in. If so, they weren't big on decorating because the curtains were ripped...

"Wait," I said.

Josh stopped the Jeep and turned to me.

"I saw something move behind the curtains on the first floor in that house," I explained, pointing to the white colonial I'd been looking at. "See?" The torn green curtain fluttered again.

"Do you think it could be a person?" Roxanne asked.

"I doubt it," Josh said. "This street is a mess and any people living here would at least board up the windows."

"What if they can't?" Roxanne continued. "What if they're stuck inside and waiting for help?"

"If that's true, now that they see us, wouldn't they at least call out or send a signal?" Josh asked. "I haven't heard or seen anything."

"You're right," Roxanne agreed. "No one's even waving."

"Then if it's not people in there, it must be touchers," I said. "But they're always outside unless it's raining—so what are they doing inside? The captain said there were six of them."

"Trying to surround us, maybe," Darryl suggested.

Manny's Jeep had stopped right behind ours.

"Usually they're not shy," I said. "They throw rocks or jump on the truck."

"But they know this Jeep with the water on top can hurt them," Josh pointed out.

"You think they're hiding?" I asked.

Josh shrugged.

"No." Darryl said. "Erin's right. They always attack. Isn't this a dead-end street?"

"Yeah," Roxanne said.

"So you think they want to get us trapped all the way in here and then come after us?" I asked Darryl.

He nodded.

"In case Darryl's right, we won't go in any further," Josh said. "We'll sit here and wait."

———

Nothing happened right away. I noticed more movement behind the green curtain, but no other signs of either a human or toucher. "Should we do something to get them to come out?" I whispered to Josh.

"No. Be patient."

"It's been a long time already," I argued. Although I didn't have a watch, it seemed like we'd been waiting for hours.

"It's not even ten minutes," Roxanne said. "So..."

"Watch out!"

When Darryl yelled the warning, I ducked and a rock smashed against my window. Inching up, I saw a woman toucher running towards our Jeep.

"She's coming here!" I yelled.

Josh switched on the water and liquid trickled onto the ground. "This'll keep them away from us," he said.

"But it won't kill them, will it?" I asked.

"No," Josh said. "We have to pour the formula all over their bodies."

"Three more on the left!" Roxanne shouted.

I turned around and saw a small toucher—I couldn't tell if it'd been a boy or girl—and two yellow men-things. The child toucher carried a rock while the adults held large pieces of glass. "Get down!" I hollered.

I heard the sound of shattering glass, but this time it was in Manny's Jeep. "I thought the water in the street was supposed to stop them from coming closer," I said.

Darryl pointed at the four touchers who now surrounded the other Jeep. "Do you see what they're doing?" he asked. "Look at their feet."

When I lowered my eyes, I saw what Darryl meant. The touchers' feet were no longer on the ground. Instead, they floated a few inches above it.

"The wings," I said. They weren't fully formed yet, but they must have started working. "Can they fly?"

Josh pushed open the door. "I don't know, but we've gotta hose them before they get closer to Manny's group. Weapons everyone— and let's go!"

———

As liquid continued to drip into the street from the first hose, Josh unhooked the second one. "Start squirting them while I set this up!" he shouted to us.

The two men touchers ran at me, luckily no longer holding pieces of glass. After I sprayed one and then the other, both moved backwards and concentrated on wiping away the water.

The child toucher, now joined by the woman-thing, came at us from the other side, but Darryl and Roxanne squirted them and they immediately backed away.

"There're supposed to be two more," I said as Josh stepped next to us, carrying the second hose. "The captain said there were six."

"I don't like not seeing all of them here," Darryl said.

A horn honked. Turning, I saw Manny dragging a hose along the ground as he and his team members joined us. "Let's finish them off!" Manny shouted.

The four touchers had dried themselves and were again moving in our direction.

"Now!" Josh yelled and he and Manny aimed their hoses at the approaching group. All four touchers fell down, writhing on the pavement.

"Keep the hose on them!" Manny shouted to Josh. "Don't let them get up!"

The rest of us held our water guns and watched the touchers lying in the street. They were obviously affected by the liquid and seemed hurt, although since they couldn't talk, we couldn't really be sure.

"No...!" The piercing scream came from behind me. "Stop!"

I turned around as Rayna desperately sprayed a toucher hovering above her head, flapping fully-formed wings. She must've gotten the thing wet because it flew away, traveling down the street until I could no longer see it.

But on the ground next to Rayna, sprawled face down, was her team member, the older man, Charlie. He didn't move.

I ran to help Rayna as she knelt on the street and together we turned Charlie on his back. "How is he?" I asked.

Rayna shook her head. "It must have touched him," she said. "He's dead."

––––––

Darryl, Roxanne, and the older woman in Manny's team joined Rayna and me. "If six of them were here, then there's still one more left," I said, glancing up at the empty blue sky.

Darryl waved his water gun over his head. "It could be another flying creature," he said.

The older woman stared at Charlie's body, rubbed her arms, and shuddered. "We should get out of here now," she whispered. "This place is giving me the chills."

Rayna pointed to Manny and Josh, who continued to spray the four touchers with their hoses. "Edith, we can't leave yet. We have to wait for the guys to finish killing them."

The touchers were still wriggling on the ground, but much less than before. They looked like wet yellow wind-up dolls whose motors were slowing down.

"We should be okay as long as we keep watching," Roxanne said. "They're five of us and only one of them and it won't be able to sneak up on us again."

I nodded. "Before, we didn't think to look up in the sky."

We stood together in a semi-circle around Charlie's body, turning our heads in all directions. I didn't see anything and the only sound I heard was the squishy noise of liquid squirting from the hoses. Then it was quiet.

"We're done," Josh said, dragging the now limp hose. "Those four are dead...What happened to him?"

"Charlie?" Manny dropped his hose and bent down to touch his team member's chest.

"A flying creature touched him," Rayna explained. "And when I squirted it, the monster flew somewhere down the block."

Manny shook his head. "Should we go after it?" he asked Josh.

"No. We're almost out of formula and we have to report what happened here—tell Headquarters about Charlie and the flying monster."

"And tell them there's still one here we haven't seen," Darryl added.

"Maybe another flying toucher," I whispered.

CHAPTER 3 – Return Trip

No one talked much on our ride back to the base. I kept thinking that the flying toucher could have killed me just as easily as Charlie because I hadn't been looking up in the sky for it. Maybe the others were thinking the same thing about themselves.

When we returned, we all watched two soldiers carry Charlie's body to Headquarters. Then, while Josh and Manny reported what happened on our mission, I walked to the Unit 4 building with Rayna and Roxanne.

Rayna shook her head. "Michelle last week and now Charlie."

"And even with the new formula, it's still hard to kill the yellow touching monsters," Roxanne said.

"At least they die," I added. "That's an improvement."

"But it takes too long," Roxanne said. "The poison has to work faster."

I stopped walking and looked at Rayna and Roxanne. "What happens when they all start flying?" I whispered. "The hoses can't reach them way up in the sky. Then the touchers can just dive at us like they did today with Charlie."

"Maybe we can use planes to drop the formula," Rayna suggested.

"Are there still planes?" I asked. "I haven't seen one since the bubbles."

Roxanne shrugged. "There probably are some planes around."

"But who can fly them?" I asked. "Are any pilots still alive?"

"I hope so," Rayna said.

———

I spent the next few minutes in the rec room with Rayna and Roxanne, but didn't feel much like talking so I excused myself and went to my room. Lying on the bed in the empty dorm, I closed my eyes and tried to figure out what we could do next. I knew I was in the army now and officers gave the orders, but I still wanted to see if I had any brilliant ideas.

Wish I could talk to Blaine. Josh was nice, but I really missed Blaine. *Day after tomorrow.* That's when Major Figueroa promised we'd come back for him. *Not even two days...*

"Are you sick or something?"

I opened my eyes and saw Lourdes staring down at me, a look of concern on her face.

"No. But we just came back from attacking a group of touchers and one of our soldiers got killed."

"Not again." Lourdes sat on her cot, shaking her head. "Who's dead?"

"Charlie."

She sighed. "I didn't know him well, but he seemed like a nice guy. How'd it happen?"

"A flying toucher so we didn't see it coming."

"They're flying already?" Lourdes looked shocked.

"This one was."

"Damn." She tossed her head back on the pillow.

It felt good to talk to Lourdes and not think that she hated me, but it was too bad our conversation was about the toucher killing Charlie. When three loud pipe clangs announced lunch, Lourdes and I walked together, like friends, to the cafeteria.

———

Nothing much happened over the next day and a half. The surviving seven of us who fought the touchers weren't given new assignments. I guess the army decided we needed to recover from seeing Charlie die like that. I don't know how the others felt, but I was glad to hang out and do nothing.

Headquarters did send another team to the street where we'd been, but they didn't find any touchers. In fact, the soldiers reported that the bodies of the four dead touchers were gone too.

We were all scared. When I was outside, I spent a lot of time looking up in the sky. But I didn't see touchers or anything else flying in the air. It had been a long time since I'd seen a bird and although there were many flying bugs, the bugs rarely bothered us—not even mosquitoes. They had so many rotting bodies to feast on.

I thought about all these troublesome things on my fourth day in the army as I walked to the Unit 1 building after breakfast. Cody was again on duty behind the desk in the lobby, his uniform as wrinkled as the first time I'd seen him.

"Hi," I said. "Remember me?"

"Sure, you're Erin. How's it going for you in Unit Four?"

"I was part of the attack team two days ago. You heard what happened, right?"

He nodded. "I'm so sorry. We're losing too many soldiers lately and Charlie Crawford was a really good man."

"That's what everyone tells me. I wish I'd had the chance to know him." I nodded towards the hallway behind Cody. "Can I speak to the major, please? He promised to go back for my friend, Blaine."

———

Major Figueroa tapped his pen on the square marked "28" on the July calendar page covering his desk. "I didn't forget," he said. "I wrote that we're picking up Blaine today, providing his wounds have healed."

"I'm sure they have," I whispered, hoping I was right.

"I'm taking food for the people on your street too," he continued. "I plan to leave at thirteen hundred hours."

"That's..." My voice trailed off. I was still trying to figure out army time.

The major smiled as he completed the sentence. "...one o'clock, after lunch."

"Can I come with you?"

"I was counting on that, Erin." He smiled again. "You can help me spot the enemy and also navigate in case I have trouble finding your street."

I don't know if Major Figueroa was being honest or just nice. But it didn't matter. What mattered was—in just a few hours—I would see Blaine, my mom, and Danny. After thanking the major, I headed back to the Unit 4 building, skipping most of the way.

————

The trip to my street was depressing—wrecks, dead bodies, rats, flies. It wasn't raining so we saw a few touchers, but they didn't come near the Jeep because they knew our attached water hoses could kill them. I didn't see any flying touchers, but I was still scared they were up there.

When we reached Walnut Lane, Major Figueroa parked in front of my house. The block was real quiet and no one was outside. "Maybe another toucher took over when you killed Cyndy Louise," I whispered.

"That's possible. Also, it's still too dangerous for people to be out unless it's raining."

Gripping my water pistol, I opened the car door.

"Erin!"

I looked up when I heard my name and saw Kyle standing behind Mrs. Perez's closed second-floor window. "Hi!" I called, waving to him.

"Watch out!" He pointed to the sky and yelled loud enough to be heard through the glass. "One of them toucher things is flying around!"

Major Figueroa grabbed my hand and pulled me forward. "To the house—now!" he ordered.

We ran to my porch and I pounded on the door. "It's me!" I yelled. "Let us in!" I heard a noise behind me and when I turned, the flying toucher—a yellow man-thing—swooped down towards us. "No!" I shouted, spraying it with water just as the front door opened.

————

"Oh, Erin!" Mom hugged me tightly and stroked my hair, acting like she hadn't seen me in years.

I pulled away when she wouldn't release me. "I'm fine, Mom," I said. "It's only been a few days."

"She's scared because of the flying toucher," Danny said. My twelve-year-old brother stood in the hallway next to Blaine, who smiled but didn't move. Muffles, however, hurried down the steps and jumped on my legs, his tail wagging.

As I reached down to pet the dog, Blaine materialized beside me and grasped my hand. "It's been really bad since that flyin' toucher showed up yesterday," he said. "Can't even keep any upstairs windows open—and it's been throwin' rocks at the roof. Gonna bust through soon if we don't kill it."

I realized the house was uncomfortably hot.

"We'll destroy it before we leave," Major Figueroa promised. "We brought the latest formula...How're you feeling?"

"I'm good." Blaine patted his left side and then raised his arm without wincing. "See?"

"Do you still want to join the army?" the major asked him.

"Definitely."

Danny looked at our mother longingly. "Can I go too? I could help them. You know I'm the best shot."

"Then who's going to protect Mom from the touchers?" I asked. "You've got to stay here."

Danny lowered his head and bit his bottom lip.

Major Figueroa stepped forward, resting his arms on Danny's shoulders. "I'm sorry, son. We are taking younger soldiers now, but not kids as young as you and your sister's right. You're needed here to help your mom."

"Maybe next year?" Danny asked.

God! Would we still be fighting touchers?

The major nodded. "Maybe then."

———

After getting himself wet, Blaine had gone down the block to the Fisher's house where he'd been living and packed a suitcase, which he now carried down the stairs. We all stood in the hallway as Major Figueroa gave each of us instructions on what to do to get the flying toucher.

"Danny," he said. "On my signal, run outside, yell, and wave your arms. Then, as soon as you see the flying thing approach, run back inside."

"Can't I be the one to lure it here?" my mother asked. "I don't like using Danny."

Major Figueroa shook his head. "Your son's much faster. He's wet so he'll be safe."

After petting Muffles again and hugging Mom, I stepped out of my house and dashed down the porch towards the Jeep as the major and Blaine followed. Then Major Figueroa and I slid into the front seats while Blaine tossed himself and his suitcase into the back.

"Erin and Blaine, get your guns ready," the major ordered.

I aimed my water pistol at the closed window.

Major Figueroa opened his window and shouted, "Now!"

Danny streaked out the front door, yelling, "Come and get me!" at the empty sky. After doing a couple of jumping jacks, he shouted again. "Here I am!"

Another door slammed shut and Kyle appeared. He ran to Danny and stood next to him.

"What's that little kid doing out here?" the major asked.

"Kyle likes to tease touchers," I said. "He's very fast."

"But he's not even wet," Major Figueroa said as he stuck his head out the window. "Get back inside, kid!" he hollered. "You can die!"

Kyle shook his head and didn't move.

———

When I saw the flying toucher, I opened my window and yelled, "It's here!"

Danny immediately ran inside our house, but Kyle waved his arms and stuck out his tongue at the thing. "You can't get me!" he shouted.

"What's that crazy kid doing now?" the major asked as he and Blaine stepped out of the Jeep.

"Kyle's gettin' the toucher to chase him," Blaine said, lifting one of the two attached hoses. "He's done it before."

"But this enemy flies," Major Figueroa said. "It can easily swoop down and kill him."

"Look!" I said, pointing to the sky. A second toucher—a girl-thing—flapping its yellow arms, flew towards the other flying monster.

"Damn it!" The major opened the driver's door and reached inside to turn on the water switch. "Be ready to douse both of them when they start descending."

The liquid from the hose poured down the street like a sudden heavy rain shower. "How high can this squirt?" Blaine asked, grabbing the hose.

"I don't know," Major Figueroa said as he removed the second hose from the Jeep and aimed it at the sidewalk. "But we're about to find out."

As the two touchers zeroed in on Kyle, who had been running down the block, he changed direction and rushed towards us.

"What's the kid doing now?" the major shouted.

"Gettin' them to come here!" Blaine yelled.

Speeding up the street, Kyle reached the Jeep and slid into the back seat, slamming the door shut and panting heavily.

"You shouldn't have done that," I said.

Kyle, still heaving, didn't answer me. He just smiled.

Outside, the major and Blaine aimed their hoses at the touchers. After Blaine's shot reached the girl-thing, knocking it to the ground near the Jeep, I opened my window and squirted the toucher in the face. I knew I couldn't kill the monster, but I could make it uncomfortable.

Dragging his hose towards the fallen toucher, Blaine continued to squirt it. He used a lot of formula, but finally, the toucher stopped moving. The flying girl-thing was dead.

The other one? I turned my head, checking for Major Figueroa and the flying man toucher.

"It fell over there," Kyle said, pointing to the sidewalk down the block, in front of Connie Chou's house. As I watched, the major squirted the man-thing again and again until it no longer moved.

"Your street's clear now," Major Figueroa said as he stepped into the Jeep and turned off the water switch. "But we used nearly the whole tank of formula."

"If it takes this much work just to kill two touchers, how are we ever going to kill them all?" I asked.

"They have to make the poison stronger," the major said as Blaine slid into the back seat.

––––––

Major Figueroa warned Kyle not to go after touchers by himself. "You'll get yourself killed," he said, waving his forefinger.

The boy nodded, looking very serious, but I don't think he got the message.

After we dropped Kyle off at Mrs. Perez's house, along with the food we brought for the block, Major Figueroa headed back to the army base. "I'm going to drive as fast as I can since we don't have enough formula to protect us," he told Blaine and me.

"Do the touchers know that?" I asked.

"Perhaps. The water tank is clear so they can see it's practically empty. If they're communicating to each other silently like we think they are, then they'd know."

"My water gun is full," Blaine said.

"Mine is half full," I added.

"We don't want to fight them like this," Major Figueroa said. "Let's hope we have an easy..."

"Toucher on my side!" I shouted. "Running with a bat!"

The major swerved the Jeep to the left, trying to spin away from the creature, but the thing—I couldn't tell if it had been a male or female—moved super fast.

"It's coming closer!" I yelled, opening my window just enough to shoot water at its yellow face. I must've hit it because the toucher immediately stopped running, dropped the bat, and stood in the middle of the street, furiously rubbing its cheeks with both hands.

"Another one!" Blaine yelled.

I turned to the left just in time to see a man-thing heave a large flowerpot at the driver's side of the car. "Watch out!" I cried, ducking with my hands over my head. I heard a thud, but no sound of cracked glass. When I looked up, Major Figueroa was still driving and the Jeep seemed okay.

"It hit the back bumper," Blaine explained.

The major drove through the next few streets without any problems while Blaine and I scanned the roads for new touchers.

"In the sky!" Blaine hollered.

Glancing up, I saw them—a squadron of touchers, flying like a formation of big yellow geese, one winged toucher in the lead and the rest lined up in rows behind it. They seemed to be following us.

"What do we do now?" I asked Major Figueroa.

"We get back to the base as fast as we can. They're too high and even if we could reach them with a hose, we don't have enough formula to fight them with."

"What if they attack us?" I continued.

"Let's hope they can't tell from where they are that our tank is empty."

"But if they're talkin' to each other like you said..." Blaine pointed out.

"It still may take time to transmit their messages," the major said. "Especially if it's a new skill."

———

Just before we reached the base, the flying touchers disappeared. "Why didn't they come all the way here?" I asked Major Figueroa as he parked the Jeep.

"Probably because they know we're a danger to them," he said. "They didn't want to risk a fight."

As the three of us walked to Headquarters, I kept thinking about those strange goose-like things. "I wonder how many touchers are flying now," I said.

"More and more as their wings develop fully," Major Figueroa said. "They'll all be flying soon so we've got to be able to attack them in the air."

"Planes," Blaine said. "We need planes."

The major stood still and shook his head. "That's not the problem. The airports are filled with planes. What we need are pilots to fly them."

I remembered my conversation with Rayna and Roxanne. *Pilots*...I'd been right to worry.

"I've always wanted to be a fighter pilot," Blaine said, smiling. "When can I learn?"

"As soon as we find the pilots to teach you." Major Figueroa grabbed Blaine's shoulder as we entered Building 1. "Glad to have you in the army, young man. Welcome aboard!"

CHAPTER 4 – Reunited Again

Major Figueroa assigned Blaine to my unit and I led him to our building. But the two of us didn't talk. I don't know about Blaine, but I felt a little funny after being apart. "Here we are," I said when we reached the entrance.

"So how're you doin'?" Blaine asked, his blue eyes twinkling.

"Fine. And you seem good too."

"Yeah, I am." Dropping the suitcase, he opened his arms wide. "Erin," he whispered. "I really missed you."

I ran into his arms, my eyes starting to tear. "Me too," I murmured, trying not to cry.

Blaine put his hand under my chin and lifted my head. Then he kissed me, long and tenderly. He didn't stop until I heard a clapping noise.

When I opened my eyes and turned around, I saw Rayna, Roxanne, Manny, Josh—and nearly everyone else from Unit 4— staring at us. Most of the soldiers were smiling, including Captain Stallings. But Josh gave me a questioning look that morphed into a sad face.

I shook my head at him. *I told you I had a boyfriend*, I wanted to say. But I kept my mouth shut.

———

Since there were no empty cots in my room, Blaine was placed in the other dorm, which now had a spare bed—the one that had belonged to Charlie Crawford. While Blaine unpacked, I sat on the cot next to his and told him what happened to Charlie.

"That's why I gotta learn how to fly a plane," he mumbled.

"But you need a pilot to train you."

"Then we'll find a pilot," he said, smiling that cute grin I'd missed.

"Where?"

"You ask too many questions," he said, grabbing both my hands. Then, pulling me against his body, he kissed me, harder than before. I closed my eyes and kissed him back.

Blaine lowered his hands until they were on my breasts, stroking them gently. It felt so good..."No," I said, forcing myself to push his arms away.

"What's the matter?"

"It's not right."

"Why?"

I flicked a strand of hair away from my eyes. "First of all, this room isn't private. Lots of people live here."

"No one's here now." Blaine ran his fingertips along my nose.

"Someone could come in at any time," I argued. "There's not even a lock on the door."

"What if I find a private place for us?" Blaine asked. "Will you be with me then?"

I thought about his question for a moment before answering. "I don't know," I whispered truthfully.

———

Thanks to Major Figueroa, I had the rest of the afternoon off so I could give Blaine a tour of the base. I tried to remember everything Rayna had said, but I'd only been in the army a few days myself. After I showed him the ground floor rooms we used in our building, we stepped outside.

"What about touchers?" he asked, staring at the clear blue summer sky.

"Like the major said, they're afraid of us here."

"Maybe they're just organizin' themselves for a big attack."

I shrugged my shoulders. "Anything's possible, but right now, touchers aren't a problem on the base."

Blaine took a deep breath and smiled. "Feels good to be outside when it's not rainin' or we're not fightin' them."

"C'mon," I said, grabbing his wrist. "Let me show you the other buildings before the dinner bell rings at...eighteen hundred hours." I was making a real effort to learn military time and I hoped my numbers were correct.

Blaine didn't challenge the time. "You're some soldier," he said, wrapping his arm around my waist. "And you're cute too."

———

At dinner, Blaine sat next to me and I introduced him to Rayna, Roxanne, Manny, Josh, and a few older soldiers.

"I've heard lots about you," Rayna said, smiling.

"All good, I hope."

Rayna nodded.

My new friends seemed to like Blaine. When Manny found out that Blaine loved cars, he talked to him about an old Chevy he'd fixed up.

Boring! Tuning out, I looked around the mess hall. Everyone seemed to be eating or socializing—except Josh, who was frowning at me like earlier in the afternoon. *What did he expect?* I'd been honest with him about Blaine. Grabbing my spoon, I concentrated on the mystery-meat stew.

I didn't look at Josh for the rest of meal, which was really hard because he sat right across. I either talked to Blaine on my left or Rayna on my right. Roxanne and Manny were also opposite, but I couldn't say anything to either of them without facing Josh so I ignored them and hoped they wouldn't be mad at me.

When dinner was finally over, I stood up quickly. "Time to go," I said, tugging on Blaine's arm.

"What's the big rush?" He swatted my hand away.

"I've got to use the bathroom," I lied.

"So just go and come back," Blaine suggested. "I'll stay here and wait."

"I'd rather use the bathroom in our building."

"Why?"

Good question. "Umm...It's a lot cleaner."

"Really?" He gave me a puzzled look.

I got the feeling nobody believed my story, but I jumped up and headed towards the exit, relieved to hear footsteps behind me. When I reached the door and turned around, I faced Rayna.

"What was that all about?" she asked.

"Josh has been giving me funny looks ever since Blaine came so I'm trying to avoid him. Speaking of Blaine, where is he?"

"Still talking to people at the table."

I stopped walking and frowned. "What should I do about Josh?"

"Tell him that he's making you uncomfortable."

"But I already told him about Blaine."

"Then tell him again."

———

I was sitting on the rec room couch with Rayna when Blaine and Manny walked in together.

"Hi," Blaine said, squeezing next to me and wrapping his arm around my shoulder. "Want to play pool?" He pointed to the unoccupied game table.

"No, thanks." I remembered the first night with Josh.

"How about a movie?" Manny asked, sifting through the box of DVDs. "Here's a good one...*Armageddon*." He waved the disc in the air.

"I don't want to see an end-of-the-world movie," Rayna said, making a pouty face. "Find something funny—or at least a happy romance."

"Comedy's good, but no chick flick," Manny muttered as he again examined the pile of movies. "How about this one—*Back to School*?"

"Okay," I said. "Are you guys good with it?"

"Sure," Rayna said and Blaine nodded his head.

So we watched *Back to School*. It had a few lines that made me giggle, but it also reminded me there was no more school. At least Blaine's arm was around my shoulder and I snuggled next to him feeling comfy and content. Then Josh entered the room.

Josh made a lot of noise, purposely I'm sure. He clomped in front of the TV screen and then stood opposite the couch, leaning against the wall, arms folded, scowling at me.

Burying my head in Blaine's arm, I tried not to think about Josh.

"What're you doin'?" Blaine whispered.

"Snuggling." I wriggled deeper into the sofa's back cushion.

"Okay." Blaine caressed my ponytail. "Go ahead and rest."

I closed my eyes. When I slowly opened them a couple minutes later, Josh was still standing in the same position so I shut my eyes again and thought about Blaine. I remembered the day we first met in the Douglas' house across the street—everybody holding knives because we thought Blaine and his friend, Zach, wanted to rob us. Then I remembered being together with him in the Fisher's house— our first kiss during the scavenger hunt, hiding in the closet...

"Hey, Erin. Wake up."

When I heard Blaine calling my name, I opened my eyes. "Hi," I said, still wrapped in his arms. "I was just dreaming about you."

"Not nightmares, I hope."

I chuckled. "Of course not. Sorry I fell asleep on you. How was the movie?"

"Pretty good."

I scanned the room, now packed with lots of soldiers. But Josh was no longer there.

———

Blaine and I walked hand in hand to my room. "I wish we could sleep in the same room," he said, pulling me close to him.

"It's not like we'd ever be alone there," I pointed out, leaning against the door.

"Still..." Lifting my face, he gazed into my eyes. "Did I tell you how much I missed you?"

"Yes," I said closing my eyes. "But tell me again. I love hearing you say it."

"I really missed you, Erin." Kissing me tenderly, he pulled me even tighter against his body. Just then, I heard footsteps followed by a loud phony cough so I untangled myself from Blaine.

Rayna stood in the hallway, smiling sheepishly. "Sorry to interrupt," she said. "But I want to get inside and you two are blocking the door."

"Oh." I felt my face turning red as I took several steps to my right.

Rayna opened the door and faced Blaine. "Good night," she said. "Nice meeting you."

"Same here. I'll be headin' to my room."

CHAPTER 5 – Back to Work

I didn't see Blaine again till breakfast. Like usual, I sat with Manny, Rayna, Roxanne, and now Blaine. But this time, Josh didn't sit at our table. Curious to find out where he was, I checked the other tables.

Josh was sitting next to Lourdes. They were both laughing and I think he was holding her hand. For some reason, that scene bothered me. *Why?* I had Blaine, the one I wanted. I took a bite of bread and thought about Josh and Lourdes.

"What's wrong?" Blaine asked.

"Nothing. I'm just thinking about something."

"Hope it's not me that's makin' you so mad," he said.

"I'm not mad."

"Really? This is what you look like." He scowled at me.

"Sorry." I chewed another small piece of bread and then smiled. "I'm good now."

Putting his arm around my shoulder, Blaine squeezed it. "I'm glad I'm not your problem."

I kissed his cheek and rubbed it tenderly. "Of course you're not."

"Ahem." Roxanne coughed loudly. "If you two lovebirds can tear yourselves away from each other, Captain Stallings is about to give out assignments."

Nodding, I turned towards the captain.

"Good morning, soldiers," he began. "Today, we're testing a new formula that our scientists say is stronger and should kill the enemy faster."

He paused and waved the folded paper he'd been holding. "A group has been spotted not far from the base so in addition to our regular surveillance patrols, we're sending two Jeeps to try out the chemical."

The captain unfolded the paper as he continued to speak. "For Jeep One, I need Andrew, Blaine, Rayna, and Margaret and for Jeep Two, let's have Manny, Erin, Dawn, and Josh. You'll all..."

I hope Captain Stallings didn't say anything important after Josh's name because I stopped listening. *Why'd Josh have to be in my Jeep? Why not Blaine?* How was I supposed to concentrate on killing touchers while working with Josh? He was acting so weird.

As we all headed to the briefing room, Blaine nudged my side. "We're goin' on our first army mission together," he said. "Pretty cool, huh?"

"We're in different Jeeps."

"So what? We're still goin' together."

"I guess."

Blaine stopped moving and stared at me. "What's wrong?" he asked. "You've got that dumb look on your face again."

I forced myself to smile. "I just wanted to be in the same Jeep as you."

"Same team, just different Jeep," he said, squeezing my hand. "No big deal."

———

I purposely took a seat in the first row of the converted classroom so I wouldn't have to look at Josh as the eight of us listened to Captain Stallings explain our mission.

"Army scouts have reported seeing an enemy group—four or five together—not far from us on Archer Road," the captain began, pointing to a spot on the large local map taped to the front wall. "You'll attack them at both ends of their location, effectively shutting off their escape route."

"Not if they're flyin'," Blaine muttered, loud enough for everyone to hear.

"That's true," Captain Stallings said. "But this group isn't flying yet."

"You can't be sure they're not hooked up with a bunch that're usin' their wings," Blaine pointed out.

"We can't be sure of anything," the captain agreed. "But our orders are to attack the enemy on Archer Road so that's what you're going to do."

I raised my hand. "Is there any way to squirt them when they're flying—longer hoses, more powerful water guns?" I asked.

"Not yet, unfortunately," the captain said. "But the army's working on it."

"They better find somethin' soon," Blaine whispered to me.

I put my finger on my lips and tried to listen to the rest of the captain's talk. But it was hard not to think about what Blaine had said. *How could we fight touchers if they were flying?* Our hoses and water guns couldn't reach them so they could easily swoop down and touch us—just like they did to poor Charlie.

———

After Blaine and I got water pistols, we stood in the hallway together. "I can't wait to kill those yellow monsters," Blaine said, aiming his gun at an imaginary toucher.

"I wish we were in the same Jeep."

"This is almost the same."

No, it wasn't. But I didn't want to argue again so I just shrugged.

"I'll meet you outside at zero nine hundred hours," Blaine continued. "That's nine o'clock."

"I know."

"You've got that dumb look on your face again, Erin."

"I'm just thinking about the touchers," I lied.

"Don't worry. We'll get them."

"I hope."

Blaine lifted my face and kissed me hard on the lips. Closing my eyes, I tried to think only of him. But it didn't work. *Josh, Josh, Josh,* my mind kept repeating. *How can I work with Josh?* Gently, I pushed Blaine away. "I've got to get ready," I said. "See you later."

44

At nine o'clock—the sun already hot—our team gathered in the parking lot and then separated into two groups of four. As we walked to the Jeeps, I waved to Blaine and he threw me a kiss.

Josh stared at me, but didn't say anything.

"Everybody in," Manny said, opening the door.

I dashed into the back seat, hoping Dawn, a quiet woman in her twenties, would sit next to me. No such luck.

"I guess we're together now," Josh said, smiling.

"Yes," I repeated, returning his smile and hoping I looked happier than I felt.

It was really awkward with Josh next to me. I didn't want to talk to him so I pretended to study the street, which looked the same as always since the bubbles—crashed cars, bodies, bugs, rats—nothing pretty. I think Josh spent most of the ride staring at me, but I didn't turn around to see if I was right.

Luckily, the trip was short—maybe five minutes—and Manny did nearly all the talking. He didn't seem to mind if the rest of us only grunted, nodded, or said an occasional, "yeah."

"Here we are!" Manny announced as he pulled the Jeep into Archer Road. "We've got the front end and Andrew's team is blocking the back. Now let's see how fast we can kill the yellow slime."

―――――

I stopped thinking about Josh and concentrated on the touchers. But I didn't see any as we prepared to step out of the Jeep. "Where are they?" I whispered.

"Hiding and waiting for us," Manny replied as he grabbed one of the attached hoses. "Josh, take the other hose," he ordered.

The four of us stood together in the street, Dawn and I holding water guns and Manny and Josh clutching hoses. Nobody talked as we checked for the enemy. The street was too curvy to see the second Jeep, the one with Blaine and the rest of our team.

"Did you hear that sound?" Dawn whispered.

"No," I said and Josh and Manny shook their heads.

"It's a scratching noise from over there." Dawn pointed across the street.

"Maybe it's one of those skinny dogs or cats looking for food," I suggested.

Dawn shrugged and we continued to monitor our part of the street—looking in all directions, including up.

That's when I heard something. "Flapping—like birds." I lifted my gun towards the sky.

"I hear it," Manny said, turning on the water and then raising the hose. "Get ready."

There were two of them—flying touchers—moving fast and heading straight at the four of us.

I aimed my water pistol, but the touchers were too high. "It's not going to work!" I shouted. "Quick! Get into the Jeep!" We'd left the doors slightly open so I ran into the back, followed by Dawn.

Then I realized Manny and Josh were both still outside.

"Get in!" I yelled. But they ignored my order and stayed in the street, each clutching a hose. Manny aimed his at the flying touchers, but the yellow things were beyond his reach.

Climbing on top of the Jeep, Josh stood next to the water tank and lifted his hose, trying to spray the touchers. "Too high!" he yelled as he jumped off the roof and got into the front passenger seat.

Only Manny remained outside.

"Look!" Dawn shouted. "They're coming from that house I told you about, across the street!"

When I turned, four touchers—all different sizes and shapes—were rushing our way.

Josh slid over to the driver's seat and started the Jeep, honking as he guided us closer to Manny, who sprayed water on his pants and legs and then squirted a circle around himself. The touchers on the ground stopped moving, but the flying ones were so close, they could almost reach his dry head.

Leaning out the window, I aimed my gun at the flying toucher nearest Manny. It wasn't a direct hit, but some water must have dripped on the yellow creature because it backed away, flapping its wings faster, probably trying to dry itself. That gave Manny enough time to get into the Jeep.

"Geez!" he yelled. "Damn yellow monsters move so fast."

"You should've wet your head," I said.

Manny just shrugged.

The touchers on the ground slowly approached us, avoiding the water Manny had sprayed like invaders might treat a moat around a castle. "The hose is in the road so the water's still coming out," Manny said.

"And what happens when we run out of water?" Dawn asked.

"You guys are forgetting something," Josh said. "The rest of our team is at the other end of the street. They'll get to us."

I looked out the window, hoping he was right. The flying touchers had landed and the six of them formed a circle around our Jeep. They all stood there—waiting.

———

"I wish we still had cellphones," Manny said. "But at least I can do this." He honked the horn three times, stopped, and then repeated the beeps. "They'll figure it out."

The touchers didn't react at all to the noises, not moving away or coming closer. Instead, they continued to stand and watch us.

"We could run them over," I suggested.

"Nah," Manny said. "They move too fast."

"We could drive away," Dawn whispered.

"And not carry out our orders?" Josh asked. "What kind of soldier are you?"

Dawn lowered her head and didn't answer.

In the quiet that followed, I heard a car's engine and through the rear window, saw the other Jeep. "Andrew's coming!" I announced.

The two-lane road was narrow and smashed cars and junk made it impossible for Andrew's Jeep to pull alongside so he parked behind us and honked the horn while Blaine, the front seat passenger, blew me a kiss.

That's when the touchers broke their circle and three of them headed towards Blaine's Jeep.

"What're they doing?" Dawn asked.

"Trying to surround us, maybe," I said.

"There's not enough of them to do that," Manny said.

"Look!" Josh pointed to the sky. "Three more flying ones!"

The new arrivals didn't land on the ground. Instead, two set down next to the water tank on top of Blaine's Jeep and banged on the roof. The other toucher must have landed on our roof because I heard footsteps above us, followed by a pounding noise.

"It's trying to make a hole or something," Josh said.

"They can't do that, can they?" Dawn asked.

Manny shook his head. "The Jeep's protected with some kind of super strong stuff."

Maybe the touchers couldn't get in that way, but knowing those yellow things were up there was scary. Also, the noise was creepy—a steady thumping over our heads.

"We gotta do something," Manny muttered.

"What?" I asked, covering my ears. The noise was getting louder. Maybe more than one toucher was on top of our Jeep.

"How about I drive around the block to try to shake them off?" Manny suggested.

"And then what?" It didn't sound like much of a plan.

"Then we head down this street again and squirt them through the windows with our water guns," Manny continued.

Dawn shook her head. "There are too many of them."

Nobody spoke. I guess we were all thinking about how we could kill the touchers without getting ourselves killed too.

"Can we signal the other Jeep that we need to figure out a way to attack them together?" I asked.

"How?" Josh looked at me.

"We've got black markers and paper." I held up my notebook from the briefing. "We could make a sign and hold it up on the back window."

"That's a good idea," Manny agreed. "Now what're we gonna write?"

The message we decided on was, "WE NEED A PLAN. LET'S WORK TOGETHER." I held the notebook page against the rear window and watched as Andrew, an older guy with glasses, nodded his bald head and Blaine gave a thumbs-up signal.

"Now all we need is the plan," I whispered.

"We gotta be able to squirt them with that new formula," Manny said.

"Do we have enough water left in the tank?" Josh asked.

"Probably not," Manny said.

"But the other team must have all its water because the touching things were on our end of the street," Dawn pointed out.

"I'll check," I said, quickly writing, "IS YOUR WATER TANK FULL?" and again holding the paper against the window.

Both Blaine and Andrew nodded.

"We need a diversion," Josh said. "Something to get them away from us so Andrew's team can set up their hoses."

"That sounds dangerous," Dawn whispered.

Her attitude was starting to annoy me. "Everything since the bubbles landed is dangerous," I said. "If you can't handle it, you shouldn't have joined the army."

Dawn lowered her head and kept quiet.

"Can we toss something out of the Jeep that they'd be interested in?" I asked Manny and Josh.

"Yeah," Manny chuckled. "One of us."

"That's not what I meant," I continued.

"I know," Manny said. "But that's what they want—us."

I thought for a moment. "You're right," I said. "Let me be the diversion. I'll run out and get them to chase me." *Like Kyle...*

Dawn looked at me as if I was out of my mind. "They'll kill you," she said.

"Not if I'm soaking wet. If I use the water in our guns and bottles on myself, the touchers won't come near me and then you guys can grab the hoses on the other Jeep and squirt them."

"Captain Stallings said we're not allowed to do that," Dawn whispered.

I frowned at her. "I don't care about breaking the rules. It's the only way."

"Are you sure?" Josh asked.

"It's always worked."

"But these toucher things are changing—growing wings, forming groups," Josh argued.

"I'm betting they still won't go anywhere near a totally wet person," I said.

"Let me do it then," Josh offered.

"No," Manny said. "I'm the team leader. I'll go."

I shook my head. "I'm smaller than both of you so I'll use less water. I have to be the one."

————

It took most of our water to get me wet enough to risk stepping outside and the rest went into my two pistols.

"Go away!" I shouted as I opened the door, squirting the toucher who stood guard. "Shoo!"

The girl-thing immediately jumped backwards and tried to rub the water off its yellow arms.

"Come on!" I yelled, dashing towards the other Jeep. "Try and catch me!"

But the girl toucher was so focused on drying itself that it didn't even look up. The flying one, who stood on the roof of our Jeep holding a rock, stared at me, but didn't move.

Taking a step forward, I waved my arms and guns at the boy toucher next to Blaine's Jeep who eyed me suspiciously. "What about you?" I asked, taking a second step in its direction.

The boy-thing rushed towards me, but stopped when it got within a few feet. "I guess you noticed I'm wet," I said, squirting its yellow face. The toucher pawed at its eyes as if the water was painful.

Sprinting away from the boy-thing, I aimed my gun at the short man toucher still standing on top of Blaine's Jeep. "Get off!" I shouted.

"Yeah!"

I turned and faced a soaking wet Blaine, who, like me, carried a pair of water pistols. "Hi, partner," he said, his curly long brown hair dripping water as he sprayed the flying toucher and the second guard. "Let's finish this mission."

————

Blaine and I continued to pester the three touchers surrounding his Jeep, squirting them with our guns and teasing them. I don't think they understood our words, but it felt good to yell.

When I sprayed one of the touchers again, I realized I was firing air. Also, after being outside in the hot sun, I was no longer dripping wet. "Blaine!" I yelled. "I'm out of water and my clothes are drying so I'm going into that house!" I pointed to a small gray building across the street.

"I'm comin' with you!" he said. "Let's make them chase us!"

Picking up a broken piece of glass, Blaine threw it at the boy toucher, who'd finally finished wiping the water from its face. The glass landed on the thing's arm, but then bounced right off—no cut, blood, or anything. The toucher looked in our direction, but remained near the Jeep.

"They're like Superman," I said as we reached the gray house, remembering that bullets didn't work either. "Nothing seems to hurt them."

"The army's water does," Blaine pointed out. "That's their kryptonite." He twisted the doorknob and when it didn't open, used a rock to smash the front window.

Blaine climbed through the window and I followed. The first thing I did was check the street. "The touchers are still by the Jeeps," I said.

"So we get ourselves wet, fill the guns, and go back." Blaine smiled at me. "I've been dreamin' about showerin' with you...Race you upstairs."

———

Five minutes later, we were again on the street—soaking wet with loaded water pistols. We rushed towards the six touchers that still surrounded both Jeeps.

"Let's shoo these three away from here so Andrew can get the hoses goin'," Blaine said, pointing to his Jeep.

I squirted at the boy toucher and when he backed off, went after the girl-thing. Blaine concentrated on the man blob that still stood on the roof, hoisting a large rock.

"Watch out!" I yelled as the man toucher flung the rock at Blaine, then flapped its yellow wings, and flew away.

Blaine ducked and the heavy stone fell harmlessly to the ground.

The Jeep's door opened and Andrew and his team jumped out. "Thanks, guys," Rayna said, standing next to Margaret, a woman I hardly knew.

I nodded at them.

"Yeah, thanks," Andrew echoed as he unfastened one of the hoses. "We're ready so you gotta get them here."

"That won't be a problem," Blaine said, tugging at my arm. "Time for a roundup."

———

The wet boy and girl touchers stood on the sidewalk intent on removing the water from their yellow bodies. "Come on!" Blaine shouted, waving his arms at the girl thing. "Wanna get me? I'm right here!"

The girl toucher looked up, saw he was full of water, and went back to drying itself. I tried to lure the boy toucher to the Jeep. "You can touch me!" I said, moving closer till I was only five feet from it.

The boy thing glanced at me for a moment, but didn't take a step in my direction. *Not interested?* Of course with no mouth, I couldn't tell what it was feeling—if these strange yellow monsters still had any emotions.

"They don't want to touch us right now because we're so wet," I said to Blaine. "So how do we get them back to the Jeep?"

"We'll figure out somethin'. There's gotta be a way..."

"Guys, watch out!"

I recognized Rayna's voice and when I turned around, she pointed to the sky where a group of flying touchers—six in a gooselike formation—headed our way.

"Like a goddamn bomb squad," Blaine muttered. "We can't stay out here any more."

"But we're still wet," I argued. "They won't go after us."

"How do you know?" Blaine asked. "They can easily swoop down and touch our heads." He fingered the hair near his scalp. "This part's nearly dry already from the sun." He tugged on my hand. "Don't be a jerk. We've got to go back inside."

––––––

Blaine's Jeep was the closest so we went there, joining Rayna, Margaret, and Andrew. The flying touchers had landed and we watched them huddle together with the other creatures. They stood ten feet from us, bunched in a large circle, their yellow heads lowered like they were concentrating hard.

"They're all planning something," I muttered.

"But it's so quiet," Margaret said.

"Since they can't talk, maybe they're communicating using telepathy like the captain said," Rayna suggested.

"We should get out of here," Andrew said. "There're twelve of them now and if we can't squirt them, we can't kill them."

"But we can't go forward." I pointed to Manny's Jeep in front of us, blocking the road. "And what about our mission? We were ordered to destroy the enemy."

"We can't hose them unless we go outside," Andrew said. "And if we do that, they'll kill us."

––––––

About five minutes later, the touchers broke up their huddle and surrounded Manny's Jeep. Several picked up rocks and pieces of glass from the street and hurled them at the windows while two flying things perched on the roof and pounded it with rocks. The others just stood silently, watching the action.

I heard the smashing sound of broken glass as one of the Jeep's back windows shattered and Manny started driving down the street as fast as he could.

"Are they still on Manny's roof?" I asked.

"I don't see 'em," Blaine replied. "They must've been blown off."

Margaret pointed to her right. "They're all coming here now," she said. "What do we do?"

With Manny's Jeep no longer in front of us, Andrew was able to move forward.

"Turn on the wipers," Blaine said.

"That won't help," Andrew argued. "There're too many of them."

"But it'll keep them away from the front windows," Blaine explained. He looked at me and I nodded. We had a little of our own telepathy. "Erin and I are goin' out again."

After using almost all the water in the pistols to soak our heads, Blaine and I opened the back door and stepped outside.

———

It was creepier this time because the touchers were everywhere and so close. But the water dripping from our heads kept them from attacking us. "They're still holding all those rocks and glass," I whispered to Blaine.

"You watch them," he said softly. "I'm gonna do this fast."

A girl toucher lifted a rock to throw at Blaine. "Look out!" I yelled, pushing him down as the stone crashed into the side of the Jeep.

Another rock whizzed past our heads, sailing over the Jeep, as Blaine untied a hose and handed it to me. "Start sprayin' them!" he ordered. "I'll free the other one."

"Oww!" A large rock hit the side of my leg. I hopped, trying to forget the pain as I aimed the hose at the touchers, squirting them back and forth like I was watering a garden. But I wanted the opposite result.

"Die!" I shouted. "All of you!" I took two steps forward and the touchers backed away. "That's right! Get out of here!" One boy-thing fell, its arms and legs flapping like a frightened chicken. I pointed the hose at it and kept the water going until the boy toucher stopped moving.

The other touchers near me frantically tried to rub the liquid off their yellow bodies, but I kept dousing them with my hose until they were soaked. One by one, the things fell on the ground, moving their arms and legs. They must have been hurt and maybe they wanted to scream, but they couldn't make any sounds because they no longer had mouths. Or maybe they didn't feel pain any more. Whatever. It didn't matter. What mattered was that they were dying.

"How're you doin'?" Blaine called from the other side of the Jeep.

"They're all just about dead," I said. "What about you?"

"The same," he shouted. "We're done here."

I looked up in the sky and saw two touchers circling above. With lots of water on the ground and on Blaine and me, they weren't attacking us. But they weren't dead. "What about the flying ones?" I asked Blaine. "We didn't kill them."

"We need planes for that. We gotta get them in the air."

Nodding, I opened the door of the Jeep.

CHAPTER 6 – Driving Lesson

A loud siren—like we used to hear from a police car or ambulance—went off in the middle of the night, waking me and everyone else in the room. "What's going on?" I mumbled.

"I don't know," Josh said. "Must be some kind of emergency."

"What time is it?" I asked, rubbing my eyes.

"Two-thirty," Rayna replied. "Better hurry, Erin. We have to report to the lunchroom immediately."

I was so exhausted. Fighting touchers the day before had really knocked me out. Although I dressed quickly, when I entered the lunchroom, everyone was already seated and listening to Captain Stallings.

"...attacked the base about an hour ago," he was saying. "The flying ones threw rocks at the water tanks while the enemy on the ground shredded car tires, pulled out wires, and damaged exteriors. Most of our vehicles are ruined."

"Isn't this base guarded?" Blaine asked.

Captain Stallings shrugged. "Not heavily," he said. "We don't have the manpower so just two soldiers patrol the property. But the enemy's never tried anything like this until now..." His voice trailed off.

"What happened to the soldiers patrolling the base and any others who were outside?" I asked.

"All dead," the captain whispered.

―――――

Our days of freedom were over. We were no longer allowed to be outdoors, walking wherever we wanted, whenever we wanted. Now we had to march together with our unit to dinner, armed with water guns, always watching for flying touchers. Except for evening meals and training exercises—or rainy weather—we stayed indoors.

I hated it. "It's like being in prison again," I complained to Rayna in the bathroom a few mornings later as we got ready for breakfast. "I love going outside in the sun and now..."

"I know," Rayna agreed, shutting me up. "You've told me about being stuck in your house all that time."

What bothered me most was that we had no chance to defeat the touchers like this. I remembered Blaine's argument. "We need planes," I told Rayna as I ran a brush through my hair. "We've got to attack them in the sky."

"And who's going to teach us how to fly the planes?"

That pesky question again—the one I had no answer for. "There's got to be a pilot somewhere," I mumbled.

"And how do we find him?"

Another good question. "We've got to start searching," I said. But I didn't know how. I just knew we had to find a pilot—and we had to find one soon.

―――――

I only half-listened to Captain Stallings' after-breakfast briefing, still trying to figure out how we could find a pilot so we could learn to fly planes.

"What's wrong?" Blaine whispered.

"Nothing. I'm just thinking."

"Those must be pretty bad thoughts," he continued. "You keep frownin'."

"Like you've been saying," I murmured. "We need pilots."

"You goin' to advertise for one on Craigslist?"

"Very funny, Blaine." *Advertise*, he said. *No Internet, no TV, no radio, no newspapers*. Still, there had to be a way to get the word out...Maybe there was.

The captain finished talking and we were dismissed. As I stood, I tugged at Blaine's sleeve. "Remember the megaphone I used at home to tell people about Cyndy Louise growing wings?" I asked.

"So?"

"So couldn't we drive around—especially near the airport—and shout out for pilots to join the army and help train us?"

"With a megaphone?"

I shrugged. "A megaphone or something else that's loud enough for people to hear the message. The army plays music every day so they should be able to record an announcement. Right?"

"I guess it could work," Blaine agreed, smiling.

———

Captain Stallings liked my idea. But this was the army so he couldn't send me on the streets without first checking with Headquarters. Late that afternoon, Blaine and I were called into his office.

"Congratulations," the captain said, standing and holding out his hand to me. "The army has approved your plan. As we speak, they're recording a message to broadcast in the vicinity of the airport."

"Great!" I said, shaking Captain Stallings' hand. "When can we start?"

He shook his head. "I'm sorry, Erin. You won't be delivering the message."

"Why not?"

"You don't drive. Day after tomorrow, we're sending cars with teams of two—and both soldiers need to be able to drive."

"But it was my idea," I muttered.

"Yes—and it's an excellent idea. The army is very grateful. In the past, you would have received a written commendation that would have gone in your file. However, these days..." Captain Stallings' words drifted off.

"What about me?" Blaine asked. "I know how to drive. Can I get the word out that the army needs pilots?"

"Yes, Blaine," the captain said. "You're on the list." Then he looked at me again. "I'm so sorry, Erin. You'll have other chances."

I was really pissed as we left Captain Stallings' office. Blaine must have understood how mad I was because he tried sweet-talking. "You should be real proud," he said. "The army loved your idea and they're gonna use it. That's so cool."

His words didn't make me feel better and I didn't bother to answer. But that didn't stop Blaine. "You're only a kid and you came up with a great plan," he continued. "I wish I'd thought of it."

I kept walking.

"I'm proud of you, Erin—and I'll make sure everybody knows it was your idea. The drivin' part's not a big deal. Anyone could do that."

"Just not me," I whispered, "because I don't know how to drive. My dad was supposed to teach me this summer, but he's dead and..."

"I'll teach you."

"How? We're not even allowed outside anymore, you don't have a car here, and you can't drive the army's cars, especially now after the touchers messed up so many of them. The working cars are all heavily guarded."

Blaine took my hand and held it as we reached my room. "Don't worry," he said, smiling. "I'll find a way."

———

After dinner that night, Blaine excused himself. "There's somethin' I gotta do," he said mysteriously. "You go on ahead with the guys." He pointed to Rayna, Manny, and the rest of our unit.

"But we're all supposed to walk back together with the guards," I argued.

"I'll catch up." Blaine gave me a gentle push on the rear and headed towards Captain Stallings' table.

Rayna studied me as our unit returned to Building 4. "Is something wrong?" she asked. "You were very quiet at dinner."

"I want to look for pilots with everyone," I muttered. "But they won't let me."

"I'm not going either," Rayna said. "And I know how to drive."

That didn't make me feel any better. "They should make an

exception for me because it was my idea," I complained.

———

I was sitting by myself on the couch in the rec room when Blaine entered. "Hi," he said, plopping down next to me.

I didn't say anything.

"Don't you want to hear what's goin' on? Aren't you curious?"

I grunted and crossed my arms.

"Okay, then, since you don't even care..." Blaine started to stand.

"Wait," I said, grabbing his shirt and holding on. "Tell me."

He sat again and smiled. "Captain Stallings said I could teach you how to drive. Lessons are tomorrow mornin' after breakfast."

"You're not kidding?" I stared at him.

Reaching into his pocket, he pulled out a key. "But we've only got the car till lunch so you better be a fast learner. Think you can do this?"

I jumped onto Blaine's lap and hugged him. "I'll be the fastest learner ever! Thank you! Thank you! Thank you!" I shouted, kissing him hard on the cheek after each "thank you."

"This can work," he said, taking my face in his hands and kissing me tenderly on the lips.

———

The driving lesson wasn't anything romantic—Blaine and me alone together—because Captain Stallings assigned Maria, a sweet lady in her fifties, to watch us in case of another touchers' attack. But even if it had been just the two of us, I would've still concentrated on learning to drive.

"This is the gas pedal and this is the brake," Blaine said as I gripped the steering wheel of the dented Honda Accord.

"I know that much," I snarled.

Blaine pointed to the stick between the two front seats. "This is what you use to change gears."

"What are gears?"

"The different things a car does—drive, go in reverse, park."

"I see the 'P' and 'R' and 'D,'" I said. "But what's 'N' and the numbers?"

"Neutral and different drive speeds," Blaine explained, inserting the key. "But you don't have to worry about those right now."

We were in the back of the parking lot, away from other cars, so I couldn't do much damage. Anyway, this car was already banged up, which is maybe why I was practicing on it. I turned the key and the engine rumbled.

"Go ahead," Blaine urged. "Move the stick to 'Drive.'"

I did what he said and the car bounced a little. Then I pressed my foot on the gas pedal and the car moved forward. I was driving! No sweat.

———

We practiced the rest of the morning. At first, I just drove around the parking lot with Blaine having me stop and turn around many times. When he told me to put the car into "Reverse," I went backwards slowly. In fact, everything I did was slow. The driving lesson felt more like a crawling lesson.

"This is boring," I complained after about my tenth slow time around the lot. "I can walk faster. Can't I go someplace where I can actually drive the car."

"Not yet. You're just learnin'."

"But I've already learned this part. I know how to drive around the lot perfectly. I haven't come close to hitting a car or a tree or anything else. To drive on a street, I've got to be able to move much faster."

Blaine turned to Maria in the back seat. "Can we go somewhere else?" he asked.

"The captain just told me to stay with you for as long as you were out driving," she said, shrugging. "It's up to you."

"Please!" I smiled at Blaine, sweetly I hoped. "I need to practice on a real road."

"Maybe we can go up to the entrance," Blaine said.

"Okay," I said, guiding the car into the driveway before he changed his mind.

———

Since it was such a long distance to the main road, I could at least drive faster than in the parking lot. "This is much better," I said as I approached the Ridgeview Corporate Park sign. "Can I go on...?"

I never got a chance to finish my question because, at that moment, three touchers rose from their hiding spots in the tall grass and pelted the car with pebbles and rocks.

"Turn the car around!" Blaine yelled.

Suddenly the driving backwards part of the lesson seemed real important. I got the car into "Reverse," twisted the wheel, went backwards, and moved the stick into "Drive."

I heard a window slide open and through the rearview mirror, saw Maria shooting touchers with her water guns. "Keep going!" she yelled when I hesitated. "Don't worry about me!"

I'd almost finished straightening the car when I heard glass shattering. "Which window broke?" I asked.

"A back one!" Blaine hollered. "Don't stop! Finish makin' the turn!"

As I got the car facing the base, one of the touchers—a teen boy-thing—appeared right in front of us, its yellow arms extended.

"Hit him with the car!" Blaine ordered.

He's not human, I reminded myself as I pressed down hard on the gas pedal and drove over the boy toucher. Then, driving as fast as I could, I headed for the parking lot.

We were halfway there when something heavy landed on the roof, jolting the car so hard that my hands fell off the steering wheel.

"Hold on!" Blaine shouted, grabbing the wheel and straightening it just before we turned off the road and into the tall grass.

Snatching the wheel from Blaine, I drove forward as something pounded the top of the car. "What's that?" I asked.

"No questions now," Blaine said as he opened his window slightly, sprayed water at the roof, and quickly closed the window. "Just keep drivin' and we'll be okay."

Although he opened and closed the window three more times, the overhead thumping continued. "Damn!" he muttered the final time, tossing his water gun on the floor.

"What's wrong?"

Instead of answering me, Blaine unlatched his seat belt and reached into the back seat. Then, from the corner of my eye, I saw him again open his window slightly and spray the roof. This time, when he closed the window, he leaned against his seat.

I didn't hear any more pounding. Whatever had been up there was gone. I knew what it was, but asked anyway. "A flying toucher?"

"Yeah."

When I finally reached the lot, I put the car into "Park" and closed my eyes, gripping the steering wheel tightly.

Blaine put his arm around my shoulder. "You said you wanted to go fast," he whispered. "Lucky for us, you're a quick learner."

I looked at the two water pistols—one on the floor and the other on the seat. "You used Maria's water pistol," I whispered. "Maria...?" The woman in the back hadn't said anything since just before I ran over the boy toucher—and she hadn't reacted at all when the flying toucher landed on the car. Blaine had taken her gun. Again I peeked into the rearview mirror, but didn't see Maria.

Blaine shook his head. "It was her open window that they busted and when you were turnin', one of them reached inside and touched her."

———

All my excitement about learning how to drive vanished the moment I found out Maria was dead. If I'd been more experienced, I could have turned faster and the toucher wouldn't have gotten her.

Blaine must have read my thoughts again because as we walked back to Building 4 with a guard, he squeezed my shoulder and pulled me towards him. "It wasn't your fault," he said. "We were trapped on the driveway and you had to turn around."

"But if I turned faster..."

Blaine shook his head. "It wouldn't have made a difference. Once they smashed her open window, Maria didn't have a chance."

I looked at his face to see if he was telling the truth. "Really?"

He nodded his head sadly.

Maria was still dead, but I felt a little better knowing it wasn't my fault.

"When we find a pilot tomorrow, we can attack them better," Blaine said.

"I only started driving this morning. Will I be able to go?"

Blaine kissed the back of my neck. "Definitely," he whispered. "After this mornin', you can be my drivin' partner any time."

CHAPTER 7 - Pilot Search

The next morning after breakfast, I sat in the lunchroom with other Unit 4 soldiers, waiting for our assignments. "We don't have many good cars left," Captain Stallings began. "But we're using eight for today's mission." He held up a CD and waved it. "Each car is equipped with one of these, ready to be played. It's our message—repeated over and over—urging pilots to come to the base to help us."

When the captain pulled a sheet of paper from his pants pocket and started reading the pairings, I crossed my fingers and wished silently. After fourteen names had been called, Blaine and I still sat next to each other at our nearly empty table, holding hands and waiting. Then Captain Stallings turned to both of us and smiled. "You'll be doing the driving, Blaine," he said. "And Erin, you'll be going with him."

I let out a deep breath. Sometimes wishes do come true.

———

Armed with maps showing our routes, the sixteen of us marched to the parking lot where eight cars were lined up. "Does it matter which car we take?" I asked one of the guards.

"I don't think so," the skinny woman said, shrugging.

"Then I want that one," I said, pointing to a sea mist green car. "I like the color." Blaine snickered at me. "With everythin' that's goin' on, you're lookin' for pretty cars?"

"So what?" I ran to the green car before someone else chose it and slid into the passenger seat.

———

As Blaine drove up the long driveway, I clutched a water gun and scanned the tall grass for hidden touchers.

"It's clear now," Blaine said. "The captain said they checked just before sendin' us out."

"But they couldn't check the sky for flying ones," I said, looking up.

After we reached the sign and made a left turn without seeing touchers, I grabbed the map. "You stay on Hazelton for about five miles and then turn right into Highcrest Parkway South."

"Okay."

As Blaine continued to drive, I studied the road. It was still full of smashed up cars, packs of scrawny dogs and cats, disgusting fat rats, and worst of all, rotting human bodies covered with bugs. The bugs were mostly flies and mosquitoes, but there were also creepy crawling things, probably beetles and roaches. All the dead people's faces were pretty much eaten away and I tried not to stare at them.

Although Blaine drove with the windows closed and air conditioning on, I could tell that it smelled really bad outside. The only good thing about the trip—aside from being with Blaine—was that there weren't any touchers.

"Where are the touchers?" I asked.

"Maybe after yesterday, they're scared of you and me."

"Sure. They used their ESP to spread the word to stay away from us because you knocked one off the car and I ran over another. Big deal. They didn't die."

"And now they've got a wanted poster out for us," Blaine said, chuckling. "'America's Most Wanted.' Remember that old show?"

"Yeah." It seemed like years ago when we watched TV.

"Right exit coming up at Laguna Road," I said, checking the map again. "That's when we're supposed to play the CD." I pushed "Start" and turned up the volume since we couldn't open the windows.

"The army needs pilots! If you know how to fly a plane, go to the army base at the former **Ridgeview Corporate Park**, located at **Hazelton Boulevard and Eagle Street**. We are making weapons to destroy the enemy, but we desperately need pilots. If you can fly a plane, we need you to train our soldiers. Help save our country! Come to **Ridgeview Corporate Park** immediately. The address is **1200 Hazelton Boulevard**."

The message repeated continuously so it didn't take long till I was sick of hearing it. But if the words reached even one pilot, then it was worth our effort.

Since we blasted the recording so loud, Blaine and I couldn't talk as he drove our set loop around roads near the airport. Although the ride continued to be creepy, the streets were all passable so Blaine didn't have to detour around smashed-up cars.

We saw one other car going the opposite way and the driver—a young guy—shook his head at us and shrugged.

"I guess he's not a pilot!" I shouted.

Blaine nodded.

"Still no touchers!" I yelled.

"Don't knock it!" Blaine hollered. "Just keep lookin'!"

I clutched both water guns, ready to shoot as soon as I saw any of them. And then, I did.

"Blaine!" I yelled, lowering the volume of the announcement. "There's a bunch of touchers coming at us!"

We were on a side street with wrecked cars blocking the other lane. "I'm backing out," Blaine said as he zoomed the car in reverse, not worrying about hitting traffic behind us since there wasn't any.

The group of touchers—I counted five—raced after us. Two held chunks of wood and others carried large rocks.

"Watch out for the rocks!" I warned just as a girl-thing tossed a stone at the hood. The rock shattered the right headlight as Blaine continued driving backwards. Then I caught a glimpse of something in the sky—a flying toucher dive-bombing at us.

Blaine reached the corner and was again driving forward as fast as he could. I no longer saw the pack of touchers that had attacked us on the ground—I guess they couldn't keep up with the car—but the flying toucher was still heading our way.

Opening my window just enough to shove the water gun through, I aimed at its ugly yellow face and squirted the flying thing right between its empty eyes. Immediately, the toucher flapped its wings and changed direction. "Got it!" I yelled, closing the window.

"Good job," Blaine said.

"Thanks. So what do we do now?"

Blaine shrugged. "We can't drive our route any more—not with all those touchers around—so we gotta head back to the base." Turning to me, he smiled. "You wanted to know where they all were and now you know. Got anythin' to say before I blast the message again?"

I shook my head.

"Okay, here goes." Blaine turned up the volume and we listened to "The army needs pilots..." as we drove away from the airport.

———

We weren't the first team back. As Blaine and I entered Headquarters, Manny and Roxanne walked out. "How'd it go?" I asked, giving both of them a quick hug.

"Not so good," Roxanne said. "We'd just started our loop when we were surrounded by the enemy. I guess they didn't like the message."

"Four of them yellow things came after us," Manny added.

"Any flying ones?" I asked.

"No," Manny said. "Just on the ground. But they threw rocks at the car and messed up a back light and a bumper."

Roxanne nodded. "We were lucky they didn't break any windows or slash the tires."

"We had the same problem," I said. "I hope the recording played long enough for some pilots to hear it."

"I'll take even one pilot," Blaine said. "We can manage with just one person who knows how to fly a plane."

"Maybe the other teams are doing better," I suggested.

"I don't think so," Roxanne said. "Major Figueroa said two teams came back ahead of us so counting you guys, that makes four—half of the eight."

———

By lunchtime, seven teams had made it back to the base. Although many of the cars were messed up, all fourteen returning soldiers were okay. But one pair was still somewhere on the streets.

I sat in the cafeteria with Blaine, Manny, Rayna, and Roxanne, eating a peanut butter sandwich and worrying. "Who's in the missing car?" I asked.

"Josh and Dawn," Roxanne said.

Josh and that wimp? Josh wasn't my favorite person, but the thought of him being trapped with scaredy-cat Dawn bothered me. "What's the army doing about finding them?" I asked.

"Probably'll send out a search team this afternoon," Manny said.

I turned to Blaine and stared at him, concentrating very hard.

He smiled and nodded. "Yeah, I know. You want to volunteer."

That ESP thing was still working. "Will you come with me?"

Blaine squeezed my arm. "Of course, Erin. Finish eatin' and we'll find Captain Stallings."

I gulped down the rest of my sandwich.

———

I don't know if there were any other volunteers, but the captain sent Blaine and me to find Josh and Dawn.

"They were driving a black Honda Civic," Captain Stallings said, handing me a folded sheet of paper. "Here's the map of their route. Take the best car you can find and get started. Good luck." He gave us both a quick hug.

To me, he sounded more like a father reluctantly letting his kids go out for a fun drive—like to the movies—than an officer sending soldiers on a dangerous rescue mission. *Here are the car keys.* But my dad would never hand me keys or anything else. And there were no more movie theaters. I shook my head, trying to erase those sad thoughts as Blaine and I walked into the parking lot, again escorted by a guard.

"I don't want the green car," Blaine said. "It drove funny after the rock hit it. Choose another one."

"Wow!" I said. "These are a mess." Every car had dents, smashed bumpers, or shattered windows. One blue van even had a crushed-in roof.

"They do look pretty bad," Blaine agreed. "But they probably still drive okay...How about this one?" He pointed to a white Toyota Camry. "It's just got some scrapes."

The "scrapes" were black gouge marks that covered the whole driver's side from door to door. It was one ugly-looking car. "Yucch!" I said.

Blaine raced to the car's passenger side. "It's good here," he said. I followed him and looked. He was right. No gouges.

"Let me make sure all the doors work," Blaine said as he opened and shut both doors on the driver's side. "Perfect!"

"I thought I was picking the car," I complained, folding my arms.

Blaine placed his arms around my shoulders. "Okay, then. Choose another."

I scanned the lot again. Every other car looked much worse than the white Camry. "All right," I said. "I choose this one." I pointed to the Camry.

———

I waved to the guard as Blaine drove out of the lot, up the long driveway with the tall grass. "No touchers here," I announced when nothing jumped out at us.

Blaine reached the main road and again turned left on Hazelton, heading towards the airport. "What next?" he asked.

"We stay on Hazelton for fifteen miles and then make a right onto Westwood Avenue."

I clutched my water guns, ready for an attack. But the roads were spooky quiet; not even the packs of dogs or cats were around this afternoon. Maybe it was too hot for them, although the rats didn't seem to mind the early August heat. They still scurried from inside the wrecked cars when we drove by. And like always, the bugs were everywhere. I tried not to think about the rotting bodies and how bad it smelled outside.

I heard a fluttering noise in the sky and since we no longer had any birds, knew what was making the sound. "Hear that?" I asked.

"Yeah. How many of them?"

I opened my window a crack and looked up. "Three—and they're heading our way."

"Damn!" Blaine muttered. "How're we gonna find the missin' car if we gotta stop and fight these flyin' touchers? Did they see us?"

"I don't think so, but I can't be sure. Can we find a place to hide till they pass?"

"Where?"

Good question. I thought quickly. "Turn into the next side street and park somewhere," I said. "Pretend we're just another abandoned car."

"Okay. It's worth a try." Blaine made a quick right and squeezed the Camry between a battered black Jeep and a silver Chevy. Then we waited.

"They're right above us," I said.

"Yeah—and still flyin'."

―――――

Leaving our hiding place, we continued to follow Josh and Dawn's route. "Go a half mile and make a right at the Shell station into Jasper Road," I said.

The Shell sign was the only thing that remained of the corner gas station. A fire had destroyed everything else.

"See that car?" Blaine asked, pointing to the burnt remains of an auto. "It must've smashed into the gas pump when the driver was touched."

I shuddered. Burning to death in a fire didn't appeal to me. But then I realized the person in the car hadn't died from the flames; he'd already been dead from the touch of one of those yellow monsters. *Was that a better way to die?*

"Erin! Why aren't you watchin'?"

Blaine's voice jolted me out of my mini-funk. Two touchers—a young girl and very tall man—were running towards my side of the car, carrying bottles. By the time I saw them, the touchers had almost reached me.

"Be careful!"

Opening the window just enough to squirt my pistol, I sprayed the tall toucher's yellow stomach and the man-thing stopped running and tried to dry itself. But the girl toucher dropped the bottle and got hold of my window, clutching it with both hands, trying to reach inside.

I pressed the button to shut my window, leaning as far back in the seat as possible, away from the deadly yellow fingers. The window closed—but not all the way—catching the girl toucher's fingers as the car dragged its body through the street.

"Blaine!" I yelled. "The toucher's hand is stuck in my window! I can't close it!"

I heard a thumping and saw the girl-thing's emotionless face and other hand as it tried to widen the opening. *Was it in pain?* I couldn't tell.

"Open the window and then shut it—fast—before the toucher gets in!" Blaine shouted.

I did what he said and when I checked again, the yellow hand was gone.

———

"That was close," I said, letting out a deep breath.

"Only 'cause you weren't payin' attention. You're supposed to be watchin' for them. That's why you're here."

"I'm sorry."

"Do it again and we'll both be dead."

After looking at Blaine's angry face, I didn't say anything else. Instead, I stared out the window, noted the names of the streets we were passing, and picked up the map, which, during my battle with the yellow fingers, had fallen on the floor.

"You make a left on Crawford Road and then take the next left—Elm Drive. That was the start of Josh and Dawn's loop."

Blaine just nodded. I think he was still mad at me.

At Elm Drive, we began following the route Josh and Dawn had taken. "See anythin'?" Blaine asked.

At least he was talking to me again. "No black Civic."

"We've almost gone..." Blaine started to say, but he never finished that thought. "Do you hear that?" he asked instead.

I did. It was our message for pilots. "It's coming from over there," I said pointing to the left.

———

Blaine followed the sound of the recording, which was a few blocks away.

"That's not part of their route," I said, fingering a spot on the map.

"They were probably chased off, like us," Blaine said.

When we reached the car, the black Civic—what was left of it—blocked most of the road. Its doors were flung open, all the windows were busted, and the tires were ripped. But the CD player still worked because the message continued to urge pilots to join the army.

"Where are Josh and Dawn?" I asked.

"I don't know, but I don't want to get trapped behind their car," Blaine said as he backed up and then positioned us alongside the Civic. "See anythin'?"

Unfortunately, I did. Dawn's body lay crumpled face down on the floor of the Honda, one arm protruding onto the street.

"Dawn's dead," I whispered.

"Josh?"

"He's not in the car."

"Then he must've escaped from them," Blaine said. "We've gotta find him."

"But what about the touchers that did this?" I asked. "They're still around here somewhere—so how do we rescue Josh without getting ourselves killed?"

———

Neither of us spoke as we each tried to come up with a rescue plan.

"If we turned off the record, I could think better," Blaine said. "It's so damn loud."

"But if we do that, the touchers will know we're here."

"Good point." Blaine nodded. "We'll leave the message on."

"Where could he be hiding?" I asked. "In one of those houses?" Four small homes lined the left side of the street while an empty lot occupied the entire right side. Maybe the grass had been mowed before the bubbles, but now the lot was filled with tall stalks, weeds — and perhaps touchers. "I don't like all that high grass," I mumbled.

"I don't like anythin' here," Blaine said. "Do you think Josh is watchin' us from one of the windows?"

I looked at the row of buildings again. Most windows were smashed and two front doors were wide open. "He could be anywhere," I said. "Maybe he's not even on this street."

"He'd stay near the car figurin' the army'd send someone to..."

Before Blaine finished his sentence, a group of touchers rushed from the end of the block towards our car. "Time to go!" he shouted, throwing the car into reverse and quickly backing out of the street.

"Want me to squirt them?" I asked.

"No! Too many. We gotta get outta here." At the main road, he shifted gears and sped away.

When I turned, the band of touchers had just reached the street and stood there, watching our car. "They're not following us," I said.

"That's because we're movin' too fast."

"What now?"

"I'm gonna turn around, come back, and park near here, but not on the block with Josh's car. Maybe those touchers'll think they've chased us away and leave."

———

We parked around the corner from the broken Civic. Although we could still hear the recorded message, it wasn't nearly as loud. "No touchers yet," I said.

"At least the noise'll keep them from hearin' our car," Blaine pointed out.

"Should we get out and look for Josh?"

"With all those touchers and just the two of us and our water guns?"

Folding my arms, I frowned at Blaine. "We can't just sit here and wait forever."

"I thought we'd wait another five minutes and then check the top of the street." He smiled at me. "Is that too long?"

"No."

"Glad you agree."

His attitude annoyed me, but this wasn't the time to start a fight. "What about the flying ones?" I asked, looking out the window.

"We haven't seen any here."

"But when we drove away, the others could've signaled them."

"If the flying touchers show up, we'll deal with them then."

We sat without talking, listening to the loud recording until I heard a new sound. "Something's happening over there," I said, pointing in the direction of the busted Civic.

―――――

As we neared the black Honda, I saw where the noise was coming from. It was Josh.

"Stop!" he shouted, waving his hands as he raced towards us. The group of touchers that had been after us was behind him, only a few feet away and gaining fast.

"Slow the car so I can squirt them!" I yelled. Opening my window slightly, I aimed at the closest toucher, a big man-thing. "Got him!" I shouted. The male toucher stopped running, grabbed its leg, and tried to scrub off the offensive water.

But the other touchers had nearly reached Josh. As one lunged for his shoulder, I squeezed the trigger again, wetting the thing's outstretched arm. Immediately, that toucher—a teenage boy— lowered its arm and shook it really hard.

Josh was almost alongside our car with the remaining touchers still trying to grab him. One dove at his leg, but I squirted the thing's hand just before it reached its target. "I'm opening the door for Josh!" I hollered as I unlocked the rear passenger door and flung it open. "Hurry!" I yelled. "Get in!"

Josh tumbled into the car, slammed the door shut, and locked it. Then he lay face up across the back seat, panting for breath. He looked like he'd lost a fight: His face and arms were scratched and bruised and his clothes were ripped and filthy. But he was very much alive.

Josh saw me smiling at him and gave a thumbs-up. Then he closed his eyes and continued to lie on the seat, still breathing hard.

———

This time the band of touchers followed us, racing to keep up with the car. I heard a loud thud as a rock bounced off the trunk and fell on the street.

"Can...you...go...faster?" Josh managed to ask.

"When I get to the main road," Blaine said. At the corner, he turned onto Hamilton, picking up speed.

I peeked out my window and smiled at Josh. "We're losing them," I told him.

Josh, sitting up now, nodded at me. Then he leaned his head against the seat and closed his eyes.

"It must've been real bad," I said.

"Yeah."

I didn't push it. "You don't have to talk about what happened."

Josh nodded again, his eyes still closed.

Except for me giving Blaine directions, no one spoke as we drove back to the base. Then something hard fell on the roof of the car, jolting us. Blaine lost control of the steering wheel and we veered to the other side of the road.

"Watch out!" I shouted as we headed for a collision with one of the many smashed cars.

Blaine grabbed the wheel and steered us back in the lane just before we crashed.

I looked out my window again, this time staring up. "It must've been another rock," I said. "There's a group of flying touchers following us and they've got rocks between their legs."

"If they keep throwing rocks at the car, the roof'll cave in," Josh said.

I glanced at the roof, which was already badly dented. "What'll we do?" I asked Blaine.

"We gotta keep movin'. But maybe there's a way to hold them

off."

———

Blaine's idea was to zigzag. "Like playin' a video game," he explained. "When you want to get around obstacles, you don't steer straight. I'm gonna drive fast, but cockeyed—so y'all hang on! It's gonna be a bumpy ride!"

Another rock hit the roof, but this time Blaine held on to the wheel and controlled the car. As I clutched the seat, he moved the car from side to side like skiing down a mountain around the flags.

One rock missed the car, bouncing hard on the road on my side, but the next hit the back edge of the roof, near Josh. "Are you okay?" I called.

"Yeah," Josh said. "But it's getting a little tight."

Part of the roof had caved in, forcing Josh to crouch low. "We're almost there," I told him. "Only about a mile to go."

There was another loud crash as a rock hit the trunk, flinging it open. "Can you still drive?" I asked Blaine.

"That's not the problem," he said. "Look behind you."

Turning around, I saw what he meant. A flying toucher stood in the open trunk staring right at me.

"Watch out, Josh!" I shouted. "There's a toucher in the trunk!" I handed him one of my water guns. "Use this."

As I ducked down, I heard water being sprayed and when I lifted my head again, the toucher was gone. "Josh!" I called. "You saved us! You squirted it just in time."

Josh lay with his eyes closed, leaning against the back seat, and didn't answer me.

"Josh...?" I repeated. Then I turned to Blaine. "Is he...?"

Blaine nodded solemnly. "I think so," he said. "It must've touched Josh as he fired the gun."

———

I had no time to think about Josh. Even though we were almost at the base, the touchers were out there and our car had a collapsed roof and an open trunk. Clutching my remaining water pistol, I checked the sky. "I don't see any more flying ones," I reported.

"Good," Blaine said as he turned into the driveway at the "Ridgeview Corporate Park" sign and began the long approach to the base.

"They could be hiding in the grass again," I whispered.

"Just a little further..."

Something moved in the grass. I opened my window a little and forced the pistol through. The grass fluttered again and a rabbit hopped out. *A bunny!* I hadn't seen any since the bubbles. This one was brown with a fluffy little white tail, like a cotton ball...

"Erin, what's goin' on? I heard you open the window."

"It's nothing. Just a cute little bunny."

We reached the parking lot and Blaine turned off the car. I looked at Josh's body in the back seat and forgot about the bunny. *Some rescue mission.* Josh and Dawn were both dead and we didn't even know what happened to them. And now we never would.

CHAPTER 8 – The Pilot

Bad news travels fast. By the time Blaine and I returned to the Unit 4 building after our debriefing, everyone knew about Josh and Dawn.

"It's so sad," Rayna said as I lay on my cot, staring at the ceiling.

"Yeah."

"It's not your fault."

"Not with Dawn. She was already dead when we got there. But we found Josh and got him into our car. He was alive..."

"It could've happened to anyone."

"But it didn't happen to anyone. It happened to Blaine and me." I turned away from Rayna. "I don't want to talk about it anymore. I just want to rest."

"Sure."

I heard Rayna's footsteps as she left the room and shut the door.

Closing my eyes, I tried to force myself to sleep, but my mind was too active. *Could've saved him...Should've saved him...*I threw the pillow over my head and started counting. When I reached one thousand, I was still wide-awake.

———

I must have fallen asleep because I was jolted awake by the loud gong signaling dinner. As I ran to join the rest of my unit for the trip to Headquarters—accompanied by two guards—I realized I was very hungry.

When I took my regular seat in the cafeteria with my friends, Manny leaned across the table. "A guy who works in Headquarters told me there's a pilot here," he whispered. "So someone got our message this morning."

"That would be great if it's true," I said. "I could use some good news."

Blaine squeezed my hand tightly.

I devoured all the food on my plate and then grabbed Blaine's leftover slice of bread. Roxanne noticed. "Wow!" she said. "You're really hungry."

I nodded and continued chewing. When I finally stopped thinking about food, I turned my attention to the room. As I scanned the tables, my eyes met Lourdes, sitting by herself. She glared at me. *If looks could kill...*

Turning my head away, I tugged on Blaine's shirt. "Lourdes is mad at me again," I whispered.

"It's probably because of what happened to Josh."

"Does she think I wanted him to die? I should talk to her and explain." As I started to stand, Blaine grabbed my arm and pulled me down.

"No."

"Blaine's right," Rayna said. "There's really nothing you can say."

I peeked at Lourdes again and she was no longer looking at me. Her head was lowered and when I squinted, trying to get a better look, I saw tears rolling down her cheeks.

———

Manny's news was true. Our messages near the airport had persuaded at least one pilot to join the army. "Please welcome our newest recruit," Major Figueroa said after dinner, extending his arm towards a pretty blonde. "This is Captain Kim Stevenson. She's a certified pilot and she's volunteered to teach our soldiers how to fly planes."

"That's a pilot?" I whispered to Blaine. Kim Stevenson was young and tall with very long legs. Even in her torn jeans, she looked more like a model than a pilot.

"I can't wait to learn how to fly a plane," Blaine said.

I poked him gently in the arm.

Kim Stevenson talked a little about her experience, saying she'd worked for the post office for three years, flying mail planes. "So I haven't flown large aircraft," she explained. "But I'd be glad to teach you the basics of flying a plane. Like everyone else, I want to destroy those yellow things. I'm so glad you guys found me..."

She stopped talking and started to cry. "I'm sorry," she said moments later, wiping the tears. "It's just that it's so hard, especially after losing my husband, my parents—everything..." She walked back to her seat and sat, head down, her long blonde hair hiding her face.

"Thank you, Captain Stevenson," Major Figueroa said. "We all understand what you've gone through." He studied the room. "Now I need volunteers for flight training. Of course it'll mean going to the airport and securing planes, which, as you know, won't be easy." He shrugged, holding out his arms, palms up. "But that's where the planes are. So who wants to be a pilot? I'll take the first ten."

Blaine's arm shot up immediately, followed by Manny's. I counted six other arms—and then, suddenly, like an independent thing, my arm rose too.

Did I really want to be a pilot? I'd dreamt of becoming a famous artist, which was now impossible. But somehow I became a member of Kim Stevenson's first flight class. Of my close friends, Blaine and Manny would be joining me; Rayna and Roxanne hadn't volunteered.

"I've always been scared to fly," Rayna explained after dinner as we returned to our building. "Every time I went on a plane, I made sure to sit away from the window so I didn't have to look out. And when the plane took off and landed, I always read a book or listened to music—anything to forget where I was." She chuckled. "I could never be a pilot unless there was a way to fly with my eyes closed."

Roxanne nodded. "I can't imagine flying a plane," she said. "I got my driver's license just before the bubbles and had enough trouble figuring out how to operate a car. It took me three tries before I passed the road test."

"You're very brave," Rayna said, smiling at me.

"Or very stupid," I murmured.

"No," Roxanne said. "You must be mechanically gifted because you learned how to drive a car so fast. That means you'll be good flying a plane."

"You think?"

"Definitely!" Roxanne put her arm around my shoulders and gave me a quick squeeze.

I still didn't know if I'd made the right decision. But having girlfriends made me feel really good.

———

Our first flying session with Kim Stevenson was set for the next morning at zero nine hundred hours. After breakfast, a guard escorted Blaine, Manny, and me to Headquarters along with Darryl, the other Unit 4 volunteer.

Darryl had been on my team when I first joined the army and I'd been scared of him then because he was so big. But he was soft-spoken and funny. "So you're gonna be a pilot, Erin," he teased. "What makes you think you can fly a plane?"

"I learned to drive a car in one morning." I liked Roxanne's reasoning.

Darryl snickered. "You think flying a plane's as easy as driving a car?"

"I hope so."

He tapped my shoulder and grinned. "You're a smart girl. I'm sure you'll do just fine."

"So you'll be my co-pilot when we go hunting for touchers?" I asked.

Darryl shook his head and laughed. "No way, girl! I'm not that brave!" He gave my shoulder another tap and walked away, making me question the good things he'd said.

Blaine, who'd been in front of me talking to Manny, turned and winked. "Why so serious?" he asked.

"I'm just wondering if I can do this."

"Sure you can. You'll make a great pilot." Reaching over, Blaine pulled me close and gave me a giant hug.

———

The pilot-training class gathered in the lobby of the Headquarters building. There were seven guys and three girls. One of the women was a chubby-cheeked lady with glasses, who looked like my biology teacher, Mrs. Hurwitz. I'd never liked Mrs. Hurwitz because she gave us surprise quizzes, but I tried to put that negative image out of my head when I introduced myself.

"Hi," I said, extending my hand and smiling. "I'm Erin."

"Flo," she replied, pumping my hand as she examined me carefully. "You don't look old enough to do this, hon." Her eyes stared through me like a doctor reading an x-ray. "Got any experience?"

"No," I said, trying not to show how uncomfortable she was making me feel. "Do you?"

"I flew a coupla times with my cousin who was a pilot and had a small plane. Kinda liked it."

I smiled again and rushed away before she could ask any more questions.

The second woman was younger, probably in her late twenties, with light brown skin and curly dark hair. She stood by herself with her arms folded, watching everyone else. "My name's Erin," I said, smiling as I reached her.

"I'm Carmen," she said. "I saw you talking to the witch."

"Flo?"

Carmen nodded. "That's her. Witch of the west, or east, or wherever we are in this new world. She's the head witch."

"Why do you say that?"

"You'll see," Carmen said. "Just make sure you never fly a plane alone with her."

———

Our first lesson was held inside the classroom where we received mission instructions. We again sat in the seats with attached desks, which had notebooks and pens ready for us.

"Good morning, class," Captain Stevenson said, smiling. "It feels weird saying that. I never thought I'd be a teacher. Everybody, please call me 'Kim.'"

I smiled back. Kim was nice so maybe training to be a pilot wouldn't be so tough.

"We're going to start by learning all the parts of a plane," she continued. "Someone found a poster that I'm going to hang up." She unfolded a picture of a plane and taped it to the wall, covering the street map. The names of the parts had been written in black marker.

"Okay," Kim said. "Let's review what makes up a plane..."

I tried to concentrate, taking notes about all the things on the plane. Some parts I knew—wing, cockpit, engine. But there were parts I'd never heard of—fuselage, slats, rudder, aileron, stabilizer.

Kim talked for about half an hour before asking for questions. When she did, I immediately raised my hand.

"There's so much to learn," I said. "Can we get written information and maybe a picture of an airplane like the poster?"

Kim shook her head. "I'm sorry. We don't have any books about planes and I don't have the time to write everything out." She pointed to the poster. "This is the only picture. But you can draw an airplane. It's really pretty simple."

Duh! I was supposed to be an artist, but since becoming a soldier, I hadn't drawn anything. Picking up the pen, I quickly sketched a plane and began labeling the parts.

"Hey, that's a great plane!" Manny said, snatching my notebook and showing Kim my picture. "Can we make copies for all of us?"

"Good idea," Kim said, smiling at me. "I didn't know you were an artist."

"I used to be," I murmured.

———

Class lasted until lunch. "That's enough for one morning," Kim told us. "I want all of you to spend the rest of today studying your notes. Then tomorrow, we're going to the airport to get inside a plane. They found a couple that seem okay and I'm checking them out this afternoon."

"Need any help?' Blaine asked.

"You need to study today's lesson," Kim said.

"I'm a fast learner. I can review everythin' tonight."

"Well..."

Before she could finish, I interrupted. "Can I go too?"

Kim smiled at me. "I know. You're another fast learner."

I shrugged, not wanting to brag.

"All right," Kim said. "The two of you can come with me. But we'll talk planes along the way."

"What about the rest of us?" Manny asked. "Maybe we should all go."

Kim shook her head. "That won't work because we're just taking one car. We'll meet tomorrow after breakfast to head out to the airport so I'll see you then."

As I picked up my notebook and turned to leave the room, Flo blocked my path. "Brown nose," she said, scowling at me.

"What do you mean?" I'd never heard those words.

"Sucking up to the teacher like that."

"Blaine asked first," I argued. "And it sounded like a good idea so I volunteered."

"Yeah," Flo snickered. "Teacher's pets—both of you."

Blaine, Kim, and I were escorted to the parking lot by Millie, an older lady with curly gray hair who reminded me of my grandma—who I'd probably never see again—and Carlos, a young guy with a slight Spanish accent, who looked really strong. But that wouldn't help us if we ran into touchers.

"Wow!" I said to Kim. "Two guards. You must really rate."

Kim shook her head. "It's not about me," she said. "It's because I'm the only pilot and the army needs me to teach you how to fly."

We reached the parking lot and Carlos waved us towards a banged-up black SUV. "Does this thing work?" Blaine asked.

"Yeah," Carlos said, his voice surprisingly soft. "They didn't have no time to fix the dents, but the mechanic said it runs real good."

As Blaine started getting into the driver's seat, Carlos stopped him. "Sorry, kid," he said. "Orders are for me to drive." He pointed to Kim. "And she's to go in the front."

Blaine and I stepped into the back with Millie sitting in the middle. "Here," she said, handing each of us a loaded water pistol. "Just in case." Millie sounded tough, not at all like my Grandma Fay, who loved to bake cookies for me and Danny.

"Erin!"

I heard Blaine and snapped out of memory lane.

"What?"

"I asked if you remembered the roads we took to the airport."

"Not really." *Grandma Fay made the best lemon cookies. The cookies were delicious warm when they were still soft and gooey. One time, I ate so many that I threw up and Mom thought I had a virus.*

"We made a left on Hazelton and then a right onto Highcrest Parkway South and we looped at...Erin, what was the name of the street where we made the loop?"

"Laguna Road." *No more Grandma...No more lemon cookies.*

———

After Carlos got past the driveway with nothing attacking us from the tall grass, he headed to the airport. As he drove, the rest of us watched for touchers.

Like always, the roads were empty of traffic and full of smashed cars, rotting bodies, packs of scrawny dogs and cats, disgusting rats, and zillions of bugs. I tried to remember what ordinary roads used to look like—cars traveling on clean clear streets with open windows and fresh air.

We reached the airport without seeing any touchers. "Why aren't they attacking?" I asked Blaine. "They must have noticed us."

"Maybe they want to find out what we're doin' first."

"See the white plane on the runway with the stairs down?" Kim said. "We're going to check that one."

Carlos parked next to the small plane.

"Let's go," Kim said, opening her door.

"Wait!" Millie ordered. "We've got to make sure it's okay."

"All right." Kim closed the door. "But please hurry."

Carlos stepped outside, aiming his water gun in front of him. Then he walked to the plane and peeked through a window. It must have looked clear because he climbed the stairs and entered the plane, shutting the door behind him.

Kim, Blaine, Millie, and I sat in the car, waiting. About five minutes passed and Carlos didn't return.

"It's been too long," Blaine said. "Somethin' must've happened."

"I agree," Kim said, opening her door.

"No!" Millie reached forward and grabbed the pilot's arm. "You're not going anywhere."

"We can't just leave him," Kim argued.

"My orders are to protect all of you," Millie said, "so no one's getting out."

"But..." Kim began.

"She's right," Blaine interrupted. "If touchers are inside the plane, Carlos is already dead."

"My plane..." Kim murmured.

"Not yet," Millie said. "Unless you want it to be your coffin."

"What are we going to do?" Kim asked.

"We're going to sit and wait," Millie replied. She pointed to Blaine. "Climb into the driver's seat and we'll watch the plane."

We sat in the car for what seemed like hours. But when I checked Blaine's watch, I saw it had just been ten minutes. The airport was totally silent and looked deserted—no dogs, cats, or rats and no disgusting bugs. I stared at the white plane again and...

"What was that?" I asked.

Blaine gave me a puzzled look.

"Something moved inside the plane."

"Carlos?" Millie asked.

"I'm not sure it was a person," I said.

We were all quiet again as we studied the plane. Something dashed in front of a window and then disappeared. "There!" I pointed to the spot. "Did you see that?"

"Yeah," Blaine said. "It was fast. But it wasn't yellow so it's not a toucher."

"It's some kind of animal," Kim said. "Light brown fur."

"Just one?" I asked. "Maybe it's a pack, like the dogs and cats."

"It looked bigger," Millie said. "And I think I saw two."

"How'd they get in if the door was closed?" I asked.

"Maybe it wasn't," Kim said. "The army unlocked the door so I could check the plane and maybe they didn't close it all the way."

"What would an animal want in a plane?" I asked.

"Food," Blaine said. "With animals, it's always about food."

"So how do we get them out?" I continued. "Does anybody have food?"

Kim reached into the pocket of her jeans. "I saved a piece of bread from lunch," she said, producing a napkin-covered lump.

"How about this?" Millie asked, waving a candy bar.

"We can try to lure the animals out with our food," I said. "But what if they think we'd make a better meal and go after us? We don't have anything to fight them with."

Millie shook her head. "Not true," she said, flashing a switchblade knife.

"Me too," Blaine said, holding a similar small knife.

"It's not enough," I said. "Those little knives won't stop a big animal."

Blaine snickered at me. "It's not a lion, Erin."

"You don't know what it is." I faced the guard. "And Millie said it looked big."

"All right," Blaine said, smiling. "You have a point. Maybe there's somethin' behind the back seats we can use as a weapon."

Climbing into the storage area, I found a black bag tucked into a built-in slot next to the spare tire. Inside the bag were a few metal tools. "What are these?" I asked, holding up a heavy diamond-shaped silver thing and then a much lighter L-shaped long black rod.

"Stuff for changin' a tire," Blaine said. "But they can double as weapons. Take them out."

I gave Kim the metal rod and rested the bulkier tool on my lap.

"Okay," Blaine said. "We're as ready as we can be."

———

Blaine quickly placed pieces of bread and candy bar on the ground near the entrance to the plane. Then he ran back inside the SUV and locked the door.

We waited again.

"Maybe they don't see it," I said when nothing happened. "The food's so small."

"We've got to get their attention," Kim said. She fingered the steering wheel. "What about honking the horn?"

"That could bring touchers," Blaine said.

"They could already be on the plane," I pointed out.

Blaine shook his head. "They would've attacked us by now, especially when I ran out."

"Millie?" Kim asked, turning to the back seat. "What do you say? Should we honk?"

The guard spread her hands and sighed. "You may as well. We can't sit here forever and Carlos is still inside the plane."

Blaine honked the horn three times. It sounded very loud, especially because the airport was so quiet.

Again nothing happened.

He honked three more times, pressing on the horn a little longer.

"If the animals don't come out, the touchers..." I started to say, but stopped when the door of the plane slowly opened.

————

There were two animals and they were much bigger than dogs and cats. Their fur was a yellowish brown, but it was loose and straggly, not healthy-looking. The creatures were so scrawny that I could make out the shape of all their bones.

"What are they?" I whispered.

"I was wrong," Blaine said. "They are lions—mountain lions, I think."

"Really?" I'd never seen mountain lions anywhere but in a zoo.

"Poor things must've been starving wherever they used to live," Kim murmured as the two animals chomped down our food in seconds. When they finished, they both turned to the car, seeming to notice us for the first time.

"Guess we're the dessert," Blaine muttered.

As if it agreed with Blaine, the larger lion trotted to my window and opened its mouth wide. Those teeth looked really sharp.

"What do we do now?" I asked. "We can't go out or they'll rip us into pieces and then eat us." I didn't know if that would happen, but it seemed possible.

"Let me honk the horn again," Blaine suggested. "Maybe it'll scare them." He pressed on the horn and both animals jumped back. But as soon as Blaine stopped honking, the creatures returned to the SUV, circling the car and sniffing the tires.

"Drive away before they bite a tire," Millie ordered.

"And leave Carlos?" I asked.

"Just for now," Millie said. "Until we can shoo the lions away."

"They could go back into the plane," Kim said.

"Or they could go somewhere else in the airport," Blaine added.

"But we..." I didn't finish my sentence because two touchers were running towards our SUV.

———

Since we no longer had a choice, Blaine drove off the runway and onto the road that circled the airport. When I turned around, I saw the touchers had stopped running and now stood in front of the plane, watching our car.

But the mountain lions had disappeared. Maybe they went back inside the plane or maybe they went someplace else in the airport, like Blaine suggested. "I don't think touchers can kill animals," I said.

"But those monsters sure can kill people," Millie said. "If they get into the plane and Carlos isn't dead already, they'll kill him."

We were all quiet because we knew Millie was right.

"We can't just leave him here," Kim finally said.

"We won't," Blaine assured her. "We just have to be better prepared."

"We've still got water and our weapons," Millie pointed out.

"It's not enough," Blaine said, shaking his head. "Not to fight both touchers and lions."

"But the lions might not be in the plane anymore," I said.

"True," Blaine agreed. "But they could be. The touchers could be gone too—or they could be in the plane. It's impossible for us to know for sure without going in there."

"How much extra water do you have?" I asked Millie.

"Why?"

"If I get myself all wet, the touchers won't bother me."

"Are you sure?"

"It's always worked."

Millie took a bottle of water from the pocket of her jeans. "Will this be enough?"

I shrugged my shoulders. "It'll have to be."

"Why should you be the one to risk your life?" Kim asked. "We should at least choose."

"No," I said. "I'm the smallest by far so I need much less water than anyone else. Also, I've done this before." I took Millie's bottle and carefully wet my body, concentrating on my shoulders, arms, legs, and hair—parts touchers could reach most easily.

When Blaine returned to the runway, neither the touchers nor the animals were outside the small white plane. Gripping the metal diamond-shaped tool, I got out of the SUV and climbed the steps leading to the plane's door.

———

The door was halfway open so I slipped inside, trying not to make noise and holding the metal tire tool in front of me, ready to use it on a mountain lion. But I didn't see or hear any animal. The only thing on the floor of the plane was Carlos, face down in a puddle of blood. His shirt was ripped apart and his back was full of animal bites and claw marks and some looked deep. Blood was still oozing from a long gash on his left arm.

I rolled Carlos over as carefully as I could. He was unconscious, but breathing softly so at least he was still alive. While I didn't know how badly he was hurt, I knew he needed help as soon as possible.

I took one step towards the exit and stopped. A toucher stood inside the doorway, blocking my escape. Hoping I was wet enough, I raised my arm and waved it at the yellow woman-thing. "Go away!"

I shouted. "I'm wet! Water!" Then I shoved my fingers into my ponytail and wrung it, flinging the drops at the toucher.

The woman-thing stepped to the side to avoid the water, but didn't leave.

Lifting my pistol from my pocket, I moved toward the toucher, again waving my wet arms. "Water!" I shouted, squirting the creature's face. "Wet!"

The woman-thing immediately pawed its face, but didn't back away.

This wasn't good. Soon my water gun would be empty and I'd be dry. "Leave!" I yelled, spraying the creature's bare legs.

Although the toucher reached down to rub its legs, it didn't move. I figured my water pistol had one squirt left so I wanted to aim for the face again, thinking that would bother it the most. But since its face was still lowered, I waited.

"Erin!"

I heard Blaine's voice outside the plane.

"Don't come in here!" I shouted. "There's a toucher right inside the door!"

"I know! Try to force it to go out and then back off!"

The toucher had finished drying its legs and took a step towards me. "This is the end of my water!" I yelled as I sprayed the woman-thing between the eyes.

That squirt really bothered the toucher. Its blank face seemed to pucker and, walking backwards, it stumbled out the door.

Moving as fast as I could, I ran to the door and slammed it shut. Since I didn't see any lock, I leaned my body against the door, knowing it wouldn't help if the toucher wanted to get inside because the yellow monster was much stronger than me. But doing something made me feel better.

"Get the toucher away from the plane!" I yelled, not knowing if Blaine and the others could hear me. "Carlos is alive, but he needs a doctor!"

Then I stood against the door and waited.

———

I heard Blaine talking, but couldn't make out his words so I ran to a window and looked outside. Two touchers—the woman-thing that had been in the plane, still wiping its wet face, and a smaller girl-thing—stood in front of the plane, keeping the others from reaching me.

I studied the cabin, looking for something that could help. There wasn't much—just four seats and a small pull-down table. In the back area behind where Carlos lay, still not moving, was a two-foot long rectangular box, attached to the plane.

Walking carefully around Carlos, I unlatched the box. It held supplies: a first-aid kit, towels, soap, a couple bags of pretzels. I pulled out mostly everything, figuring I could use towels and first-aid stuff for Carlos and stashed a bag of pretzels in my pocket.

Then I dug further. *Yes!* On the bottom were two bottles of water! After emptying most of the contents of one into my gun, I shoved both bottles into my pocket and returned to the window.

The touchers were heading towards the SUV. Kim and Millie sat inside, but Blaine stood in front of the car, holding just the long tire tool.

Running out of the plane, I fired at both touchers, hitting them squarely in the backs of their heads. They turned and I squirted them again, getting the woman in its face and the girl in its hands. As they concentrated on scrubbing off the water, I ran to the SUV.

"Quick!" Millie said, opening the back door for me.

Blaine slid into the driver's seat and started the car. As he drove off the runway, the touchers were still wiping away the terrible water.

———

"Good timin', Erin," Blaine said as he reached the road. "I thought I was done."

"Lucky I found two bottles of water. But we've got to get Carlos out."

"What happened?" Millie asked. "Is he alive?"

"Barely. The lions attacked him so he's unconscious and there's lots of blood."

"How can we save him?" Kim asked.

"I don't know," I said. "Those touchers are right there and if they go inside..." I stopped talking and tried to remember if I'd closed the plane's door when I ran out. I wasn't sure.

Blaine stopped the car and made a U-turn. "We'll go back and try again," he said. "Erin, you said you found water. Did you use it all up?"

I shook my head. "No. I've still got one full bottle and some of the other. Think that'll be enough?"

"It better be," Blaine said.

———

Blaine again drove the SUV onto the runway next to the small plane. "I don't see those touchers," he said, shutting off the car.

I didn't see them either, but that didn't mean they weren't inside the plane. "We have to take a chance and go in," I said.

"Give me the water," Blaine said, stretching his arm towards me. "I'll do it."

"No." I moved the bottle out of his reach. "I'm still damp from before so I'll go again."

"Both of you, stop arguing," Kim said. "It's my plane so I'm going in there."

Millie spoke next. "Two of you should go and you should choose who goes," she said.

"We don't have enough water to protect two of us," I pointed out.

"If there's no toucher inside and Carlos is still alive, you girls won't be able to haul him out of the plane and into the car," Blaine argued.

"We don't have to get him out," Kim whispered.

The rest of us stopped talking and looked at her.

"What do you mean?" I asked.

"The army fueled the plane for me," Kim explained. "I can fly it to the base."

"What about checking it?" Blaine asked.

"If you two cover me, I can do a quick outdoor inspection and then check the instrument panels inside."

"What do you think?" I asked Millie.

The guard shrugged. "I've been staring at the plane while you've all been talking and nothing's moved inside," she said. "Of course they could still be there."

"We're goin' in anyway," Blaine said. "Can you drive the car back?"

Millie nodded. "Just give me directions."

I did.

————

The three of us made it to the plane without meeting any touchers or lions. As Blaine and I stood watch, Kim examined the plane's body. "It's all good," she said, caressing the wing and smiling. "Let's go in."

We climbed the steps to the door, which was closed—hopefully because I'd been the last one inside and remembered to shut it. With each of us aiming our water guns, Blaine flung the door wide open. It was quiet and the plane seemed empty, except for Carlos, who still lay on the floor in the rear.

Kim rushed to the cockpit as Blaine and I checked Carlos. He looked the same: His eyes were still closed and he was breathing softly. The only difference was the bleeding had almost stopped.

I pointed to the first aid kit, on the floor where I'd left it. "Can we use anything from that to help him?" I asked.

Blaine opened the box and rummaged through it. "Not really," he said, shaking his head. "We need big bandages, not these little things." He held up a few band-aids.

"Maybe we can at least clean him," I suggested, grabbing one of the towels. Carefully, I patted the bite and claw marks and added water to wipe the blood from the gash on his arm.

"How're you doin'?" Blaine called to Kim.

"Almost done!" she shouted.

"Is the plane okay?" I asked.

"Yup!" Kim shouted. "Get into the seats and fasten your belts. We're flying back to the base."

————

I'd been on a plane twice in my life. When I was twelve, I'd gone with my family to visit Grandma Fay in Florida and I remember looking out the window and being amazed at how little the houses and cars looked—like toys. The only other time I'd been in a plane was when I was three and I don't remember that ride at all.

But this was different. The plane was small and Kim wasn't flying very high so I had a good view of the ground. Things below didn't look tiny, but everything looked broken, even most of the houses. Cars were stopped in strange positions along nearly every road and from the sky, they looked even more smashed and twisted.

"How long will this ride take?" I asked, turning away from the window.

"Less than five minutes," Kim said. "And most of that time will be in the landing. We're approaching the base now."

As she spoke, I saw the executive park ahead.

"Where are you goin' to land?" Blaine asked.

Kim pointed to the long driveway. "There's plenty of room in the field surrounding the base," she said. "That's where I'm heading." She pulled a lever and the plane started dropping.

"Isn't the grass too high?" I asked.

Kim shrugged. "I don't have much choice."

"The parking lot would be better," Blaine suggested.

"Yes. But I didn't tell them I was bringing the plane so cars are parked there."

I caught a glimpse of the lot and there wasn't room for any plane, even a small one.

"Hold on tight," Kim said. "We're ready to land."

———

It felt a little bumpy as the plane skidded through the tall grass until it finally stopped. Through my window, I saw the parking lot and the buildings a few hundred feet away.

"We've got company," Blaine said, pointing to his window on the opposite side. Three touchers ran towards us, each holding rocks and branches.

"We can't make it to the base," I whispered. "It's too far for us to run—and they're much faster."

"Can you take off again and circle around till it's clear?" Blaine asked Kim.

"I could except..." The pilot turned her chin to the front of the plane where two more touchers were flying right at us.

"We're trapped," I said. "There's no place to go." I pulled my pistol and extra bottle of water from my pocket. "I guess we can wet ourselves and fight them. Maybe it'll work for a while." I didn't believe my words, feeling like Butch Cassidy and the Sundance Kid in that old movie my dad loved. They had gone down fighting.

Blaine unbuckled his seatbelt and walked to me. "I'm sorry, Erin," he whispered, leaning down and kissing my cheek.

"Me too," I said, trying not to cry.

The touchers had reached the plane and were pounding the sides with their rocks and sticks. Then the flying ones must have landed on the top because we heard and felt banging above us.

"They're breaking my plane," Kim said, her voice quivering. She had left the pilot's seat and stood next to us, watching the touchers. "I so wanted to help."

"You tried," I said, taking her hand.

The three of us huddled together, waiting for the inevitable.

———

The pounding continued as the touchers concentrated on breaking the door. "Can we put something in front to jam it?" I asked, looking around the cabin.

"What's the use?" Blaine asked. "They're still gonna get in."

"I know," I agreed. "But we can at least make it harder for them." I didn't see anything strong. In fact, the only loose piece of equipment was the supply box so I squirted the box with water and stuck it in front of the door. "At least they won't like it," I whispered.

The banging on the door got much louder as the touchers threw their bodies against it.

"Get ready," Blaine said, aiming his gun.

*My last fight...*I pointed my pistol at the door and waited.

The door flew open and a small man-thing fell against the box.

As the toucher picked itself up, rubbing the water from its arms and legs, Blaine rushed towards the yellow creature and squirted its face. The toucher took a step back and continued to wipe away the water.

A bigger man-thing and young girl toucher entered together. I squirted the girl's face while Blaine hit the man's arm. The girl-thing stopped, but the man toucher kept walking, heading for Kim, who stood motionless, like in a trance.

"Squirt him!" I yelled, trying to spray its face. But my aim was bad and I hit nothing.

Kim woke up and squeezed the trigger, spraying the toucher in its eyes. The man-thing dropped to the floor, pawing at the water with its yellow hands.

Having dried itself, the smaller man toucher rushed at me and I squirted its head with the last of my water. "My gun's empty!" I yelled.

"Mine too!" Blaine shouted. "Kim?"

"One or two shots left!"

"Make them good!" I said as two touchers with flapping wings stepped into the crowded plane.

Kim sprayed the teen boy-thing in the forehead and the big woman-thing in the neck and both stopped to wipe off the water. But the other three touchers were now dry and they surrounded us.

"Bye," I whispered, clutching Blaine's arm.

———

While I waited to die, a hose appeared in the door followed by a heavy stream of water, drenching Blaine, Kim, me, and all the touchers.

"I got it now!" a familiar voice yelled. "This is the good stuff!"

As we scrambled away from the touchers and rushed to the doorway, Manny stepped inside, still aiming a hose on the five things that now lay on the floor of the plane, arms and legs swinging.

"What took you so long?" Blaine asked. "They were just about to touch us."

"When we saw the plane land, we had to get the Jeep set up," Manny explained. "But I'm here now." He smiled at Blaine as he continued to hose the touchers.

The girl and smaller man-thing were no longer moving. "Are they dead?" I asked.

"I think so," Manny said. "But just in case..." He gave them another dousing and then went back to squirting the moving touchers.

"Hurry," I told Manny. "Carlos, the guard, is in the back of the plane and he's hurt." I pointed to the rear where his legs were visible.

"Almost done." The two flying touchers and bigger man-thing had stopped moving, but Manny continued to soak them with the formula. "Okay!" he called. "Shut it off, Rox!"

As the water stopped flowing, Manny dropped the hose. "Get Carlos and then we're outta here," he said, hugging Blaine and me.

Sloshing through the plane, the guys gently picked up Carlos and carried him to the Jeep, stepping around the bodies of touchers. Kim and I followed behind them. Outside, I hugged Roxanne while Blaine and Manny placed Carlos on the back seat. Then Kim and I scrambled into the storage area.

As Manny drove to the lot, Kim looked behind her. "My poor plane," she murmured.

CHAPTER 9 – The Hike

While the army worked on fixing, cleaning, and drying the plane, I heard that scientists had taken the dead touchers to their lab. They were still trying to figure out what happened with the bubbles—how normal people had been turned into yellow monsters.

As I waited to start flying lessons, I hung out with Blaine, Manny, Rayna, and Roxanne. The first thing we did during free time the next morning after breakfast was go to the infirmary to visit Carlos.

The infirmary was in the Headquarters building. The army had taken two upstairs offices and torn down the walls to make one big hospital room and right now, Carlos was the only patient. He lay in the bed nearest the door, his body wrapped in bandages like a mummy, with two tubes attached to his arms.

"I didn't expect nothing like this to happen," he said, slurring his words as he motioned to his bandaged body.

"Us neither," Blaine said. "A couple of mountain lions got you."

"That's what they told me," Carlos said. "But I don't remember. Just woke up in this room looking like this." He took a deep breath and groaned. "Those must've been some mean cats."

At least he's alive, I thought, remembering Josh. "You're going to be okay," I whispered, hoping my words were true.

Carlos nodded. "That's what the doctor said. She promised I'm getting out of here next week."

It took the army five days to fix the plane. When it was ready, Kim herded her students into the classroom after breakfast. "I want everyone to go inside the plane now," she said. "It only seats four plus the two cockpit chairs so it'll be crowded. But it's important you're all familiar with the interior. After today, we'll split the class in half for flight lessons."

The army had stationed two guards by the plane, which still rested in the tall grass along the driveway where Kim landed it. We walked along the road with two other guards and then cut through the grass. That's when I heard a flapping noise in the sky and looked up as a group of touchers in their gooselike V-formation approached us.

"Everybody down!" the male guard shouted.

I scrunched low and grabbed my water gun.

"It's not far to the plane," Blaine whispered to me. "We can make it there."

"And then what?" I asked him. "We'll be trapped inside again while they rip the plane apart."

The flying touchers dropped lower, tossing rocks and diving at our heads. After wetting my hair as much as possible, I tried to squirt them, but they were too high.

"We can't stay here," Blaine said. "They'll pick us off, one by one. They don't even have to land. They can just touch us lightly."

Like Charlie. I remembered the street attack as I studied the sky and dodged a large rock.

I heard the sound of tires as a Jeep with a water tank appeared and two soldiers unraveled an attached hose and shot water into the air. They hit three low-flying touchers, knocking them to the ground, and continued to douse the yellow things with the deadly formula. The others—I counted four—quickly flew away.

Getting to my knees, I shook off the loose blades of grass. "Is everyone okay?" I asked Blaine.

He pointed to a group of people, including Kim and Manny,

standing in a crooked circle. "I don't know," he said. "Let's check what's goin' on over there."

When we reached the others, I realized someone was lying on the ground between them, not moving. As I got closer, I saw light brown skin and curly dark hair and recognized the face of the woman who had warned me about Flo. "Her name is Carmen," I whispered.

"Was," Blaine said. "She's dead."

Manny walked up to us. "I seen it happen," he said. "Damn thing flew down and tapped her on the head. Not hard, but that don't matter. I tried to squirt it, but..." His voice faded out and he shrugged.

Darryl had been listening and now spoke in the soft voice that didn't fit his huge body. "But you didn't see why it happened," he said to Manny.

"What do you mean?"

"Carmen wasn't watching the sky." Darryl pointed to Flo, who stood by herself across from us, staring at the body. "That one," he continued. "She gave Carmen a push and when Carmen turned around to find out where the shove came from, that's when the flying yellow thing killed her."

I looked at Flo, who still stared at Carmen's body, no emotion on her face. *Witch.* That's what Carmen had called her. Then Flo lifted her head and smiled at me.

———

The two soldiers in the Jeep took Carmen's body back to Headquarters and the flight class—now just nine—stepped into the plane for our lesson.

I didn't know what to do about Flo and had no time to discuss it with Darryl and Blaine. *Should we say something to Kim or Major Figueroa?* All we had was what Darryl said he saw and he could have been wrong. Maybe it was an accident. Maybe she didn't mean to push Carmen. But what about Carmen's warning?

I shook my head, trying to clear away thoughts of Carmen and Flo so I could concentrate on Kim's lesson. She was touching each part of the plane, explaining what it was, and then questioning us. Although I tried to listen, I couldn't stop watching Flo and when I looked at Blaine and Darryl, they were watching her too.

Kim called my name once to identify some airplane part and when I mumbled the wrong answer, she frowned. "Haven't you been paying attention, Erin?"

"I'm sorry. I'm still thinking about Carmen." *That was true.*

"Yes," Kim said. "What happened to her is very sad. But you need to listen so you can learn how to fly a plane and destroy those yellow monsters."

"I know," I agreed. "I'll do better." I lowered my head, hoping I was telling the truth. When I looked up, Flo was staring at me. Our eyes locked for just a moment and then I turned away. But before I did, Flo smiled again.

I got through the rest of the lesson without any more goof-ups, mostly because I forced myself not to look at Flo. Instead, I glued my eyes to Kim and listened to her words like they were the most important things on earth. And at that time, they probably were.

———

When Kim finished, we walked through the tall grass with the guards, trailed by the Jeep. No touchers attacked us. But I knew the trip would be okay because it had started to rain.

It was the first rain we'd had in a long time and the army must have realized we needed a break because after Carmen's funeral, Major Figueroa gave everyone the afternoon off.

As I stood with my friends, still feeling down, Rayna smiled at me. "Let's do something fun," she suggested. "How about a picnic?"

"A picnic in the rain?" I asked.

"It's not raining that hard," she pointed out. "We could take umbrellas and cover everything."

"I'd rather go on a hike," I said.

"A hike in the rain?" Blaine laughed. "You won't do a picnic, but you want to hike?"

"Yup."

"Where can you hike?" Blaine asked. "There's no woods here."

"Maybe we can leave the base," I suggested.

"And what if it stops rainin' when we're out?" Blaine continued.

"This rain is light, but steady," I said. "It looks like it'll go on all day."

"The captain won't give us permission to leave the grounds," Roxanne said.

"Do we have to tell him?" I asked, smiling at her. "It's just a little hike in the rain. We'll only be gone about an hour."

Roxanne and Manny didn't want to go. "I can't walk that far," Roxanne explained. "I get tired fast."

"Speaking of tired, I just wanna sack out," Manny said, stretching his arms and yawning. "I'm gonna head back to the bunk."

That left Rayna, Blaine, and me. "It's okay if you two want to be by yourselves," Rayna said, her eyes darting back and forth at both of us.

"No," I said, quickly. "We'd really like you to come."

Blaine shot me a dirty look that I pretended not to see. I was a little afraid of being alone with him right now. I knew he wanted to do more than just kiss and I wasn't ready for more so Rayna hiking with Blaine and me seemed like the perfect solution.

———

The three of us went back to Building 4 to get extra water bottles—just in case I was wrong about the weather and the rain stopped. When we met again, Rayna held an umbrella. But I let the rain drip onto my hair, face, and clothes because the mid-August temperature was so warm. Also, it was safer to be wet.

Blaine wore a baseball cap that didn't cover most of his hair. "Which way, girls?" he asked.

"This hike was your idea," Rayna said to me, smiling. "So you choose."

"Okay. Since walking on the street isn't hiking, let's see what's behind the buildings." I pointed to a treed area in back of the lawn where we practiced.

"As long as we don't get lost," Blaine said.

"If we keep going straight, we shouldn't have a problem," I said.

Rayna started walking through the grass to the cluster of trees I had pointed to and Blaine and I followed.

"Why didn't you want to hike just with me?" Blaine whispered.

"Rayna would've felt bad."

"That's so important?" Blaine frowned, then dashed ahead until he caught up to Rayna.

———

I hiked behind Blaine and Rayna, sorry I'd upset my boyfriend. I guess I'd made Blaine feel that Rayna was more important to me than him. The two of them walked closely together, sharing Rayna's umbrella. And they were laughing. Maybe Blaine wanted to make me jealous. If he did, his plan was working.

The trees I'd seen from the base were part of a small neighborhood park and there was enough room for all three of us to walk side by side. But I didn't rush to join Blaine and Rayna because they seemed to be having a great time without me. Rayna said something to Blaine and he chuckled and poked her in the ribs. It was like they'd forgotten I was there.

We left the park and entered a street a lot like mine, with small houses and backyards. Blaine and Rayna stopped next to a parked car and waited for me.

"Where to now?" Rayna asked when I reached them.

"I don't know." I didn't feel much like hiking anymore.

"This is your hike," Blaine said. "You decide."

I studied the silent street. There were no signs of people, just empty cars and houses. Up a hill, in the middle of the road, was a smashed silver car with a zillion bugs circling it. I could even hear the buzzing. *Dead body?*

"Not there," I said, pointing to the wreck. "Let's try this way." I headed in the opposite direction.

"We're not going straight any more," Rayna said, "so we better remember where we are."

I glanced at the street sign. "This is Heath Street," I said. "Everyone remember the name."

———

A few blocks later, we reached a small grocery store with broken windows. The place reminded me of the Stop & Shop I'd gone to with

Mom, Danny, and our neighbor, Mrs. Perez. I smelled rotten food and heard rats scurrying around inside so I rushed past the building.

Blaine, however, stopped at the store. "Maybe we should check inside for food," he suggested.

"It'll be full of bugs and rats, dead bodies, and maybe even touchers," I said. "That's what we found in the supermarket—and that was pretty soon after the..."

"Oh, my God!" Rayna shrieked, dropping her umbrella as three rats dashed out of the store and ran over her foot. The rats continued on the sidewalk until they scooted around the corner and out of our sight.

"Gross," I muttered, remembering the creepy feeling of a rat crawling up my leg.

"Look!" Blaine shouted, grabbing my hand.

A toucher stood in the doorway of the ruined grocery store, watching us. Then the yellow man-thing leaned forward and raised its arm towards Rayna.

"Rayna, run!" I yelled as Blaine and I rushed ahead.

She caught up and we all turned at the brown house on the corner, just like the rats had done.

"Is the toucher following us?" I asked.

Rayna peeked from behind the house. "No," she said. "I guess it won't go out because it's still raining."

———

We all agreed we'd had enough hiking so we headed back to the base. But first we crossed the street to avoid the grocery store.

The rain had been soft and steady, but now it was barely a drizzle. "We'd better hurry," I said. "The rain's almost stopped."

"The park is up ahead, right behind that house," Blaine said, pointing to a gray house with black shutters.

I heard something behind me and when I turned, I saw three touchers rushing towards us. "Run!" I shouted.

We passed the gray house and dashed through the park, but now the touchers were only a few feet behind.

"Gotta...squirt...them!" Blaine panted as he stood still and aimed his water gun at the closest toucher, hitting its yellow chin. The man-thing stopped and tried to remove the water.

I didn't know how much experience Rayna had fighting touchers. "Aim...for...head," I advised between gasps.

A teen boy toucher lunged at me. But when I sprayed it on the cheek, it immediately backed away, pawing its wet face. Then Rayna squirted a woman-thing on the arm and that toucher also stopped moving forward as it worked on drying itself.

"Now run!" Blaine shouted. "We've only got a couple minutes!"

The three of us raced through the park and onto the lawn surrounding the base. When we reached Headquarters, we banged the door. It opened and we tumbled inside, standing in the entrance and gasping for breath.

———

"What's wrong? Do you need help?" Cody asked, a look of concern on his pimply face.

"Touchers," Blaine blurted out. "Chasing us."

"Here?" Cody asked, turning towards his desk. "On the base?"

"I don't know if they followed us in here," I said. "They were on the street and then in the little park near the back of the buildings."

Cody stared at us. "What were you doing out there?"

Rayna glanced at me before answering. "We just went for a little walk," she explained. "It was raining so it seemed safe..." Her voice drifted off and she shrugged.

"Wait here, all of you," Cody said, frowning at Rayna before racing down the hall.

"What's going to happen to us?" Rayna asked. "I've never gotten in trouble in the army."

"I don't know," I said. "I just hope those touchers didn't follow us inside the base."

———

Cody returned with a serious-looking Major Figueroa. I smiled at the major, but this time he didn't return my smile. "I'm disappointed with all of you," he said. "It was a stupid thing to do and you should know better."

"Sorry, sir," I whispered.

"Now we have the additional concern that the enemy may have infiltrated the base again," Major Figueroa continued, ignoring my apology. "We have to risk lives by sending soldiers to inspect everywhere to make sure we are still secure."

"The hike was my idea," I confessed.

"Even so, your friends didn't have to agree." The major looked at Blaine and Rayna.

"I thought the rain would..." I stammered.

"That's not the point," Major Figueroa said, interrupting my explanation. "You are soldiers and you need permission to go off base. Did Captain Stallings give you permission?"

I shook my head.

"If this was the old U.S. army, all of you would be brought up on charges," Major Figueroa said. "But in our current state, we have to be more lenient." He wagged his forefinger at us. "That doesn't mean I'm not pissed off at the three of you. What you did was stupid and thoughtless and could endanger the entire base. You know we're trying to keep those damn yellow things away while we figure out how to destroy them."

The major stared at me. "Erin, I thought you wanted to learn how to fly a plane."

"Yes, sir."

"A fighter pilot has to obey orders."

"Yes, sir." My voice sounded like a croak as I fought to hold back tears.

"Dismissed."

Accompanied by a guard, the three of us returned to Building 4 in silence.

CHAPTER 10 – Flying Lessons

The next week went by quickly. I should say time flew by since during those days, we had lots of flight training.

After our hike, the army found two touchers that'd chased us, but I'm not sure what happened to them. Some soldiers said they were just killed, while others said scientists were experimenting on the bodies.

I didn't have much time to think about the touchers' fate because I was busy practicing flying and it was awesome being a pilot. We had three planes now because Kim flew two other small planes from the airport to the base.

Our fleet was guarded 24/7 by four soldiers and two Jeeps with water tanks. We were afraid touchers would attack again and destroy the planes because flocks of them constantly circled the base overhead, watching us. Every day, we saw more and more touchers in the sky.

"Maybe they're all flying now," I said to Blaine as we marched into the field for one of our lessons.

"Could be," he said, shrugging his shoulders. "They've all got wings."

"So why don't they just swarm down and kill us?" I asked, looking up. "They're so many of them." I counted at least thirty.

"Because they know we've got this," he said, pointing to the water tanks.

"They could bust the tanks," I said.

"Not without lots of them gettin' killed. Guards would squirt them with whatever formula's left and there are extra supplies in the planes."

"Oh." I didn't know that. "So they're just waiting."

"Yeah," Blaine agreed. "Waitin' and watchin'."

———

The army stopped sending soldiers into the streets to kill small bands of touchers. "We're losing too many people on those missions," Captain Stallings explained one day after breakfast. "Instead, we're going to attack them in the air and in large groups."

He surveyed the room. "We're starting a second pilot training class and I'm looking for new volunteers."

I saw two hands raised—Marty, an older man, and Yolanda, a woman with glasses. I didn't know either of them well.

Frowning, Captain Stallings stared at us. "What about the rest of you?" he asked. "Blaine, Erin, Manny, and Darryl are well on their way to flying planes. I'm sure they'd be glad to tell you what a great experience it's been. Right?" He smiled at Blaine, Manny, and me, sitting together at our regular table.

"He's waiting for one of us to talk," I whispered to Blaine.

Blaine nodded and then stood. "It's been great and Kim's a terrific teacher."

Captain Stallings smiled at him. "Thanks, Blaine. That's what I've been saying. Look, I know we'd all like everything to be the way it was before the bubbles. But since that's not happening, you have a wonderful opportunity—one you never would've had in your previous life—to become an airplane pilot. Now I'll ask again, who wants to volunteer?"

Three more hands shot up.

"That's better," the captain said. "Members of the new flight class remain in your seats. Everyone else is dismissed until ten hundred hours."

———

We had longer lessons and took turns flying a plane alone with Kim. But she was just one person so she could only be in one place at a time. She was trying to get nine of us ready to fly planes by ourselves and now she was training a new flight class. And the second group was even larger—fourteen students. She worked with them every night.

"Are you going to be able to teach so many people?" I asked Kim as I sat in the pilot's seat, ready to begin my flight.

"It's tough," she admitted. "We really need more teachers."

Unfortunately, no other pilots had shown up at the base.

"Enough small talk," Kim said. "Let's get started. Go through your checklist." She let out a huge yawn.

"You're exhausted," I said, stating the obvious. "When do you sleep?"

She shrugged. "I get a couple hours a night and drink lots of coffee."

"You need more help," I said. "Can I do something to make it easier?"

She examined my face for a moment. "Maybe you can. You're a quick learner and you understand the principles of flying. If you could teach the new class the basics, then I could concentrate on individual flight lessons. I want to get the nine of you in the air without me next week."

"I don't know..."

"I've got lesson plans and I'll give you all my notes and you'll use the poster. You know the parts of the plane and it'll only be till I'm finished training your class." Kim took my hands in hers and squeezed them. "Please, Erin. I know you can do it."

I didn't know if I could, but she looked so desperate. "Okay," I whispered.

"Thank you!" Kim gave me a huge hug.

A few months ago, I'd been a high school student and now I was going to teach grownups how to fly a plane. *Wow!*

———

My first class was that evening. I'd studied Kim's lesson plans, read her notes, and reviewed the poster, but was still nervous. All my students were older than me and I was just a kid, not a real pilot. Why would they listen to me?

But they did. I don't know if it was because the members of this class really wanted to become pilots or felt sorry for me. Whatever the reason, I talked—and they listened.

After explaining what the stabilizers did, I asked if anyone had a question.

"There's too much stuff to learn," Marty, the guy from my unit said, shaking his head. "You're young so it's easier for you, but I can't remember all these parts. Maybe I should quit."

"No," I said. "Please don't give up. I felt the same way when I started, but you'll get it and then when you go into the plane and fly, it'll be worth the effort. You'll see."

"I don't know..." Marty stammered.

"If I can do this, so can you," Clarissa, a gray-haired black lady, said. "I haven't been to school in fifty years, but this is important. Think about it: You're alive and most everyone else is dead. Why are we still here? I think it's God's wish that we rise up and kill those yellow monsters and take back our country and the best way to do that is by flying planes."

"Amen!" shouted Hector, a scrawny guy with a goatee. "You got it right, Clarissa!" He started clapping and everyone else joined him.

As I finished the lesson, I kept thinking about Clarissa's words. *If all this was God's wish, why had He sent the touchers? To test us? To punish us?* None of it made any sense to me. But since the bubbles, nothing made sense.

———

The following week, I alternated between taking flying lessons and teaching the class. I really enjoyed doing both. Then, after I landed the plane one day at the end of August, Kim smiled at me. "You won't be doing any more teaching," she said.

I frowned at her. "Why? Did I do something wrong?"

"Not at all. From the reports I've gotten from the class, you've been great."

"I don't understand..."

"I'm taking over teaching the class because you're ready."

"Ready for what?"

"You've graduated. Congratulations! You're ready to fly a plane without me."

"I am?"

"Yes. You and the other graduates—the ones I think are ready to be pilots—will begin flying planes in pairs, without an instructor."

"Wow!" I leaned back in the seat, stunned. I felt like I was doing okay, but to actually be considered a pilot... "Is Blaine also ready?" I asked.

Kim nodded. "He sure is. I've arranged for the two of you to fly together starting tomorrow."

———

The next day, as Kim promised, Blaine and I did our first flight together. The plan was for us to spend about ten minutes circling the area and then return to the base.

We chose who would go first—high card in a deck we found in the rec room. Blaine got a king to my seven so he was the pilot and I was the co-pilot. Tomorrow we'd switch roles.

"When do we start flying for real?" I asked as I checked the instrument panel.

"Huh?"

"You know, fighting touchers from the sky."

"Captain Stallings said it depends on when Kim gives him the word."

"She already said we could fly in pairs."

"That's not the same as bein' fighter pilots, usin' the plane to attack the touchers."

I leaned back in the seat and sighed.

Blaine chuckled. "You're just pissed because I'm pilotin' the plane and you're not."

"That's not true at all," I said, crossing my arms.

When he chuckled again, I stuck out my tongue at him.

———

Being the pilot was much better. "There's the base," I pointed out when we flew over the former executive park.

Blaine looked at his watch. "You've got about five minutes left so use it well.

"I want to fly over my house and make sure everything looks okay."

"Can you find it from up here?"

"I think so." We were only a couple hundred feet in the air so I could make out landmarks. "Here it is," I announced as I located my street.

No one was outside, probably because it wasn't raining. Even without Cyndy Louise, it still wasn't safe. "I hope they have enough food," I whispered as I circled the neighborhood.

"The major stocked your street with food when you came back for me," Blaine said.

"How long ago was that?" It was hard to remember time without Mom's calendar. Although the captain announced the day and date every morning, I didn't pay much attention because each day was pretty much the same.

"Today's August thirtieth so it's been about a month. They should be good for at least another month."

"Still..." I stopped talking as two flying touchers swooped down and landed on Walnut Lane, right in front of my house. "Did you see that?" I asked.

"The touchers? Yeah."

"Of all the places to pick, why would they come here?"

"Maybe they know."

"Know what?" I stared at Blaine, confused.

"You've been flyin' over this street and maybe they've been watchin'. But there's nothin' you can do about it now. We can't land here and we're not prepared to attack them. It's time to go back."

I returned to the base feeling awful. *Did I accidentally lead the touchers to my house?*

———

I was home with Mom and Danny and we were all eating lunch when I heard a knock on the front door. "I'll get it," I said, rushing to the entrance. When I flung the door wide open, two flying touchers ran inside, ignoring me as they headed straight for my mother and Danny, their yellow hands reaching out...

"No!" I shouted, sitting up in bed and clutching the thin blanket.

"What's wrong?" Rayna murmured.

"I had a scary nightmare about touchers," I whispered. "It was so real."

"But it's not real," Lourdes mumbled, slurring her words. "Talk about it in the morning. It's middle of the night."

"Sorry," I said. Although I tried to go back to sleep, I kept thinking about touchers coming into my house and running at Danny and Mom, ready to kill them. The touchers were there so it could happen.

I knew I had to go back home.

CHAPTER 11 – Walnut Lane Mission

I spoke to Captain Stallings the next morning after breakfast. "I have to go home right now," I began.

The captain shook his head. "This is the army and we're at war. You can't just leave whenever you want."

I explained what I'd seen yesterday.

"I understand why you're upset," he said. "But I still can't give you permission to leave. Besides, you're training to be one of our first fighter pilots."

"Only today—this one time," I begged. "I'll walk if I have to. Just let me go. I think my dream last night was a sign that my mom and brother need me...Please!"

Captain Stallings studied my face before speaking again. "I have an idea," he said. "Let me talk to Major Figueroa and Captain Stevenson and see if it's possible."

"When will you let me know?"

"Within the hour." He gave me a small smile. "Can you wait till then or are you going to start walking home right this second?"

He knew I'd been bluffing. There was no way I could make it home alive on foot. "I'll wait," I whispered.

———

Captain Stallings agreed I could wait at Headquarters so I stood near the front desk watching Cody talk to people. He was really good at handling everyone's problems without calling an officer. Too bad he couldn't help me.

Less than a half hour later, Captain Stallings returned and escorted me to Major Figueroa's office. Kim was there too and they both smiled when I entered.

"Here's what we're going to do," Major Figueroa said, leaning on the chair behind his desk and nodding at Kim. "I've spoken to Captain Stevenson and she confirms that you're doing an excellent job as a pilot. You've reported seeing the enemy on your street and insist on going home. We were going to wait a week, but we've decided to give it a try now."

I gave him a puzzled look.

"The plane," the major explained. "You're going to fly the first mission carrying the formula. We're attacking the yellow bastards from the air—and we'll begin with your block."

I stared at him, my mouth wide open. "I don't know if I'm ready," I whispered.

"You are," Kim said, nodding vigorously. "I wouldn't have given the okay if I didn't think you could do this."

"All by myself?" I asked.

"No," Captain Stallings said. "Blaine will be with you. You'll carry out this mission together."

———

After Blaine joined us, Major Figueroa explained the plan: We'd leave the next morning after breakfast and fly directly over Walnut Lane to search for touchers. As soon as we located them, we would release the formula.

I was going to pilot the plane while Blaine would be the bomber pilot, in charge of weapons. Only in this case, the weapon was water, not bombs.

"What if we fly by my street and don't see any touchers?" I asked.

"Then you return to the base," Major Figueroa said. "We'll try again when we have the proper conditions."

"But my family..."

"As I've told you, Erin, you're a soldier now," the major

continued. "You take orders from the army and can't run off whenever you feel like it to check on the ones you love. Other people have family still alive too. I'm only giving you an opportunity to take action because you spotted the enemy by your house. Understood?"

"Yes, sir."

———

Our mission began at zero nine hundred hours. Blaine and I were escorted to the plane after breakfast and we checked the outside and then the instrument panel, following the steps Kim taught us. Everything was fine so we prepared for takeoff.

"Did you make sure the formula was in there?" I asked, pointing to the water tank the army had built into the back of the plane.

"It's there."

"What about the lever? Are you sure it'll work?"

"I can't test that without releasin' the stuff," Blaine said. "We've got to assume the army guys tried it out."

"I hope so."

"Erin, take it easy." He touched my shoulder. "It'll be okay."

"How can you be so sure?"

Blaine gave me his cutest smile and poked me gently on the side. "Because I know it'll be. Now stop stallin' and get this plane up in the air, girl. We got places to go."

"Aye, aye, sir." I took off and we soared into the sky, heading for Walnut Lane.

———

The day was bright and sunny with hardly any clouds so we had a clear view of the ground as I flew over my street. "See any touchers?" I asked.

"No."

Not the answer I'd hoped for. "Is anyone outside?"

"No."

"I'm going to keep circling. How long can we stay here?"

"Thirty minutes tops." Blaine shrugged. "If nothin' happens by then, we've got to head back."

"Well, it's still early," I said as I swung past Walnut Lane. "This is just the first look. They could be someplace on the street where we can't see them."

"I don't think so. We're low enough for me to see everythin' down there and nothin's goin' on. Erin, you've got to be prepared to leave if touchers aren't on your block."

"What if they're inside one of the houses—maybe my house?"

"They're almost always outside unless it's rainin'."

I didn't say anything else and circled my street again. But no one was outside—no people and no touchers.

———

"Half hour's up," Blaine said as I circled Walnut Lane for the umpteenth time.

"I can't go back without doing anything."

"You have no choice. Even if you wanted to check out the street, there's no place here to land."

"What about Fern Crest Park? It's just a few blocks away."

"Listen, Erin," Blaine began. "Even if there's room in the park, you can't just land the plane, leave it unprotected, and go through streets searchin' for touchers. We'll get killed and even if we somehow make it back, they'll destroy the plane. Also, we can't be sure we've got enough fuel to take off again. This is supposed to be a thirty-minute deal and it's already been longer. We have to..."

"Wait a minute," I said, interrupting Blaine. "Did you see that?" We were flying over my block again and something darted through Mr. Muldare's backyard.

"Yeah," Blaine said. "What was it?"

"I don't know. I'm circling again."

"Last time 'round, no matter what. If you don't see it again, we're headin' back."

I returned to Walnut Lane hoping what I saw was a toucher.

———

"It's not a toucher; it's a boy!" Blaine called out as we flew over the street.

"Danny!" I shouted, spotting my brother behind Cyndy Louise's house. He was dripping wet as he waved and pointed towards the back of the block, mouthing words I couldn't hear. When we flew past, he cupped his hands and shouted at us.

"Can you understand what he's saying?" I asked Blaine.

"'Woods'—and he was pointin' that way."

"Maybe he's trying to tell us touchers are in the woods," I suggested. "But we've been flying over there all this time and haven't seen them."

"They could've seen the plane and been hidin'..."

"Where? The fire burnt most of the trees."

"There's still broken trunks. And what about all the garbage bags people on the block dump there? They could be under the piles."

"Yucch! But I guess it's possible." I looked at Blaine. "So if that's true, let's finish our mission."

"Aye, aye, Captain," Blaine said as he fingered the lever that controlled the hatch.

———

After making another circle and returning to the block, I no longer saw my brother in any neighbor's yard. "Is Danny still out there?" I asked.

"I don't see him," Blaine said.

"Good. He must've gone home...Ready?" I asked as we reached what was left of the woods.

"Yup."

"Then here we go." As we flew over the burnt trees and stacks of garbage bags, I heard the click of the lever signaling the release of the poison.

"Bull's-eye!" Blaine shouted.

"Anything happening down there?"

"Not yet."

"I know it's past thirty minutes," I said. "But we should fly over the woods one last time to see if touchers were hiding there."

"Agreed," he said, nodding. "One last time."

Returning to Walnut Lane, I flew above the woods and there they were—seven touchers sprawled on the ground with yellow arms, legs, and wings flapping.

"Awesome!" Blaine hollered. "Let's go..."

He stopped talking as something hard hit the plane. Even with my belt on, I almost fell out of the seat. "What was that?" I asked, grabbing the control wheel to steady us.

"I guess we didn't get them all," Blaine said, pointing to the winged creature that stared at us from the front window as it gripped the plane with one hand and pounded on the glass with its other yellow fist. "Can you fly like this?"

"I don't know." Lifting my rear end, I stretched so I could see around the man-thing.

"Want to change seats?" Blaine asked. "I'm taller."

"No, I can do this." At least, I hoped I could.

"I'll try to guide you."

"It would be better if you could get the toucher off the plane."

"And just how do I do that?"

"Squirt it?"

"This isn't a car where I can open a window."

"What if I suddenly dive down real fast?"

"Erin, this isn't the time to test a new trick. You're not an experienced pilot. Just fly back to the base and when we land, the guards will take care of the toucher. They've got more formula there."

———

Although the toucher continued to hold onto the plane and bang on the window, with Blaine's help, I made it to the base and landed the plane on our runway: a mowed strip in the tall grass by the entrance.

"Good job," Blaine said.

Ignoring his compliment, I stared at the cockpit glass. "The toucher's gone," I said.

"Must've flown away. Maybe it got scared about landin' here."

I looked at the empty field. "Where are the guards?" I asked. A Jeep was parked nearby, but I didn't see any soldiers.

"That's strange," Blaine said. "They should be patrolin' this area. Maybe they're by the other two planes." He pointed to the left side of the field, which held the rest of our fleet.

"But we were the ones flying and they knew we'd be back soon."

Blaine nodded. "You're right. It doesn't make sense that nobody'd be here now...What's makin' that noise?"

The clanging sound over our heads was so loud that it rattled the cockpit. Outside, a yellow leg walked by the window. "Touchers," I whispered. "They're smashing the plane."

———

I couldn't tell how many touchers were attacking us, but I saw two yellow creatures. "We can't let them continue to do this," I said, hearing thumping noises on both sides. "They'll break the plane."

"What weapons do we have?" Blaine asked.

I patted the pocket of my jeans. "We've always got our water guns."

"But we don't have any formula. I dumped it all in the woods."

"We don't have to kill them, just slow them down enough so we can escape and get help. We can do that with the water guns."

Blaine looked at the rear of the plane. "We need to get ourselves wet first. There's more water back here." The pounding noises continued as he rushed to the rear and returned with two bottles. "It's not much so pour carefully."

We each used a bottle of water. After dabbing the last drops on my chest, I nodded at Blaine and said, "Let's do this."

———

I pointed my gun in front of me as Blaine slowly opened the door, trying to make as little noise as possible. With all the loud thumping, we hoped the touchers wouldn't hear us.

It worked. We scooted out the door without being seen and Blaine signaled me to go around the side while he attacked the roof.

I tiptoed towards the pounding noise until I reached a pair of touchers—a teen boy and a woman—who were smashing the plane with heavy branches, so focused on what they were doing that they didn't see me approach.

When I squirted both in the face, they immediately dropped the sticks and began rubbing their smooth doll-like faces.

I turned my attention to the top of the plane where a man-thing was bashing the plane with a heavy piece of metal. Blaine had positioned himself behind the toucher, ready to shoot. But he didn't see the girl toucher that fluttered directly above him.

"Jump!" I shouted as I sprayed the diving toucher, hitting it in the neck and the thing landed where Blaine had been a moment ago. As it squirmed on the ground, I squirted the toucher again, but nothing happened. I was out of water.

"Thanks," Blaine said, pushing me forward. "We better get out of here before they all dry off and come after us."

We sprinted to the base, running as fast as we could.

CHAPTER 12 – The Attack

Headquarters was eerily quiet. "Where...is...everyone?" I asked, my words coming in gasps.

"And...no...guards." Blaine pointed in all directions.

It was late morning, a time the base should have been bursting with activity. I tugged at the front door, but it was locked. "It's Erin and Blaine!" I shouted. "Let us in!"

Blaine pounded his fists on the door and I joined him. But no one appeared.

Leaning my ear against the entrance, I listened for sounds inside. "Nothing," I said.

"We can't stay out here any longer," Blaine said, pulling me away from the door. "We've got to get inside before they reach us. Look!" He motioned to the sky. "They'll be here in a minute."

When I glanced up, I saw the squadron of flying touchers. Blaine took my hand and we ran to our building accompanied by the sounds of wings flapping over our heads.

"Watch out!" Blaine hollered, tossing me to the ground as he fired his water gun at a diving toucher, spraying the man-thing's yellow neck. While the toucher dropped to the ground and concentrated on drying itself, we rushed to the entrance of Building 4.

"It's locked!" I shouted, twisting the door handle. "Please open up!" I was sobbing as I banged my hands hard against the door. The sounds of moving wings were much louder now, like they were right above us.

"I'm out of water," Blaine said, grabbing my arm. "We're still a little wet so maybe..." Before he finished his sentence, the door opened and the two of us tumbled inside.

"Move back!" Lourdes ordered, pushing me away from the door and locking it.

As I waited for my heart to stop pounding, I looked at the hallway. I didn't see anyone else and it was creepy quiet.

Blaine spoke before I did. "What's goin' on?" he asked. "Where's everybody?"

"Come with me and I'll explain," Lourdes said, walking towards one of the first floor offices. Opening the glass door, she motioned us inside.

————

Blaine and I took seats in the waiting area of what had been a lawyer's office. Framed diplomas and photos of people in suits filled the walls. The magazines on the glass table were covered with dust and I etched lines in the dust while waiting for Lourdes to speak.

"They came here less than an hour ago," she began. "Hundreds of the yellow things flew onto the base and attacked us, killing the guards before anyone could stop them."

"The formula?" I asked.

Lourdes shook her head. "They smashed all the water tanks. There's nothing left."

"What about the rest of the soldiers?" Blaine asked. "Where are they?"

"The yellow monsters killed a lot of people—anyone who was outside and couldn't make it into the buildings."

"We didn't see any bodies," Blaine continued.

"They tossed most of the dead people in the back," Lourdes said. "But that was after they used them for something—holding their arms or legs like they were draining energy or..."

"I've seen that," I interrupted. *My neighbor, Mr. Ortega...*

"What about the soldiers that survived?" Blaine asked.

"I think they locked themselves inside the other buildings like we did," Lourdes said.

"We tried Headquarters first," I said. "But nobody came to the door."

Lourdes stared at me before she spoke. "Maybe they didn't hear you," she said very softly.

"I hope so," I said. But we'd been real loud.

"How many people are in this building now?" Blaine asked.

"About fifteen."

"The touchers didn't try to follow you inside?" I asked.

Lourdes shook her head. "It happened fast and when they finished with the bodies, they flew away. That was only a few minutes ago. When I heard you banging on the door, I opened it, but no one's gone outside. We've all been too scared."

"Captain Stallings?" Blaine asked.

"I don't know if he's alive," Lourdes said. "But he's not here."

"Rayna, Roxanne, and Manny?" I whispered.

"Rayna and Manny are safe," Lourdes said. She shook her head. "I'm sorry. Roxanne didn't make it."

———

As Lourdes walked Blaine and me to the other survivors, I tried to understand what had happened. "How did you hear us all the way from the lunchroom?" I asked.

"I wasn't with the others," she explained. "I was at the front desk."

"What were you doing out there?"

"Trying to reach Headquarters on the walkie-talkie, but I couldn't get through." Lourdes shrugged. "Then I just stayed at my desk. Habit, I guess."

Maybe that's why no one in Headquarters came to the door. If Cody wasn't at his desk and they were all hiding somewhere...

"Erin!"

I snapped out of my hopeful daydream as Rayna threw her arms around my shoulders and hugged me tightly. "Thank God, you're alive!" Then she seemed to notice Blaine. "And you too, of course," she said to him.

Blaine gave Rayna a little salute. "Glad you feel that way," he said sarcastically.

Before Rayna could respond, Manny rushed up to us and poked Blaine in the ribs. "Hey, buddy," he said. "You decided to join us here, huh? Thought maybe you guys would fly away from all this."

"And miss the action?" Blaine asked.

"What action?" Manny shook his head. "We ain't done nothing except watch them damn yellow things touch and kill. I seen one get Roxanne..." His voice faded.

"There'll be action," Blaine said. "We've still got soldiers and we're gonna win this war."

"Right," I agreed. But as I looked around the lunchroom and saw just a few frightened people, I didn't believe Blaine's words could come true.

CHAPTER 13 – Plane Trouble

I was telling Rayna and Manny what happened to Blaine and me in the plane when Lourdes banged on the wall, hushing everyone. "We finally caught a break!" she said, smiling. "It's pouring like crazy!"

In a flash, everyone rushed out of the lunchroom and into the dorms to get raingear. It was warm outside so I just grabbed an umbrella and headed for the door with the rest of what was left of Unit 4.

Blaine, who'd waited for me, ducked under my umbrella. "We should check the plane," he said. "We don't know how badly it was damaged."

"They could've wrecked it more after we landed," I whispered. "With no guards to keep touchers away, the plane could be ruined." Then I had another bad thought. "And what about our other two planes...?"

Without another word, we changed direction and walked quickly towards the overgrown field surrounding the driveway.

———

The plane looked worse than when we left it, with dents all over the roof, both sides, and even the wings. Although the glass wasn't broken, the whole outside was a mess.

"Maybe it's not as bad as it looks," Blaine suggested.

"You think?"

He tapped one of the dents. "It could be okay mechanically, like a banged-up car that still runs fine."

"But this is a plane, not a car." Again, I had a bad thought. "What if Kim is dead? Then who's going to check out the plane and tell us how to fix it?"

"She's alive." Blaine nodded his head. "I'm sure of it."

"How can you be so sure?" I stared at him as he continued to nod.

"I just know."

"Should we go inside and see if they wrecked the controls too?" I asked, pointing to the open door.

"No." He tugged at my tee-shirt sleeve, pulling me back. "They could be sleepin' in there. And if they are, we're makin' too much noise. Let's go to Headquarters and report what happened to us."

———

This time, as Blaine and I walked to Building 1, we saw people outside. And we also saw bodies—lots of them—as soldiers moved victims of the touchers' attack to the field for burial.

Roxanne...She's out there too. My eyes started tearing.

In front of Building 3, I stopped two men carrying the body of a middle-aged woman. "How many people in your unit died?" I asked the blond guy with glasses, who held the woman's legs.

He gave me a shrug. "I'm not sure yet, because there're more bodies near the woods," he said. "But we found twelve so far and three soldiers are missing."

"I'm sorry," I said, wiping my eyes as I moved out of the way.

When we reached Building 2, soldiers were doing the same thing with what looked like even more bodies. As I took a step towards a skinny woman standing in the entrance with a clipboard, Blaine grabbed my arm. "Don't ask," he said.

"Why not?"

"It's just gonna be the same bad news. Why do you need to know the number of dead people? We got a job to do. We were on a mission—remember? And we're supposed to report what happened. Come on." He pushed me forward.

But as I walked, I looked back at the victims that still lay on the grass. "Wait," I said, turning around.

"What now?"

I reached the body I'd recognized. It was Flo, the woman from our flight class—the one Carmen had called a witch, who Darryl thought...But it didn't matter any more. Flo was dead so we'd never know if she'd gotten Carmen killed.

I counted fourteen more bodies before we left.

———

There was less activity at Headquarters than the other buildings we'd passed, just a couple soldiers in front keeping guard and no dead people on the grass. "It's better here," I said.

"So far."

Inside the building, a young black woman I'd never seen before sat at Cody's desk. "Hi," I said. "Where's Cody?"

She shook her head sadly.

I shouldn't have been shocked by her response, but somehow I was.

"Is Major Figueroa alive?" Blaine asked.

"Yes," the woman said.

"And Kim Stevenson?" I whispered, crossing my fingers.

The woman smiled at me. "The pilot lady? Yeah, she's fine too."

Blaine gave me a little poke in the ribs. "Told you," he said.

"I'm Erin Fredericks and this is Blaine Erstad," I explained, pushing Blaine's hand away. "We're supposed to report to the major and Kim about our mission. Can we see them?"

"My name's Yvonne Adams," the woman said. "Wait here while I check."

———

Five minutes later, we stood in front of Major Figueroa. "I'm so glad you're both okay," he said, hugging us. "We lost too many good soldiers."

"How many?" I asked, ignoring Blaine's dirty look.

"Nearly sixty so far. But we're still counting bodies and searching for the missing."

"How did it happen?" Blaine asked.

The major stepped behind his desk and shook his head. "We misjudged the enemy," he said. "We figured they were too afraid of the formula to attempt an all-out attack on the base. But obviously, we were wrong." Turning to the window, he stared outside. "It happened so quickly that we couldn't even issue a warning."

"Cody?" I whispered.

"He died a hero," Major Figueroa said. "As soon as he heard flapping wings and realized what was going on, Cody ran outside to warn the other soldiers. His actions saved many lives, including mine."

The major clutched his desk with both hands. "When I heard Cody shouting, I ran to the entrance. But Cody was on the ground, already dead, and all I could do was lock the door before the enemy got inside."

"We banged on the door," Blaine said. "But nobody came."

"I ordered everyone into the lunchroom so no one was at the front desk and we didn't hear you," the major explained. "I'm very sorry."

———

Major Figueroa listened to our story. "And you think the plane is in bad shape?" he asked afterwards.

Blaine shrugged. "We don't know. The outside's full of dents and the door was open so we didn't go in because touchers could've been hidin' there."

"Kim should check the plane," I suggested.

Major Figueroa nodded. "Right now, Captain Stevenson is working with mechanics to repair the other planes," he said. "The creatures damaged them too."

"Can those planes be fixed?" I asked.

"I don't know yet," Major Figueroa said. "Meanwhile, I'm sending soldiers with you to make sure the enemy's not inside your plane and I'll have Captain Stevenson meet you there."

———

Millie was one of the guards who accompanied us to the plane. "How're you two doing?" she asked as she and a young bearded guy named Ken walked with us into the wet tall grass.

"We're good," I said. "We were on a flying mission when the touchers attacked the base so we missed the whole thing."

"It wasn't fun," Millie said from underneath her red umbrella. "Damn yellow monsters are so quiet that unless you're looking up, you never see them."

"You were inside?" Blaine asked her.

"Yeah, lucky for me."

We reached our messed-up plane. "You flew in this pile of crap?" Millie asked as she studied the damage.

"Most of that happened at the end when some touchers attacked us," I explained. "But we were able to land and escape."

"How'd you get away?"

"We had enough water to wet ourselves like when we were with you and Carlos."

She nodded. "We're gonna check the plane...Ken!" The bearded guy joined the three of us. "Time to go inside. Get your guns ready."

Closing his umbrella, Ken aimed two pistols. "I'm good."

"Maybe you should both stand in the rain first to get wetter," I suggested. It was no longer pouring, just drizzling steadily.

"Nah," Millie said, pointing her guns at the door. "Move back and wait for one of us to wave you inside."

———

"I don't like this," I said as Blaine and I waited for Millie and Ken. "I keep thinking about what happened last time a guard checked a plane."

"You mean Carlos," Blaine said.

"Yeah, the mountain lions." I looked at him. "But if there're any touchers inside..."

"It'll be okay," Blaine said. "I've got another feelin'."

"What's with all these feelings?"

"I don't know." He shrugged. "I just feel sure about some stuff and..."

"Hey, you guys!"

Blaine stopped talking when he heard Ken's voice.

"It's okay to come in," the guard, standing by the door of the plane, said.

As we stepped inside, I scanned the cabin. "It looks pretty much the same," I said.

"What about the instrument panel?" Blaine asked as we headed to the cockpit.

Everything looked all right. "I don't think touchers have been in here," I said. "Maybe the plane can be saved."

Millie, who stood near the controls, smiled. "That's good to hear," she said. "And I could use some good news."

————

There wasn't much to do in the plane as Blaine and I waited with the guards for Kim, so after picking up the stuff that had fallen from the storage box, I stepped outside and Blaine followed me.

"Why'd you want to wait in the rain?" he asked.

"I felt kind of trapped in there."

"Because of what happened to us before?"

I shook my head. "I think it's more what happened at the base when the touchers attacked from the air and no one saw them." I looked at the drizzly sky. "It creeps me out, the way they do that."

"Everythin' about those yellow monsters is creepy," Blaine said, putting his arm around my shoulders and pulling me close. "Come here."

Lifting my chin, he kissed me tenderly on the lips. I shut my eyes and tried to forget where we were and concentrate on feeling good. I was just starting to succeed when Blaine moved away. "What's wrong?" I asked, blinking my eyes and staring at him.

"The rain," Blaine said. "It's stopped—and look." He pointed to the sky behind me. When I turned, I saw that it was filled with flying touchers.

————

Blaine and I had no choice; we had to go inside the plane. Although it was warm, I felt chilly and rubbed my shoulders to get rid of the cold. But it didn't work. Moving to one of the passenger seats, I peeked out the window. "I don't see anything," I reported to

Blaine as he sat next to me.

"Maybe the touchers are goin' someplace else," he suggested.

"Like Headquarters?"

Blaine shrugged and the two of us sat quietly, thinking our separate gloomy thoughts.

"Hey, you two," Millie called. "Stop looking like you just failed your science test."

Science test. When was the last time I'd taken one of those? I slid out of my seat and met Millie, who stood in front of the cockpit. "You've got something to be happy about?" I asked.

"We're not dead," she said. "That's good."

Ken, sitting in the pilot's seat, turned to face me. "And the flying things just passed over us," he added. "See?"

A few wings fluttered in the far distance. "They're leaving the base," I whispered. "I wonder why."

"Just be glad," Millie said.

"We've got less soldiers now so why aren't they attacking?" I continued. "And where are they going?"

"Away from here," Blaine said, joining us. "That's what matters."

———

As Blaine and I waited inside the plane with Millie and Ken, the afternoon continued to brighten. "It's not going to rain again," I said as the sun broke through the clouds. "And there're no touchers around right now so why can't we leave?"

"Captain Stevenson's supposed to meet you here," Millie pointed out.

"But that was when it was raining."

"True." Millie checked her watch. "We'll give her another fifteen minutes and if she doesn't show up, we'll all head back."

I stared out the window, waiting. "It's got to be time to leave," I said to Millie after what seemed like forever.

She glanced at her wrist. "Almost, but we can go now."

It wasn't a long walk to the buildings, but without the rain to protect us, it was scary. Ken led the way with Blaine and me in the middle and Millie behind us. We all had water guns, but no other weapons. "Shouldn't we use our water to wet ourselves?" I asked.

"Not enough water," Millie snapped. "Just walk fast."

"What's that?" Blaine said, pointing to the other side of the field, where the grass hadn't been mowed.

I looked in the direction of his finger. "I don't see anything," I said.

"Listen." Blaine held onto my shoulder.

I heard something: a faint cry for help. For a moment, Blaine and I glanced at each other. Then we both started running towards the sound.

"Wait!" Millie shouted. "What're you two doing?"

"Someone needs help!" I yelled back.

"But we're supposed to be guarding you!"

"Then you better come with us!" I called. I didn't say anything else because I saw what was happening—and it wasn't good.

———

There were touchers on the ground—at least five—and they were closing in on two men and a woman, who were running fast, but not fast enough.

"It's Kim," I whispered to Blaine as we crouched in the grass so we couldn't be seen. "We've got to save her." Jumping up, I waved my arms. "This way!"

Kim immediately turned and rushed towards us, followed by the pack of touchers.

"At least they're not flying," I said, aiming my water gun at the nearest one, a huge man-thing.

"You spoke too soon." Blaine nodded to the sky as he sprayed the second toucher. The other three were now up in the air, heading right for us.

"Move it!"

I heard Millie's voice and water being squirted behind me. But I didn't turn around because I was too busy running for my life.

With the sound of flapping wings very close above, I fired the water pistol at a boy-thing's face before its yellow arm reached my hair. The toucher fell to the ground in front of me, poking at its wet eyes.

"Don't slow down to look!" Blaine ordered. He shoved me forward and I ran through the parking lot towards Headquarters, moving faster than I ever thought my legs could go.

———

I knocked on the door of Building 1 and Yvonne let me in. "You're safe now," she said, taking my hand.

Panting hard, I just nodded. I was still heaving when Blaine pounded on the door, shouting, "Open...now!"

As I continued to crouch on the floor, Blaine and Kim rushed into the lobby and joined the heaving party. The door burst open again and Millie threw herself inside, immediately shutting and locking it. Then she pointed behind her.

I looked outside, saw two touchers, and got my voice back. "Where's Ken?" I asked Millie.

She shook her head and reached out with one arm, wriggling her fingers.

"The two men with me?" Kim whispered.

"Don't...know," Millie said between pants. "Didn't...see...them."

Lowering my head, I closed my eyes and said a silent prayer.

CHAPTER 14 – Energy Boost

The next few days were really depressing. We'd lost so many soldiers, our planes were in bad shape, and the word was that the supply of formula was low. But worst of all, we were trapped inside, not allowed out—except for dinner—unless it rained. And the weather was clear and sunny.

"It's like being stuck at home after the bubbles," I complained, remembering the long months in Walnut Lane.

"Not quite," Blaine said. "This is an army base with lots more ways to fight the touchers."

"Oh, yeah?" I put my arms on my hips. "Then why aren't we fighting?"

Blaine shrugged. "I guess the army's not ready yet."

"What are they waiting for?"

"I don't know."

It was evening and we'd been watching a movie in the rec room with other soldiers, but left when neither of us could concentrate. Now we stood in the hallway outside my room.

"I wish we could at least be together," Blaine whispered, taking my hands in his and squeezing them softly. "Can I come in with you?"

"You know you can't." I wriggled out of his grasp. "It's not exactly private." Opening the door quietly, I looked inside. "Two people are already in bed," I whispered.

Blaine took my hand, whirled me into his arms, and kissed me hard on the lips. Then he turned and walked away.

———

Kim and a couple of repair guys were fixing the planes. But unfortunately, they weren't plane mechanics. One man had worked on cars and the other knew everything about washing machines and dishwashers.

"How's it going?" I asked her the next day after dinner.

"You mean the planes?"

"Yes."

Kim shook her head. "Sorry, Erin, I'm in bit of a fog. The planes are coming along. Since we don't have the parts, we're trying to improvise."

That didn't sound good. "Will the planes fly okay?"

"I hope so. I'm going to test them before I let you or any other student fly."

I grabbed her arm. "Please be careful," I said. "You can't let anything happen to you because..."

"I know," she interrupted. "I'm the only pilot here."

"Yes."

Kim stared at her hands. "It's getting so hard to do this. There's so much pressure."

Just what we needed—a depressed pilot. "It'll be okay," I said, hoping I was telling the truth. "We'll help you." *How?* I had no idea, but it seemed like the right thing to say.

———

I didn't get much sleep that night and neither did anyone else. When the loud crashing noises started, we all jumped out of bed. After dressing, I grabbed a water gun and ran through the hall with the others to find out what was happening.

"It's coming from down there," Rayna said, pointing to her left as we reached the entrance.

Lourdes stood in front of the door, blocking our way out. With Captain Stallings gone, Corporal Lourdes Avilla was now in charge. "No one's allowed to leave," she said. "My orders are that you stay inside until I hear from Headquarters."

"But that's where the noise is coming from so maybe they can't get word to us," I argued. "Did you try to contact them?"

"Yes. All I got was static."

"Then we should check it out."

Lourdes shook her head. "You have to wait."

Soldiers from the other dorm room had joined us and Blaine worked his way through the crowd to stand next to me. "It doesn't make any sense to wait here if Headquarter's in danger," he said to Lourdes, his arm draped around my shoulder. "Listen."

When we stopped talking, we heard the buzzing and pounding sounds.

I tried again. "Please, Lourdes. Give us permission to go. Otherwise, we're going to leave anyway. Right?" I turned to the people behind me.

"Yeah! C'mon!" angry voices grumbled.

Nodding, Lourdes stepped away from the door and we all tumbled out into the black night.

———

Blaine and I and the rest of the soldiers from Building 4 followed the loud noises, which were definitely coming from somewhere around Headquarters. A few people carried flashlights that they switched on and then quickly off, not wanting to alert whoever—or whatever—was out there.

"Do you see anything?" I whispered to Blaine as we approached Building 3.

"No. It's much too dark."

"What if they're flying?" I looked up at the empty-looking, practically moonless sky and shivered. "They hardly make any noise," I mumbled.

"We'd hear the wings."

"Not always."

Blaine poked me lightly in the ribs. "If you'd shut up, we'd have a much better chance of hearin' them."

———

When we got close enough to Headquarters to see what was going on, our group numbered at least forty. I crouched on the ground next to Blaine and watched. But I didn't understand.

In front of the building, five touchers were dumping trashcans and sifting through the garbage. "Why are they doing that?" I whispered.

"They're lookin' for somethin'."

Duh! "I asked why, not what."

Blaine shrugged. "I can't explain their reasons."

Rayna and Manny crawled behind us. "What're we gonna do now?" Manny whispered.

"That depends on who's in charge," I said. "Did Lourdes come?"

"No," Rayna whispered. "I saw her stay behind and close the door."

"What about the other units?" I continued, turning my head. "There must be an officer here."

"It don't matter," Manny said. "We got no orders so it's up to us to figure this out."

"But..." That's all I managed to say before someone sneezed. The sneeze was so loud that all five touchers stopped what they were doing and charged at us.

———

"Run!" Blaine shouted.

I'd already figured out that strategy and rushed towards the other buildings.

"No!" Blaine yelled again and pointed to the sky. Two touchers were flying in my direction.

"Where?" I shouted, hoping Blaine could hear me. All around us, soldiers screamed and scattered like a panicked herd of cattle, everyone desperately searching for a place to hide.

"Plane!" Blaine yelled, pointing to our little white plane, which still rested in the mowed grass of the long driveway.

Since I didn't have a better idea, I followed Blaine. As I ran, I checked the sky and then the road for touchers. But they didn't come after Blaine and me; they were too busy attacking the others, who mostly remained by the buildings.

When we reached the plane, I was totally out of breath as Blaine attempted to open the door. It didn't budge. "Locked," he muttered.

I collapsed next to the plane, not having the strength to run any further.

"In there!" Blaine motioned to the high grass that hadn't been mowed for the runway. Then, grabbing my hand, he pulled me forward.

———

Blaine and I sprawled under the cover of the tall grass, hidden from anyone—or anything—approaching on the ground. I stared at the sky, which was no longer pitch black. "Flying...see...us," I panted.

Blaine understood and must have agreed because he immediately scooted on his hands and feet and ripped off large clumps of grass. Crawling backwards, he tossed me a handful. "Cover yourself," he ordered.

Taking the grass, I dumped pieces on top of my chest and legs. It didn't hide me completely, but it helped. As I worked, Blaine threw another batch of grass at me. I was starting to resemble a green mound.

I watched Blaine camouflage himself and then I closed my eyes, intending to rest for just a moment.

———

"Wake up!"

When I heard Blaine's loud whisper, I opened my eyes slowly and blinked. It was daytime and the bright sun was beating down on me. "What time is it?" I asked as I wiped away damp grass that was sticking to my face and bare arms.

"I don't know. But it's been quiet for a while so I think they're gone."

"Sorry I fell asleep," I said. "I didn't mean to. Were you awake the whole night?"

"Yup."

"You could've woken me and we could've taken turns sleeping."

"It's okay, Erin." Blaine smiled at me. "You looked so peaceful—

and you were exhausted." Taking my hand, Blaine helped me up. "It's dangerous out here. We've got to get back."

———

As we trotted to Headquarters, we saw some casualties of the night—bodies sprawled on the grass near the entrance. I counted seven.

"Not again," I said, thinking I was whispering. But I must have spoken pretty loud because just after my words, two touchers sprang out from behind the building and rushed at Blaine and me.

I fired my water gun at the attacking man-thing, hoping Blaine would squirt the girl toucher heading his way. "Got her!" Blaine yelled as he reached the front door and banged on it. The door opened and we both stumbled inside.

Yvonne quickly locked the entrance and then turned to us. "How'd you manage to escape?" she asked. "We thought everyone outdoors was dead."

"We hid in the tall grass," Blaine explained, "and waited till it was quiet to come back, not figurin' the touchers were still here."

"Yeah," Yvonne said. "We've all been trapped."

"Major Figueroa?" I asked.

Yvonne nodded. "He's okay."

"And Captain Stevenson?" Blaine asked.

"She's inside too."

———

The touchers didn't leave. Blaine and I watched from a window as the two creatures rummaged through the garbage they'd emptied all over the lawn, ignoring the dead people around them.

"They're still looking for something," I said.

"Obviously."

"What could be so important?"

"Probably somethin' else to use against us."

"But all they have to do is touch us and we die. Why do they need anything else?"

He nodded. "That's a good point. Maybe they're not killin' us fast enough so they're lookin' for a quicker way."

"In our garbage?"

Blaine shrugged.

The touchers continued to sift through stuff we'd thrown away. "They don't care about the food," I said, pointing to a black plastic bag that had been opened, emptied slightly, and then tossed aside. Pieces of bread crust and vegetable cans were scattered nearby.

"Why should they? They don't eat."

"They don't do a lot of things," I said. "Look!" The girl toucher held a small object in its yellow hand and showed it to the man toucher. "The small one found something."

"And seems kind of excited," Blaine said. "Arms are wavin' up and down."

Before we could figure out what the toucher had taken, both spread their wings and flew off.

———

We told Major Figueroa about the curious thing the two touchers had done. "You couldn't see what they found?" he asked.

"No," I said. "It was small and we were too far away."

"Maybe we can still discover what they took," the major continued. "Can you point out the bag it came from?"

"I think so," I said.

With two guards flanking us, the major, Blaine, and I stepped into bright sunlight. Although soldiers were already at work, removing the dead from the lawn, they hadn't touched the garbage and the spilled food was under heavy attack by those disgusting crawling and flying bugs.

"It wasn't food," I said, avoiding the gross black bag and leading the major and Blaine to the white half-spilled plastic bag where the girl toucher had found something.

Kneeling on the ground, Major Figueroa dumped the rest of the stuff in the white bag on the grass. "This is just office garbage," he said.

I saw sheets of paper, a couple pens, busted rubber bands, scissors missing a blade, crumpled pieces of tape, black wires, and a tiny cardboard box.

"It wasn't paper or a pen," I said.

Blaine picked up the unmarked square box and gave it to Major Figueroa. "Do you know what was in this?" he asked.

The major held the empty little tan box in his hand and examined it. "The only thing I can think of is a small light bulb, maybe for a desk lamp." He turned to me. "Could the creature have been holding a bulb?" he asked, shoving the box into the pocket of his jeans.

"Maybe," I said.

———

"Find out if anyone recently changed a small light bulb and threw out the old bulb and box," Major Figueroa told Yvonne.

A few minutes later, she returned to his office, shaking her head. "I asked everyone."

"Did any people from this buildin' die last night?" Blaine asked.

"Two soldiers," Yvonne said softly. "Corporal Logan Collenza and Private Myra Davis."

I knew Myra a little—a quiet woman in her thirties who always smiled. "I'm so sorry," I said. "Did either of them work in an office that had a desk lamp?"

Major Figueroa nodded. "Corporal Collenza kept track of our supplies. He had a desk, which must have a lamp. Follow me."

Blaine and I sprinted to keep up with the major as he marched down the hall and opened a glass door with an etched silver sign that read, "Permosafe Insurance: Protection for Life."

The inside office was filled with many small cubicles and Major Figueroa led us to the second one. "This was Logan's workspace," he said, pointing to a neat area containing only a small desk, gooseneck lamp, and trashcan. "Let's check the light," he said, lifting the lamp and unscrewing the bulb. Then the major reached inside his pants pocket, set the little box Blaine had found in the trash on the desk, and placed the bulb inside. "We have a fit," he said.

———

"So the touchers took the light bulb," I said to Blaine as we headed back to Major Figueroa's office. "Why?"

"Somethin' to do with the electricity, maybe."

"But the bulb wasn't working," I continued. "Otherwise it wouldn't have been in the garbage, right?"

"Yeah."

"They're collecting bad old bulbs?"

Blaine shrugged as I followed him into Major Figueroa's office.

"I need you two to find out what the creatures are using this for," the major said, pointing to the little box with the bulb that now sat on his desk.

"Yes, sir," Blaine said. "What do you want us to do?"

"One of our plane's been repaired. I need you to fly over the latest location we have for them and see what's going on—if they're using light bulbs or anything else. Maybe you'll learn something that can help us fight them."

"Can't we kill them?" I asked. "They're killing us for no reason." *Charlie, Carmen, Josh, Roxanne, Cody, Captain Stallings, and now Myra...*

"Sorry, no." Major Figueroa shook his head. "There's not enough formula left."

"Can't we get more?" I asked.

The major rested his hands on the desk and stared at them for a moment. "I don't know," he said, speaking very quietly.

"Why not?" Blaine asked.

"We haven't gotten a shipment from the scientists in over a week."

"You think they're all dead?" I whispered.

"I don't know," Major Figueroa repeated.

———

Blaine and I grabbed Milky Ways and water bottles and then, escorted by two guards, headed for the repaired plane. It wasn't the white one we had flown earlier. This was the pale blue plane we'd practiced on with Kim.

The sun was still shining brightly, but no touchers sprang out of the high grass or dove at us from the sky. "So who's going to be the pilot?" I asked, trying to sound casual.

"Let's choose," Blaine said. "Pick a blade of grass. Tallest one wins."

I plucked the highest blade of grass I could find and we measured. Blaine's was an inch longer. Ripping the grass, I tossed the pieces on the ground.

When we reached the plane, the guards unlocked the door and looked inside. It was clear so we did our flight checks. After signaling our escorts to leave, Blaine took the pilot's seat and prepared for takeoff. "Ready?" he asked.

"Yes." I secured my seat belt.

"Then here we go." Blaine pulled back on the control wheel and the plane zoomed across the grassy runway and up into the sky.

I opened the map Major Figueroa had given us and checked the circled area. "We've got to fly over Dunham Street, near the park. That's where this group of touchers is supposed to be."

"How do we know they're the ones that took the bulb?" Blaine asked.

"We don't."

"So why are we doin' this?"

I thought quickly. "If one toucher took a light bulb, it figures others took bulbs or something else they needed. We have to find out what they're looking for and what they're doing with the stuff."

Blaine nodded. "I guess that makes sense."

It made as much sense as anything else about the touchers.

———

Blaine flew over Fern Crest Park and I recognized Dunham Street by the bank on the corner. "Go lower," I said. Kim had told us planes weren't allowed to fly below five hundred feet—but that was before the bubbles.

Blaine dropped the plane so we were just three hundred feet above the ground. "See anythin'?" he asked.

Leaning against the window, I saw a yellow creature scooting around wrecked cars. "One toucher's down there." Then three more joined it, all of them hurrying along the street. "They're four now and they're in a rush to go somewhere."

"I see them," Blaine said, turning the plane to follow the band of touchers.

They entered the park, ran to a large open area, and then stopped. "Oh, my God!" I shouted. "Do you see that?"

"Yeah," Blaine said. "I just wish we had formula so we could kill them."

There must've been a hundred touchers on the grass. They were standing, huddled together, some holding objects, and all looking at each other. "What're they doing?" I asked.

"Communicatin'?"

"Without words—using telepathy?"

Blaine shrugged. "They can't talk without mouths so that's the only way."

I pressed my head against the window and squinted. "I can't make out what they're holding," I complained.

"I'm gonna go a little lower," Blaine said as he dropped the plane. "Is this better?"

I focused on a big man toucher's hands. "That one's got an electric cord with a plug," I said. "I can see some of the other stuff now. A girl-thing's holding an iron and another one has a toaster."

"Appliances and power cords—all electrical energy."

I turned to Blaine. "But the electricity can't work here so that stuff's useless, right?"

He paused for a moment before speaking. "Maybe not to them."

———

We circled the park a few more times, but didn't see anything else except more touchers joining the group. They were so caught up in whatever they were doing that they weren't interested in our plane. They never even looked up.

"We gotta go," Blaine said as he hurriedly turned the plane around.

"Why?"

"Over there." He pointed to the right.

A flock of about twenty touchers was heading our way. "Maybe they're just going to the park to be with the others," I said.

"Maybe. Or maybe, when they get here, they'll want to kill us first."

Good point. "I guess we should be getting back," I agreed.

Something hard hit the plane above my head. "What was that?" I asked, although I pretty much knew the answer.

"Probably rocks. I'm increasin' our speed."

Another object hammered the plane, jolting me. "Hurry," I said.

"I can't go any faster, Erin. This plane was just fixed and we don't know how much more it can take."

Gripping the seat with both hands, I closed my eyes and prayed. But the rocks—or whatever the touchers were throwing—kept coming. When I opened my eyes, lights were flashing everywhere on the screen and Blaine was fiddling with the controls. "Can I help?" I asked.

"Not unless you can figure a way to stop them from poundin' us."

I didn't say anything until I heard a new sound. The engine was making a puttering noise, like it had swallowed something the wrong way and was choking. "What's happening?" I asked.

"One of those rocks must've hit us bad," Blaine said. "Engine's dyin' and we're goin' to crash so I'm lookin' for an open spot to land."

We were already close to the ground as I scanned the streets for a place that wasn't full of smashed-up cars. "There!" I said, pointing to an empty lot.

"Hold on tight!" Blaine shouted and muscled the falling plane towards the green space.

Again I lowered my head and held onto the seat. I felt a huge thump and then everything went black.

CHAPTER 15 – Strangers

"Erin, wake up!"

Blaine's voice sounded like it was coming from far away as I slowly opened my eyes and saw his handsome face. "What happened?" I asked. But my mouth felt like it was full of cotton balls and my words came out slurred.

"Welcome back." Blaine exhaled deeply and smiled.

"What do you mean?" As I tried to stand, I got woozy and slumped down into the seat.

"Easy." Blaine helped me sit. "You've been unconscious at least fifteen minutes."

Then I remembered. "The plane...it crashed."

Blaine nodded.

I looked around. Everything was crushed and broken, with pieces of glass and metal covering the floor. "We're still inside the plane?"

"What's left of it."

"We've got to get out before they come." Again I tried to rise. This time, I managed to stand, but my legs behaved like they were made of rubber and wouldn't hold me up. Groaning, I tumbled into the seat.

"You could have a concussion," Blaine said.

"Thank you, doctor," I whispered. At least my mouth was working and the slurring had stopped. "We have to find a place to hide from the touchers."

"Not until you can walk."

I closed my eyes. "That might not be for awhile."

———

The next time I opened my eyes, I felt much better. "How long was I asleep?" I asked Blaine as I stretched my arms and legs.

"About an hour. Gave me a chance to clean up so we won't trip over all the broken stuff."

It still looked bad, but at least the pieces of glass and metal were mostly off the floor. "No touchers?"

Blaine shook his head. "It's been real quiet here—kind of creepy. No sounds at all."

I stood and this time I wasn't dizzy, although my legs still felt a bit wobbly.

Blaine must have noticed. "Take it slow," he ordered, grabbing my hand. "We don't have a deadline."

"Yes, we do," I said. "We have to make it back to the base before it gets dark."

"And if we don't?"

"Do you want to stay here at night—in a busted plane with no protection from the touchers?"

He shrugged. "It might be safer than anywhere else."

"You don't really believe that."

"No one's bothered us."

"Still..." I stopped arguing when I realized Blaine held the map in his other hand. "Do you know where we are?"

"I think so." He pointed to a circled area. "Right here. See?"

"Then we're trapped," I said, sinking into the seat again. The park with all the touchers was just two blocks away.

"It's not as bad as you think."

"Yes, it is." I sat with my eyes closed, hands resting on top of my head, feeling awful again—and not because of a concussion. I didn't see how we could escape.

"Listen to me, Erin. The touchers must still be in the park, concentratin' on their energy convention and the flyin' ones that attacked the plane must have seen it crash. If they haven't come lookin' for us yet, maybe they won't come at all."

"Right."

"I may be right. We could be able to leave."

"And go where?" I asked.

"To an empty house. I'm sure we can find one."

"How far are we from the base?"

Blaine checked the map again. "Just a couple miles, I think. We could walk."

"We could do it in the rain. What's the weather outside?"

"Sunny."

"How much water do we have?"

"The two bottles we took and our filled guns."

I covered my head with my hands again. "We'll be dead in a half hour," I mumbled.

———

I was pretty good at coming up with ideas, but this time I didn't have a clue. "Does the door of the plane still lock?" I asked.

Blaine shook his head. "I stuck a piece of metal in there so we'll hear if someone's tryin' to break in."

"Great. So we'll know just before we're going to die."

"Erin, what's wrong with you?" Blaine frowned at me. "You never give up like this."

"It's hopeless," I said, my eyes starting to tear. "We're trapped in a busted plane with touchers all around. I can't think of any way to escape."

Blaine put his arm around my shoulders and held me tightly. "You gotta have faith that we'll get out of here," he murmured. "We'll figure somethin' out."

"What?"

He nuzzled my hair with his tongue. "Shh, I'm thinkin'."

"No, you're not."

"Doin' this helps me think," he said, kissing my cheek softly. "Aren't you feelin' better?"

I nodded.

"Good. Now just relax..."

Blaine opened the zipper of my jeans and began pulling down my pants. This time, instead of stopping him, I closed my eyes again.

———

Blaine had taken off my jeans and was kissing my stomach as he slowly slid my underpants down my thighs. *At least I won't die a virgin*...That's when I heard a noise—a soft clang on metal. "Something's tapping against the plane," I said, sitting up.

"Huh?" Blaine looked dazed.

"Listen." In the quiet, I heard the sound again. "It's coming from the door," I said, pointing.

"Someone's knockin'?"

Swiveling away from Blaine, I quickly pulled up my panties and jeans. "Touchers don't knock," I said, "so it's got to be a person."

"Great," Blaine said, although he didn't sound pleased. "We have a guest."

I checked the window near the door. "You're wrong," I told him. "Actually, we have guests—two people."

A man and a woman stood at the door of the plane. When they saw me, the woman—maybe in her thirties, with long tangled black hair—waved and smiled. "Do you see any touchers out there?" I asked Blaine.

He checked the other windows. "It looks clear."

"How about a car?"

"No."

The two people knocked again, this time louder, and the woman looked at me again. She was still smiling, although somehow the smile seemed phony.

"Blaine..." I started to say.

"I know. I'm not gettin' good vibes either."

"But we can't leave them outside, not with all the touchers around." I smiled and waved to the woman as I spoke. "What should we do?"

"Let them in," Blaine said. "We'll just have to be ready."

The woman, looking anxious, kept pointing to the door. But I stalled so Blaine could prepare for the couple. "One second!" I shouted as I stood by the entrance, pretending to tug on the handle. "It's stuck."

"Hurry!" the woman said. Her companion, a short older guy with a mustache, stood next to her, frowning and not saying anything.

"Okay, let them in."

When I heard Blaine's words, I slowly pushed the door open and the man and woman rushed inside. "Thanks," the woman said. "I was getting real nervous standing out there."

"Sorry for taking so long," I apologized. "But as you can see..." I waved my arm at the wreckage.

"This plane's a mess," the woman agreed. "But it's still better than being out in the street with them."

"You mean the touchers?" I asked.

"That's what you call the yellow things?"

I nodded.

"Those monsters..." She looked around the compartment. "You guys got any food?"

Blaine, who now stood next to me, shook his head.

"Water?" the man asked. He had a slight Spanish accent.

"Just a few bottles," I said. "But we need them for drinking so there's not enough to protect us."

The woman looked confused. "What do you mean, 'protect'?"

"The touchers—they don't like water," I explained, wondering how she'd managed to stay alive this long without knowing that. "They won't come near you if you're all wet."

"Really?" She glanced at her companion. "You hear that, Luis?"

"Yeah." For the first time, the man smiled. "Gimme all the water," he demanded.

Blaine gave him a dirty look. "We let you in and that's how you thank us? If we're gonna be stuck here together, we've got to share the little stuff we have."

"No share," the man said. "We take the water." Reaching into the pocket of his jeans, he pulled out a gun—a real one, not a water pistol. "This is the last time I ask nice. Gimme the water."

Blaine pointed to a dented cooler on the floor in the back of the compartment. "All our water's in there," he said, walking to the rear with Luis' gun aimed at his back.

I turned to the woman, who stood next to me, watching Blaine. "Why are you doing this?" I asked.

"It's all about survival, hon." She gave a little shrug. "We gotta do what we gotta do."

Blaine had reached the foam chest and now dragged it towards us as if it was very heavy.

"Leave it," Luis ordered. "Just take out the water."

"Sure," Blaine said, reaching down. But instead of opening the cooler, he lifted it and flung the contents at Luis. Scraps of broken metal, glass, and other junk from the crash flew at the man, a bunch striking his head and arm.

"Oww!" the man screamed, his hand groping for a piece of glass stuck in his cheek. As his eyes rolled upward, he collapsed, the gun falling from his hand and landing near my feet.

"Some guests!" I shouted, tripping the startled woman, who tumbled to the floor. Then, grabbing the gun, I pointed it at her. "I thought we just had to fight touchers," I said to Blaine as he stood over Luis, who lay on his back, motionless.

"The world's still got bad people," Blaine said. "Must be more around like these two."

"What are you going to do with us?" the woman whispered.

"We should dump you outside," Blaine said.

"Please..."

We didn't have any rope or string so Blaine took off the man's tee shirt and slit it into pieces with his pocketknife. Using the shirt strips, he tied the woman's hands and feet while I continued to aim the gun at her and then he bound the unconscious man's hands and feet.

"Shouldn't we clean him?" I asked. Blood oozed from the glass in his cheek and cuts on his head and left arm where chunks of metal had hit him.

Blaine shrugged. "If you want, but he's not worth it." He ran to the window and peeked outside. "It looks clear so maybe the touchers are still busy and we should take a chance and go."

"You can't just leave us here," the woman whined.

"Why not?" Blaine asked.

"They'll kill us."

"So what? You were ready to kill me and Erin. You're no better than the touchers—and you're still human."

"But I didn't do anything," the woman argued, twisting the cloth on her hands. "It was him—Luis. Leave him here and take me with you."

"Sure," Blaine said. "I can see you're a real nice lady, someone I'd trust to watch my back."

The woman bit her tongue. "I'm sorry. It's been so hard—finding food and trying to stay alive and I've only been together with Luis for a week so..."

"That's enough," I said, waving the pistol. "I don't believe anything you say and you're not coming with us."

Blaine walked to the window again. "It's still clear out there," he said. "Let's use one bottle of water to wet ourselves and find a place to hide."

"At least untie us," the woman whispered. "Please."

————

Before we left, Blaine didn't untie the woman, but he did loosen the binding on her hands. "You should be able to take this off," he told her as I wet my hair, face, arms, and legs.

"Here," I said, giving him the rest of the bottle. We were leaving our other water bottle for Luis and the woman—my idea. Blaine wanted to leave them nothing. But I didn't clean the man's wounds because that would have used up too much water.

"Let's get away from the scum," Blaine said as he slowly opened the door of the plane and looked around. "Still quiet."

We scooted outside and started jogging, making as little noise as possible as we headed in the direction of the base, away from the park with all the touchers. The streets were as disgusting as ever—full of crashed cars, decomposing bodies, and zillions of bugs. But there were no dogs, cats, or rats and more importantly, no touchers.

"Where do you want to stop?" I asked, keeping my voice low.

"On a street where the houses don't look like this," Blaine said. He nodded towards the block we were passing, which was full of chunks of glass, wood, and metal from broken windows and bashed in doors.

The houses on the next few streets looked just as bad so we kept going. Since it was sunny and warm, all the walking was making me real thirsty and exhausted.

"How about here?" I asked as we approached a street with houses in pretty good shape.

"I guess so," Blaine said. "Pick a place."

"How about this one?" I asked, turning into the block and running to the second house, a white two-story building with green shutters and no broken doors or windows.

"Not so fast," Blaine said, pulling me away from the entrance. "I'm checkin' it out first."

"Not without me." I took out my water pistol and climbed the step that led to the front door.

Since the door was locked, we tugged on the ground-level windows and when none opened, hurried to the back of the house. The rear door was also locked. "Should we throw a rock in a window?" I asked.

Blaine shook his head. "This house's in such good shape that I'd hate to bust it. Also, that's a lot of noise. I think we should..."

Before Blaine could finish his thought, the back door swung open.

A tall black girl about my age stood in the doorway, swinging a sharp carving knife at both of us. "What do you want?" she asked, her brown eyes flashing.

"Whoa!" Pushing me behind him, Blaine raised his arms. "Easy now. Put that knife down before you hurt someone."

"No!" The girl lunged at him. "Go away!"

"Please," I said, sticking my head out. "We just need a place to rest. We're not the bad guys."

"Really? Then why were you sneaking around my house, trying

to open windows and doors?"

"Because we didn't think anyone was still alive in here," I continued. "Like almost everywhere else."

"And if I let you in, how can I be sure you're not going to steal stuff—like the others?"

"I don't know who robbed you," I said. "But all we want is water and a couple minutes to rest and then we'll leave. We're soldiers— going back to the army base."

"If you're soldiers, where are your uniforms?" The girl pointed the knife closer to Blaine's throat.

"Nobody wears uniforms anymore," I explained as Blaine took a step backwards. "But we really are soldiers, fighting the touchers."

"The yellow monsters?" She lowered the knife to her side.

I nodded, leaving my safe spot behind Blaine and stepping next to him. "You can come with us. It's a lot better than staying here by yourself."

The girl shook her head. "I'm not by myself," she whispered.

"Who's here with you?" I asked.

"My brother and sister, but..." Her voice trailed off.

"What's wrong?" Blaine asked.

"The people who robbed us, one man pushed Curtis and he fell against the kitchen table. It's his leg. I think it may be broken."

"When did this happen?" I asked.

"About a week ago. I'm not sure exactly." The girl shrugged. "It's hard to remember days any more."

"I know." I smiled and held out my hand. "My name's Erin."

"Camille." She put the knife on the floor, took my hand, shook it, and moved away from the door. "Come in," she said. "We don't have much food left, but we do have water."

———

Blaine and I followed Camille through the back door. After passing a room with a large table filled with bottles, tubes, and wires that reminded me of chem lab, we reached the kitchen. A cute black girl with bushy hair—maybe nine or ten—sat at the table with crayons, drawing flowers. When she saw us, the girl snatched her paper and ran out of the room.

"It's okay, CeeCee!" Camille called. But the girl didn't return. "After everything that's happened and then with Curtis..."

"We understand," I interrupted. "It's all scary right now."

Camille nodded as she took two glasses from a cabinet and turned on the faucet. "At least we still have water," she said, handing each of us a full glass.

I guzzled the cold water. I must have been thirstier than I'd realized.

Camille reached into another cabinet above the counter and took out a box of Triscuits. "We've been saving these," she said, passing the crackers to me. "Sorry I don't have more."

"No, thanks." I gave back the box without opening it. "We've got food at the base." I gazed around the room, which, although it was daytime, was already partly dark. "And electricity too."

"Really?" She frowned. "I wish we could go with you."

"About your brother," Blaine began. "I've got a little EMT trainin'. Want me to look at his leg?"

Camille quickly agreed and Blaine and I followed her up a flight of stairs. As we walked past one room, I caught a quick glimpse of CeeCee before she jumped off the bed and slammed the door shut.

Camille knocked on the next door before slowly opening it. "Curtis," she said. "I've got two people here—and one of them wants to check your leg."

A big black guy, wearing glasses and an angry expression, was sprawled on top of the bed, holding a book. "Who're these people, Cam?" he asked in a deep voice that reminded me of Darth Vader.

"They're okay."

"How the hell do you know that?"

Camille slid over to the bed and sat next to her brother. "I just know." She pointed to me and Blaine. "They're in the army. And he knows some medicine so let him see your leg."

Curtis glared at me. "Do you have to stay and watch like a voyeur?"

"No, sir," I said quickly. "I'll wait outside." I hurried out of the room and slid into a sitting position in the hall floor. Seconds later, the door next to Curtis' room slowly opened. "Hi," I said. "I'm Erin and you must be CeeCee."

The door stopped moving. "How'd you know my name?" the voice behind the door asked.

"I heard your sister call you."

"Oh."

"Can I come in?"

"No!"

"Then why don't you come out?"

I didn't get an answer so I closed my eyes, trying to relax. When I heard the door move again, I kept my eyes shut. Soft footsteps and breathing followed, but I pretended to be asleep.

"Who are you?"

"I'm Erin," I said, opening my eyes.

"Not your name. You already told me that. I mean, what are you doing in my house?"

"My friend and I needed some water and some rest. We're soldiers and still have a long walk to the army base."

Backing away, the girl stared at me. "You're a soldier? You don't look like one. And where's your gun? Are you hiding it?"

"This is a different kind of army so I don't wear a uniform." I reached into the pocket of my jeans and took out the water pistol. "And this is the only gun I have—to squirt water at the monsters. I call them touchers."

CeeCee took a step forward, her eyes focused on my water gun. "Can it kill the yellow monsters?"

"Plain water, no. But it does slow them down."

CeeCee sat next to me. "That's not good enough. They all have to die."

"The army's got a special kind of water that can kill them," I explained. "But it takes a long time and a lot of water so they're working on new stuff."

"I want to join the army," CeeCee said, jumping up. "Can I go with you?"

Before I could answer her, the door to Curtis' room opened and Blaine came out, followed by Camille, who slowly closed the door.

"So?" I looked at Blaine.

"I don't think the leg's broken," he said. "But it's a bad sprain. He's got to keep off it till the swellin's gone."

"That's good news," I said to Camille. "Your brother should be better soon." *And less grumpy*, I hoped.

She nodded. "I like what you said about the army base—especially the part about electricity and food."

CeeCee jumped up. "They've got lights in the army? I want to go!"

"There aren't any kids on the base," I explained.

"Then I can be the first one."

I wondered how Major Figueroa would react.

"We can't leave now," Camille said, putting her arm around her sister's shoulders and leading the girl to the staircase. "We have to wait until Curtis can walk."

"When can we go?" CeeCee asked.

Camille gave Blaine a questioning look.

"Maybe another four or five days—but I can't swear to it. Just make sure he doesn't walk on the leg. Does he have crutches?"

"I found a pair," Camille said as she reached the bottom step. "But he doesn't like to use them."

"Make him," Blaine said.

———

I stood next to the kitchen table and scribbled the address of the base for Camille, along with a sketchy walking map since Curtis was the family's only driver. "The sign still says Ridgeview Corporate Park," I explained. "When you come in, follow the driveway all the way down to the buildings."

"But watch out for touchers," Blaine added. "They like to hide in the tall grass."

"Wait for a rainy day," I said. "That's the safest time."

Camille clutched the paper and nodded. "We'll do it as soon as Curtis is able to walk."

"Yay!" CeeCee yelled, jumping up and down. "I'm going to help his leg get better." She dashed to the staircase and raced up the steps.

Camille gave us a half smile.

"Is your brother okay with that?" I asked, remembering his snarly attitude.

"Oh, he's fine with his little sister," she said. "It's the rest of us he doesn't like so much. Are you guys going to be okay?"

"Yeah," Blaine said. "After we take showers. Thanks for letting us."

"No problem," Camille said. "As long as you don't mind cold water."

Blaine and I took turns stepping in the shower with our clothes on and soaking ourselves. When we traipsed down the steps afterwards, Camille giggled.

"You look like drowned rats," she said.

And we probably did. "We should go before we get your house any wetter," I suggested, glancing back at the staircase.

"Don't worry about that," Camille said. At the front door, she gave me a hug and shook Blaine's hand. "I hope we'll see you next week," she said.

"I hope so too," I said, returning the hug.

CHAPTER 16 – On the Run

Blaine and I again walked the smelly streets, which were quiet except for the buzzing sounds of bugs and an occasional whine or growl from a scrawny dog or cat that ran away as soon as we got close. We didn't see any live people or moving cars, just wrecked ones, some with rotting bodies inside—a constant reminder of what happened after the bubbles fell.

"How much longer to the base?" I asked.

"Maybe a mile and a half."

I stopped walking and leaned forward. "I don't know if I can make it," I said. "It's so hot and I'm still tired." Also, my head was hurting again, but I didn't mention that because I didn't want Blaine to worry. I just hoped the pain would go away.

Blaine grinned at me. "What happened to Supergirl? I thought you could do it all."

"All but this." I found a small patch of grass that wasn't filled with disgusting bugs and sat. "Give me a minute."

"I'm timin' you," Blaine said.

As he glanced at his watch, I heard a roaring sound. "What's that?" I asked.

"Lots of footsteps, like a herd of cattle." Blaine pulled me up. "No more restin'. Only one thing could be makin' all that noise."

Touchers. Their convention in the park must have ended and they were hurrying our way.

I tried to forget my tiredness and headache as we ran. But the sounds of footsteps grew louder. "It's...no...use," Blaine panted, grabbing my hand and nodding towards the sky.

When I looked up, I saw flying touchers in their V-formation. Touching my tee shirt, I realized it was no longer soaked, only a little damp and my arms and legs were mostly dry too. "Get...off...street...hide," I managed to say.

Blaine pointed to the street we were approaching. "Here."

It was another block filled with small houses, most with smashed-in doors and windows. "All...a...mess," I complained as we raced down the block.

The steps behind us sounded very close, like the touchers were on the next street.

Blaine yanked me across the road to a blue house in the middle of the block. "Best...one," he said.

The place he picked wasn't going to win any beautiful home awards, but at least it still had an unbroken front door and only one partly-busted window. Unfortunately, when Blaine twisted the knob, the door didn't open. "Damn," he muttered.

The footsteps were now as loud as thunder.

Picking up a rock, Blaine threw it at the broken window and I didn't even hear the noise. Then he stepped into the jagged hole and pulled me through.

"Shh." Blaine put his forefinger next to his lips as he held the water pistol in front of his chest.

I did the same, walking carefully on the stained gold carpet. We were standing in what had been someone's living room, but now it was filled with disgusting brown beetles. Lifting my legs, I stared at my feet, trying to avoid stepping on the beetles or even worse, having them crawl up my legs.

"Erin," Blaine whispered. "Forget about the bugs and concentrate. We have to make sure no toucher's inside here with us."

"How can I concentrate on anything? Those beetles are gross. If this is the best house, I don't want to see the others."

"Stop complainin' and follow me. I want to check all the rooms."

"I can't wait," I muttered, still staring at the floor as I walked behind Blaine. The brown bugs must've liked the living room more than the rest of the house because they didn't come with us on the tour.

The kitchen was dusty, but not real dirty. There were flies buzzing around, but nothing worse so I grabbed a glass and drank water from the sink until black bugs came through the drain. I backed away, but my stomach was grumbling from lack of food. "Blaine," I said. "I'm starving. Can you find something to eat?"

"If you're so hungry, why can't you?"

"Because of them," I said, pointing to the disgusting tentacled things crawling in the sink.

"You can kill touchers, but you can't handle little bugs?"

"They're gross."

After Blaine smirked, he opened cabinets until he found a couple bags of potato chips that were still sealed. "Here," he said, tossing me one.

We munched chips as we continued walking through the ground floor. But when I flung open the bathroom door and tons of black ants scattered, I quickly closed the door. *I'm never using that room. I'll pee in my pants first.*

"We're done down here," Blaine whispered. "Let's go upstairs."

———

The first bedroom was okay, just dusty. We headed towards the second bedroom, but before we got there, I screamed.

"What's wrong?" Blaine asked, grabbing my outstretched arm.

All I could do was point to the doorway—at the skeleton fingers on the floor, protruding into the hall. "That," I finally mumbled.

Blaine took my hand, but I pushed him in front of me as we entered the room.

The skeleton belonged to a woman because it had long brown hair and was still wearing a pink tee shirt, jeans, and one white sandal. But the body didn't have a face or skin anymore. "It's so sad and creepy," I whispered.

"Yeah," Blaine agreed. "But at least it doesn't smell."

Dad. I hadn't thought of him in weeks. *Is that what he looked like now except with a suit and short hair? Just a dressed up skeleton?* I looked at the dead woman and started crying, slowly at first and then louder, until soon I was bawling.

"Erin, you've seen much worse than this. Why're you gettin' so hysterical?" Blaine hugged me tightly and stroked my hair. "Please don't cry," he whispered.

"Sorry." I took several deep breaths and forced myself to stop. "I'm okay now." After wiping my eyes, I smiled sweetly at Blaine, who still looked concerned.

"What was that all about?"

"Nothing."

"Are you sure?"

"Yes. I guess it all built up, everything that's happened." *Partly true.*

———

There was nothing else in the skeleton lady's house, just more empty, dusty rooms. But the upstairs bathroom was pretty clean and didn't have ants so Blaine and I took quick showers with our clothes on.

I didn't mind getting this house wet; the skeleton lady didn't care. Whenever I thought of her, it reminded me of my dad. I shook my head, trying to wipe away that terrible image.

I noticed Blaine watching me, a puzzled expression on his face. "Just shaking water out of my ears," I lied.

Blaine shrugged and took my hand. "Come on," he said. "It's gettin' late and when it's dark, besides gettin' cooler, it'll be much harder to find the base."

"And it'll be harder to see touchers."

"That too."

Blaine opened the front door slowly and we listened. It was quiet again. "Let's go," he whispered.

———

The sun was low in the sky and it did feel colder, especially since I was so wet. But wet was safer so I tried not to think about the temperature as we dashed through the streets.

"Turn left," Blaine ordered.

"I've lived here my whole life and I'm not sure that's the way—so how do you know?" I asked.

"I remember drivin' it."

As I followed him, I wiped some water off my arms, trying to stay warm and hoping I wouldn't regret doing it. But a couple of minutes later, I did.

Hearing fluttering above me, I looked at the sky knowing the sound wasn't coming from any birds. "Oh, no," I mumbled, rubbing my hands on my tee shirt and using that water to wet my arms. "They're flying this way."

"We should still be wet enough," Blaine said. "Move faster."

So we ran. Every time I glanced up, I saw the touchers overhead, following us. "Are...we...leading...them...to...base?" I asked, panting.

"They...already...know...the...way." As we turned into Hazelton, he pointed to the office park sign.

That's when the touchers landed. There were about fifteen of them and they formed a half circle, flapping their yellow wings and completely blocking the driveway to the base. To get inside, we'd have to pass them.

———

For a moment, we both just stood there. "We should be wet enough," Blaine repeated. But he didn't sound real confident.

"And if we're not?" I asked. My arms were damp, not wet.

"What other choice do we have?"

"Why aren't they attacking?" The yellow creatures stood in place like we were their friends and they were waiting for us to visit.

"Maybe they remember us—and all the stuff we've done to them."

"They've done much more to us."

Blaine shrugged. "Maybe when they all got together in the park, they came up with a new way to kill us."

"The old way was working pretty well."

"Hell, Erin. Stop arguin' with me. I don't know why they act like they do. C'mon—we've gotta get to the base." He grabbed my arm and the two of us walked towards the touchers.

As soon as we took a step, the touchers moved closer to us, slowly at first and then faster until they were just a few yards away. "Blaine," I whispered, squeezing his hand.

"It's okay. We're wet and we've got our guns. They'll leave us alone."

"I hope you're right," I said, shaking my hand and squirting water in their direction as I walked.

And Blaine was right. They backed off and didn't come after us. When we reached the end of the driveway, the touchers were still watching, but not following.

I ran the rest of the way to the parking lot. I was going to live!

CHAPTER 17 - Grounded

Soldiers were finishing dinner when Blaine and I reached Headquarters. As everyone left the mess hall, we grabbed cold stew and leftover bread and sat at the officers' table with Major Figueroa. While Blaine told him about the plane crash and everything that happened afterwards, I nodded occasionally, concentrating on the food. By the time Blaine was through talking, my eyes were practically shut.

"Thanks for the rundown," the major said to Blaine. Then he turned to me. "Go to bed, Erin."

I nodded again, too tired to speak.

"I'll walk you to your room," Blaine said. "I don't think you can make it by yourself."

I didn't argue.

He half carried me to Building 4, deposited me on top of my cot, and kissed me lightly on the cheek, saying, "Sleep well."

"Umm," I murmured, snuggling under the cover and closing my eyes. I didn't open them until the following afternoon.

———

Our crashed plane was empty when the army found it—well, not exactly empty—because before they left, Luis and the woman, whose name I never learned, trashed everything that wasn't already broken. But, unfortunately, it didn't matter.

"Since we don't have the tools to fix the plane, we're just leaving it where it is," Kim told Blaine and me.

"I'm sorry," I whispered.

"Why? It wasn't your fault you were attacked."

"But now we only have two planes."

"When can we fly again?" Blaine asked. "We need to find out what the touchers are up to after their meetin' in the park. And why they followed Erin and me here."

"I don't know about flying right now," Kim said. "The major told me he's not risking more soldiers in another plane until we've got weapons to fight the enemy with."

I sighed heavily. "I guess that means we don't have any formula."

"I guess so," Kim agreed.

———

I felt okay and Dr. Wexler—a first-year medical school student—wasn't sure I had a concussion, but Lourdes made me stay inside and rest. "I've got my orders," she said.

Maybe because I was mad, I finally got up the nerve to ask a question that'd bothered me since joining the army. "Why don't you like me?" I blurted out. "Is it because of Josh?"

Lourdes shook her head. "I don't blame you for that because I know how fast the monsters can kill. I was with Michelle when they touched her."

"Then why?"

She took a deep breath before speaking. "From the minute Major Figueroa brought you here, it was like you were different, better than the rest of us..."

"Not true," I whispered.

She shrugged. "But that's over now. You're a good fighter and we all have to work together."

I nodded. She said it was over. That would have to be enough.

———

The next two days I didn't leave Building 4 except to go to Headquarters for dinner. In the mornings and afternoons while the other soldiers were working, I read old *People* and *Us* magazines about movie stars and singers who were all probably dead, napped a little, drew lots of pictures, and played solitaire. When I got sick of sitting, I walked up and down the halls for exercise.

Nights were a little better. I hung out with Blaine, Rayna, and Manny, watching dumb old movies and playing pool. But it was still boring.

Then, on the third day, it rained, which was like a holiday because everyone was given free time. I sat on my cot as Rayna and the others hurried outside. "Can't I go too?" I begged Lourdes.

"Sorry, Erin," she said. "The doctor insisted you rest here for three days."

"But I feel fine now. My head doesn't hurt at all."

"Sorry. Those are my orders."

Lourdes was such a good soldier. As soon as she closed the door, I stuck out my tongue. Then I lay down because my head did hurt a little.

———

Everyone was still enjoying the rain day and I was alone in the dorm feeling sorry for myself when the door opened and Lourdes came in.

"I've got a surprise for you," she said, sounding a lot like my mother.

"I bet." That's what I'd say to Mom when she talked to me like I was a baby.

"Oh?" Lourdes smiled. "Does that mean you don't want to go to Headquarters?"

"Really?" I jumped off the bed. "You mean it?"

"Hurry and get dressed. Major Figueroa wants to see you and Blaine right now."

"Do you know why?"

Lourdes shook her head. "I'm just following my orders."

———

"It feels so good to be outside," I told Blaine as he held an umbrella over my head. It was pouring and I was getting wet even under the umbrella, but I didn't care. The rain meant freedom and we didn't even need an escort to Headquarters.

"What's this all about?" Blaine asked. "Did Lourdes tell you anythin'?"

"No."

We reached Building 1 and checked in with Yvonne. "Go ahead to the major's office," she said, smiling.

The door was wide open so Blaine and I walked in.

"Surprise!" a voice behind the door shouted and then a pair of small brown arms grabbed my waist.

"CeeCee!" I shouted, leaning down to hug the girl. "You made it!"

"We sure did," Camille said as she entered the room, wheeling a large office swivel chair that held her brother.

"Hi," I said to Curtis, not sure how to greet the big grumpy guy.

But this time Curtis smiled at Blaine and me. "Good to see both of you," he said.

"Did you walk all the way here?" Blaine asked.

Curtis pointed to his sisters. "They walked and I rode the chair."

"We got real wet!" CeeCee said. "But it was fun!"

"I'm so glad you made it," I said to Camille.

"Us too," she replied.

———

Major Figueroa stepped into his office and put his arms around Blaine and me. "I have to thank the two of you for talking the Wilsons into coming here."

I gave the major a quizzical look.

"Why?" Blaine asked. "Do you know them?"

Major Figueroa chuckled. "Does the name Curtis Wilson mean anything to either of you?" he asked.

"No," I said and Blaine shook his head.

"Do you want to tell them, Curtis," Major Figueroa asked. "Or should I?"

"It's not that big a deal," Curtis said, speaking very softly as he lowered his head and squirmed in the swivel chair.

"Curtis Wilson is a world-famous inventor," the major explained.

"He's invented a bunch of products, things you probably used, like scorch-free Oven-O Gloves."

"My mom always used those gloves," I said, staring at Curtis, who still looked embarrassed.

"Don't forget Bug-gone," Camille said.

"The bug spray?" Blaine asked.

"And a lot more," Major Figueroa said.

A thought popped into my head. "Is that why the touchers didn't attack you?" I asked Curtis. "Did you invent something to keep them away?"

He shrugged. "Well..."

"Yes, he did," Camille said. "It didn't kill them, but the yellow monsters never bothered us."

"What was it?" Blaine asked.

"A spray deterrent," Curtis said. "Adapted from the bug spray."

————

We hadn't had many lucky breaks since the bubbles, but now I leaned against the wall, closed my eyes, and reviewed what had happened. Out of all the houses Blaine and I could've picked to hide in, we chose an inventor's house—the home of a guy who might be able to help us.

When I opened my eyes, Major Figueroa was looking at me. "That's right," he said, like he knew what I'd been thinking. "We're going to use Curtis' spray in our water guns right away." He turned to the man in the swivel chair. "And then Curtis will try to tweak his invention."

"I'll see if I can make it lethal," Curtis said.

Suddenly, the whole idea made me laugh out loud.

"What's so funny?" Blaine asked.

"Bug spray," I managed to say. "We're gonna squirt the touchers with bug spray—kill them like they're a bunch of roaches."

"We can't kill them yet," Curtis reminded me.

"I know," I said, forcing myself to be serious. "But you'll make the spray stronger."

"That's the plan," he said, nodding.

Running to Curtis, I kissed him on his forehead. "I love you!" I shouted.

The big guy quickly lowered his face and stared at the tiled floor like something interesting was happening there.

CHAPTER 18 – Surrounded

Before Curtis' arrival, most of us figured we were trapped and had only weeks or, at most, months to live. It was already late September—getting too cold to wet ourselves for protection when we went outside.

And we had a more urgent problem. Although no officer said anything, the rumor was that the base was running out of food. We noticed the portions at mealtimes were a lot smaller. But Curtis and his bug spray gave us hope.

That didn't mean we weren't still worried about the touchers. They had disappeared and not seeing them was very scary.

"We haven't seen any touchers since they followed us here after the plane crash and that's more than two weeks ago," I said to Blaine one evening as we walked with the rest of Unit 4 to Headquarters for dinner. "Do you think they're gone?"

Blaine shook his head. "No such luck. People who've been hidin' would've come out."

"Then where are the touchers—and what're they doing?"

Blaine just shrugged.

———

I didn't have to wait long before my questions were answered. The following day, most of our unit was working behind Building 4 when I heard flapping noises. I looked up and there they were—

hundreds of touchers.

"Get inside!" I shouted, rushing for the rear door. After everyone made it into the building, people scattered into different offices. Rayna, Lourdes, and I stood by one window while Blaine, Manny, and some others ran across the hallway.

"They're not landing here," Rayna said.

Lourdes nodded. "They're still flying."

"What about touchers on the ground?" I asked.

Lourdes looked at me and shrugged. "Maybe all of them are in the air and none walk anymore."

The three of us pressed our faces against the glass for a few more minutes, but we didn't see anything else. "I guess the show's over," I said, walking towards the doorway.

That's when I heard Blaine's voice. "Touchers!" he yelled. "Marchin' outside."

Rayna, Lourdes, and I ran into the hall and followed Blaine's voice until we reached a dentist's office. Others from our unit were right behind us and everybody stood near the window, trying to understand what was happening outside. Since I couldn't see over all the people's heads, I hopped on the patient's chair and kneeled on the seat. The view was much better.

The touchers were more organized than before. They now moved in straight lines, one behind the other, like a yellow army. But they no longer looked anything like humans.

Yes, they still had eyes, ears, arms and legs with hands and feet, and came in different sizes—from the very large to the very small. But I couldn't tell anymore if they'd once been males or females. Their bodies were just shapeless blobs—things to hold their arms, legs, and wings together—reminding me of yellow Mister Potato Heads.

As we watched, the touchers reached our building, stopped, and formed a circle, facing us.

"What are they doing?" Rayna whispered.

"Makin' a barricade," Blaine said.

"So we're trapped again," I murmured as another army of touchers marched towards Building 3.

Blaine squirmed away from the window, reached the dentist

chair, and helped me down. "It's not so bad, Erin," he said. "At least they're not breakin' down the door and attackin' us."

He was right. We had time to work out a plan.

———

"They must've jammed our communications because I can't reach Headquarters," Lourdes said from her seat at the head of the long black table in the conference room.

Since we hardly used this room, there weren't enough seats for everyone so about ten soldiers had to stand, most leaning against the wall. I sat next to Blaine as we all tried to come up with a way to escape the touchers' barricade.

"Do we have any water formula left?" I asked.

"No," Lourdes said.

"What about the spray Curtis is workin' on?" Blaine asked.

Lourdes shrugged. "I haven't heard anything about that being ready."

"Couldn't we get real wet and use the water guns?" Manny asked.

"It's too cold," Blaine said. "We're all wearin' jackets. It's gotta be in the forties."

"Maybe a few of us could sneak out to see what's going on," I suggested. "Like a scout party."

"No," Lourdes said. "We already know what's going on. They've surrounded our building and want to keep us inside, probably till we run out of food. Then, when we try to leave, they'll kill us."

"But we should see if all the buildings are surrounded," I argued.

"And what good will that do?"

"It'll tell us what we're up against."

"Erin's right," Darryl said. "We should at least find out what the yellow monsters are doing."

"No," Lourdes repeated. "And that's an order."

———

"I can't do this anymore," I told Blaine and Rayna as I curled myself into a ball on the rec room sofa, my hands gripping my knees.

"What can't you do?" Rayna asked.

"I can't just sit here till I'm starving from no food and then run outside to the touchers. If we don't act soon, we'll be too weak to fight them. That's like committing suicide."

"But Lourdes gave us an order," Rayna pointed out.

"If Captain Stallings was here, he'd do something right now," I argued.

"He's not here," Blaine said. "And Lourdes is in charge."

"I don't care!" I shouted, jumping up. "I'm going outside. She can have me arrested—or do whatever the army does to soldiers who disobey orders—but I'm not staying here and doing nothing."

Running to the bathroom, I splashed sink water on my face, body, arms, legs, and hair until I was pretty wet. Then I loaded my water pistol and headed for the back door.

"Wait!" Blaine caught up to me, water dripping on the floor as he ran. "I'm not lettin' you go out there by yourself."

———

Before leaving the building, Blaine peeked through the blinds of an office window facing the back. "Touchers are still everywhere," he reported.

"We should be wet enough," I said.

"Then here we go." Blaine flung open the door and we rushed outside.

Two yellow creatures stood just a few feet from us. But when they saw how wet we were, both backed off.

"That's right!" I yelled. "Get out of our way, you creeps!" As the touchers continued stepping backwards, I laughed. "Afraid of this?" I shook my wet hand in the direction of the smaller yellow thing and it took another step back.

Blaine grabbed my arm. "Erin, stop actin' like Dorothy with the Wicked Witch. We're supposed to be checkin' what's happenin' out here."

"Sure." I yanked my arm out of Blaine's grip, knowing he was right. But I really liked teasing the touchers.

As we walked, the wind gusted and I shivered. Summer was definitely over. But I could take being wet and cold; it was a lot better than being dead.

———

Before Blaine and I reached Building 3, I saw them. "It's the same here," I said. "Touchers all around the building."

"Talk quietly," Blaine whispered. "We don't want them to hear us."

"It doesn't matter. We're still wet."

"Erin, what's with you?" Blaine asked. "Stop tryin' to get the touchers all worked up."

"I'm sorry." It felt so good to bother them.

"We've seen enough," Blaine said, taking my hand. "Let's keep movin'."

The only place we saw touchers was around the buildings. Maybe they figured we were all inside so they didn't need to be anywhere else.

"This one's also surrounded," Blaine whispered as we approached Building 2.

"I think there are more of them here," I said. Just after speaking, I heard footsteps and turned as three touchers charged at us. Although I tried shaking my arm like before, I wasn't wet enough for water to drip. Then I lifted my gun to squirt them.

"No time!" Blaine shouted. "Run!"

So that's what I did. I ran.

———

I didn't know where to run. I just knew I had to get away from the touchers. But none of the buildings were safe and neither were the trees and bushes. When I turned, the touchers were closer because they were so much faster than any human.

"I...can't..." I mumbled, dropping to my knees. I felt my hair with my free hand and it was practically dry. As Blaine grabbed my arm, the touchers had almost reached us.

Then I saw someone. "Look!" I called, pointing to a girl running towards the touchers with a sprayer, the kind the exterminator used last summer to kill the ants that invaded our kitchen.

As the biggest of the three touchers stretched its arm towards me, I had just enough strength to crawl backwards, barely out of its grasp. That's when the girl got near enough so I could recognize her: It was Camille.

"Oh no, you don't!" she shouted, spraying the toucher, which crumpled to the ground. The other two yellow creatures immediately backed off. "Are you okay?" Camille asked.

I nodded and Blaine gave her a quick hug, getting soaked in the process.

Hoisting the sprayer, Camille giggled. "Curtis wasn't sure this stuff would kill them so I took a shower first." She motioned to the nonmoving toucher. "But I guess it worked."

———

Blaine and I walked to Headquarters under the protection of Camille and her spray gun. "Did the touchers surround your building?" I asked. Camille and her family were living in Headquarters.

"Yeah."

"Did you squirt them when you went out?" I continued.

"Didn't have to," she said. "They saw I was wet and ran away."

"So this was the first time usin' Curtis' new bug formula?" Blaine asked.

Camille nodded and then rubbed her arms. "Man, I'm cold," she said.

"I know," I agreed. "Being all wet worked better in the summer."

When we reached Headquarters, touchers weren't all around the building. Instead, they'd gathered together near the entrance. "What are they doing?" I asked.

Blaine stared at the creatures for a moment. "Those old toasters and other appliances they were carryin' in the park," he said. "They've got them workin'."

"But there's no electricity or plugs out here," Camille said.

"The appliances are all broken," I pointed out. "They wouldn't work even with electricity."

Blaine shook his head. "Somehow they're usin' their bodies to make those machines work. But the more important question is why?"

———

Camille, Blaine, and I stood near a bush, watching the touchers. They paid no attention to us as they continued to tinker with the broken appliances, turning them on and off. One toucher lifted an electric mixer above its head and I saw the blades spinning.

"So what do we do now?" I asked.

"I'm still wet," Camille said. "If you two hold on to me, we can go in here. The monsters will probably run away—and if they don't, I'll zap them." She raised the large spray gun.

"I vote for the back entrance," Blaine said. "I don't know what they're doin' with those machines. Maybe they want to electrocute us."

"Blaine's right," I agreed. "Let's try the back door first. If all the touchers are together here, it'll be clear."

Camille nodded. "Okay, then."

As she walked, Blaine and I held on tightly. But this time the touchers didn't ignore us. They ran in our direction, still holding the can openers, toasters, and other machines, most of them on and noisy.

The three of us stood still. "I don't like this," I whispered.

"I'm gonna spray them," Camille said.

"There are too many," Blaine argued. "You can't hit them all."

Grabbing my hand and Blaine's arm, Camille pushed us behind her. "I'm gonna try. Hold on tight 'cause here we go!"

———

I felt like a small piece of meat in the middle of a sandwich, wedged between the much taller Camille and Blaine. Peeking from behind Camille's shoulder, I saw the touchers form a circle around us.

There were eight of them, standing about ten feet away, most carrying broken toasters and other old appliances. But they didn't come any closer. The group of yellow, shapeless things without mouths and noses just stared at us. Only their eyes still looked human.

"I can squirt them," Camille suggested again.

"Will the spray reach?" I asked.

Camille shrugged slightly. "I'm not sure."

"Then don't try," Blaine said. "You'll just waste it."

"Maybe we can all walk together to Headquarters, holding on like this, and see if they move out of our way," Camille suggested.

"And if they don't?" Blaine asked.

"Then I'll spray them."

"It's better than just standing here," I whispered.

"Okay," Blaine agreed.

"We walk at the count of three," Camille said.

———

Camille, Blaine, and I did our impression of a six-legged caterpillar, inching our way towards Headquarters. We moved very slowly, concentrating on keeping in sync with each other.

The touchers didn't attack us, but they didn't go away either. They moved along with us, maintaining their circle. The ones in front walked backwards and the ones behind and by our sides stepped forward.

"Why are they coming with us?" I asked.

"Maybe they're trying to figure out what we're doing," Camille said. "At least they're not getting any closer."

"Oww!" I screamed as a hot light bulb hit my right leg before landing on the grass. Then a ton of appliances flew at us. Covering my head, I tried to stay close to Blaine and Camille.

"Get down!" Camille ordered, lifting the sprayer. "I'm gonna zap them!"

As a can opener whizzed towards me, I pressed my head to the ground and stayed there. The sound of squirting was followed by silence and when I looked up again, old appliances and light bulbs were scattered all over the grass, none of them working anymore. And the touchers were gone.

CHAPTER 19 – Bug Spray

Blaine, Camille, and I stood behind a large tree near Headquarters figuring out our next move. Although the touchers following us had disappeared, Building 1 was still surrounded by yellow monsters.

"Can you zap them?" Blaine asked.

Camille shook the sprayer. "I don't have much stuff left," she said. "And there are lots of them."

"But if they run away..." I started to say.

"...and if they don't?" Blaine interrupted.

"We can't just stand here and wait for them to attack us," I argued. "There're touchers everywhere and we don't know where the ones following us went."

Camille shook the sprayer again. "I have enough to squirt some of the monsters," she said. "Just not all."

"We should run straight at them," I said.

Blaine looked at me. "Either you're super brave or super dumb," he whispered.

"I prefer super smart." I pointed to the spray gun. "I'm thinking they already know what this is so when they see it, they'll get out of our way."

"Anybody have a better idea?" Camille asked.

No one said anything.

"Then let's do it," Camille said.

With me holding on to Camille's waist and Blaine holding on to me, we ran at the touchers. And I was right. Camille didn't even have to squirt them; she just waved the sprayer and they scooted out of our way.

When we reached Headquarters, we pounded on the front door. "Let us in!" Blaine shouted. "Hurry!"

Yvonne opened the door and the three of us rushed inside. "How'd you get past them?" she asked, giving us a befuddled look as she locked the door.

"With this," Camille said, hoisting the sprayer. "I've gotta tell Curtis that the new stuff works and he needs to make more—lots more."

"We'll fill our water guns with it," I said. "It's much better than the other formula."

Blaine nodded. "It kills them right away."

Yvonne led us to a room that had been part of a lawyer's office— the sign on the door read "Delgado and Klein, Attorneys at Law"— but was now a lab with bottles and tubes everywhere.

Curtis leaned against a counter, wearing goggles and holding a jar filled with a clear liquid. "So how'd it go?" he asked, looking up and smiling.

"You know damn well how it went or we wouldn't be standing here," Camille replied. "It killed the yellow monsters fast, but we need more."

"That's what I've been doing," Curtis said. "I just had to be sure the spray worked."

"Do you have enough for all of us?" I asked.

"Yup."

"Then let's load up and kill them," I said.

———

Except for Curtis, everyone else in Headquarters—even Major Figueroa and Kim—filled water guns with the new formula and then we all went out, hunting for touchers. "It feels good not to run away from them," I said to Blaine as we walked towards Building 2, armed with the powerful new toucher-killing water.

"It sure does," he agreed. "But we gotta be fast. If one of them gets through and touches us, we're still gonna die."

"I don't think that'll happen," I said. "They run away now as soon as we come near. Watch me."

Building 2 was still surrounded by several touchers. Rushing toward a big fat one, I squirted its legs and it crumpled to the ground, its bright yellow color quickly fading. As I predicted, the others quickly dashed away. "See," I said, standing next to the pale yellow dead thing. "The others all left immed..."

I stopped talking when I heard a fluttering noise above me. When I looked up, the darkening sky was filled with touchers, more than I could count.

"Run!" Blaine shouted. "Back to Headquarters!"

Again we ran. But with flying touchers diving right at us, I wasn't sure we could make it there, even though the building was so close.

One toucher flew at Blaine's head. "Duck!" I shouted as I squirted it and the yellow thing plopped onto the grass.

Another toucher came at me, but Blaine sprayed it and I carefully stepped away from the falling flying thing, not wanting to take a chance that it didn't die instantly.

Then three flew down together, dive-bombing at us. As we continued to run, Blaine and I turned and squirted them. We hit two and heard thuds as they dropped onto the walkway. The other toucher must have flown away because when I looked up, I didn't see it. In fact, I didn't see any of the flying monsters.

"Where'd...they...go?" I panted.

"Scared...them...off," Blaine answered as we reached Head-quarters.

I leaned heavily against the door and nearly fell to the floor when Yvonne opened it. "What happened to you two?" she asked.

"Touchers," Blaine said. "Flyin' ones. We need a better way to kill them."

Nearly everyone made it back safely. But one soldier's water gun jammed and before he could reload, a toucher got him. "Alfonso

Perry was a wonderful man," Major Figueroa told us at dinner.

We were in the mess hall with soldiers from Headquarters and several from other units, but not everyone. Although touchers no longer surrounded the buildings—some had been killed and most of the rest had either run or flown away—we hadn't gotten them all. There were still touchers on the base. And it was almost dark, making it more dangerous to be outside.

"We have to spray them when they fly," Blaine told Major Figueroa.

He shrugged and shook his head. "With our limited air force, that's impossible. Remember, we're down to two planes."

I remembered, still feeling guilty about wrecking plane number three. But then I had an idea. "How much formula can Curtis make?" I asked the major.

"Why is that important?"

"Maybe we can spray all the outside things on the base—the ground, the buildings, the cars—make a safe zone."

He nodded. "It could at least buy us some time."

———

Blaine and I spent the night in Headquarters—but not together. Major Figueroa separated us so our rooms were at opposite ends of the hall. "I'm just doing what your mother would want," the major told me, half-smiling. "You're under my supervision here."

I didn't argue because what he said about my mom was probably true. Besides, I still didn't know how I wanted to handle the sex thing—and this way, I didn't have to decide.

By morning, Curtis, assisted by Camille, had made more toucher-killing spray so after breakfast, Blaine and I squirted the roof of Headquarters while other soldiers sprayed the sides and the surrounding lawn and walkway. We didn't have enough stuff yet to protect the entire base.

"What do you think of my idea?" I asked Blaine, who'd been pretty quiet.

"It's very temporary," he said. "Only until it rains."

I looked up at the sunny, cloudless sky. "There's no chance it's going to rain today," I pointed out.

"Still, it's not a permanent fix."

I smirked at him. "Do you have a better plan?"

Lowering his water gun, Blaine grabbed my waist and pulled me to him. "I missed you last night," he whispered, nuzzling my neck.

"I missed you too," I said.

"But you didn't complain to Major Figueroa. You could've fought to stay with me."

"And disobey orders?"

Blaine kissed my ear lightly. "To hell with the orders." Then he turned my mouth to his and kissed me hard on the lips.

———

By afternoon, Curtis had made enough spray to protect the rest of the buildings on the base as well as the sidewalks, cars, both planes, and most lawns. Major Figueroa decided not to spray the front lawn, parking lot, or driveway. "It's too much," he told me. "We've got the main area covered and no one's trapped inside. That will have to do for now."

We still weren't allowed to walk freely around the base because flocks of touchers flew overhead, circling, but not landing. Just before dinner, I looked out a window in Headquarters and turned to Blaine. "They're just watching us," I said.

"Yeah," he agreed. "Watchin' and waitin'."

"For what?"

"Figurin' out how to get to us."

While we worried, it was good to see everyone from Unit 4 and the other units together at dinner again. "We missed you guys," I said, hugging Rayna and Manny.

"We missed you too," Rayna said, squeezing my shoulders.

"Speak for yourself, girl," Manny said. "I missed the food. All we had was cereal and candy bars and I'm starting to get zits again!"

I laughed. Manny was a good guy.

CHAPTER 20 – On the Attack

Two days later, it rained. Of course that was both good and bad: The good news was we could move around the base without guards. The bad news was the rain washed off Curtis' spray.

"There must be something else we can do," I said as I walked with Blaine, under his umbrella.

"I told you this wasn't the answer," Blaine said. "It's a waste of spray."

"But Curtis says he won't run out of the ingredients to make it so that's not a problem."

"It's still a waste of his valuable time. He should be workin' on a better way to kill them."

I shook my head. "This way works fine and it's fast too."

"But this way doesn't kill them when they're flyin'. And just about all of them fly."

They did fly. *But not when it rained.* Then they stayed inside, not wanting to get wet. I stopped walking and tugged on Blaine's jacket. "Let's go back to Headquarters," I said. "I have another idea."

———

"So why won't you tell me your idea?" Blaine asked for the third time.

"I told you, I want to see your reaction. We're almost at Major Figueroa's office and you can hear it then."

"I'd rather hear it now."

I poked him gently in his side. "Just be patient."

"What are you afraid of—that I'll steal your idea?"

"Of course not. I just want you and the major to hear it at the same time."

"Fine."

But he didn't sound like it was fine. He sounded pissed.

When Blaine and I entered his office, Major Figueroa smiled. "I thought you two would be outside, enjoying the chance to wander around by yourselves."

"We were out," I said. "But then I thought of something." After taking a deep breath, I began. "Although Curtis' spray works great, it can't reach the touchers when they fly. But when it rains, like today, the touchers never fly. They stay inside, usually sleeping—a lot of them together—so if we go after them then..."

"...we can spray them like a bunch of roaches in their nest," Blaine finished. "Simple, but smart." He smiled at me.

"Thanks," I said, glancing at Major Figueroa, who hadn't said anything. "Do you think it could work?"

"Possibly, but I have a number of concerns." The major stood, resting his hands on the desk and facing me. "Your plan would require sending a large number of soldiers into the streets to attack the enemy," he finally said.

"I guess."

"We don't have many soldiers left and it would mean risking their lives..."

"But Curtis' new spray works great," Blaine interrupted. "It kills them immediately."

The major shrugged. "That's true, but what happens if you spray a large group and miss hitting one?"

"We won't miss," Blaine said.

"I love your confidence." Major Figueroa chuckled.

"We can do it," I said. "I know we can."

"Erin, we're only sure of a few indoor locations where touchers, as you call them, tend to stay."

"Let Blaine and me do the job," I continued. "We'll start with the places you have. Then we'll scout the rest, find the touchers, and kill them. You won't need to risk any other soldiers, just us."

Major Figueroa stared at me again and then turned to Blaine. "You want to do this? Just the two of you?"

Taking my hand, Blaine held it. "Give us enough spray and we'll get rid of all the touchers around here," he said. "Right, Erin?"

"Right." I squeezed his hand.

"Okay, then," the major said. "We'll give it a try."

It was still raining later that morning as Blaine drove one of the "new" cars the army had found—a dented red SUV—out of the base. In addition to our water guns, we both carried large bug sprayers. Blaine had Camille's and mine was made from plastic pipes and metal by a soldier. My sprayer looked funny, but I'd tried it and it worked fine.

We also carried bottles filled with extra spray, candy bars, and bottles of drinking water. After stuffing our backpacks, I'd given one water to Blaine. "We'd better not drink the spray," he'd said when I told him about the bottles.

"I put big X's in black marker all over the spray ones."

Major Figueroa had given us a map showing three places where touchers had recently been seen. "The first target is just a couple miles from here," I said. "Turn left on Berne Drive and then continue till you get to Calcutta Road."

Dodging wrecked cars, Blaine drove along the deserted streets while I looked out the rain-streaked window. Besides keeping the touchers indoors, the wet weather also kept the bugs away. When I opened the window a little to sniff the air, it smelled better. The rain made everything better.

"See the next light?" I asked. "That's Calcutta Road. Make a right and go three blocks. The touchers should be in one of the houses on the next block."

Blaine nodded, drove to the dark traffic light and turned, maneuvering around wrecked cars like an expert racer. Then he parked in the beginning of the fourth block and we got out to hunt for touchers.

———

Walking as quietly as possible, Blaine and I traipsed through the rain, neither of us holding umbrellas because we needed our hands free for the sprayers. Unfortunately, even though I wore a raincoat, I felt wet and cold. Summer was definitely over.

We were on a residential block with broken glass all over the street, but not much other damage to the houses. Blaine tried the doorknob of the nearest house and it opened so we walked inside, aiming our sprayers in front of us.

We checked each room on the ground floor and didn't find anything unusual except more broken glass, which we carefully avoided. Then we climbed the staircase to the second floor.

Blaine walked ahead of me into one of the bedrooms. But he quickly backed out and pushed me away. "Don't go in there," he whispered.

"Why? What's inside?"

"Dead people."

"How many?"

"I saw two."

I was curious, but didn't need to see more bodies like the skeleton lady so I compromised. I didn't go inside; I just took a quick peek. Although I couldn't see faces, I could tell by the clothes that a man and woman were on a bed and he had his arms wrapped around her like he was trying to protect her. Unfortunately, his strategy didn't work. *So sad...*

———

The second house on our side was bigger than the first, with a wooden fence that now lay in pieces in tall grass that used to be a lawn. "Here goes," Blaine whispered as he tried the front door. But this time the door didn't open so he backed away and pointed to a large broken window facing the street.

After Blaine climbed through the window, he helped me inside and we tiptoed around the glass pieces, trying to make as little noise as possible. But it was difficult because the room was a disaster.

It had been a living room. A table, lamp, two chairs, and sofa were now upside down and a bookcase had been knocked over so tons of books covered most of the blue carpet. There were no dead bodies or sleeping touchers.

We worked our way out of that room and into the kitchen, which was also also a mess, with an overturned table and two upside-down chairs. That room was empty too.

Then we came to the dining room—and it wasn't empty. Five touchers huddled together, holding hands underneath a large table. Their eyes had been closed, but we must have made noise because all their eyes opened at once and they crawled towards us.

"Now!" Blaine yelled.

I think I began squirting even before Blaine shouted. I sprayed and Blaine sprayed and the touchers never got close. They stopped moving and fell down around the table. As I watched their bright yellow bodies fade to a lighter yellow, I heard footsteps on a staircase. "Do you hear that?" I asked.

"Yeah," Blaine said. "I shouldn't have yelled. There must be more of them upstairs."

"Do we have enough spray?" I whispered as we rushed to the staircase.

"I hope so."

I hoped so too because we didn't have time to refill the sprayers.

When we reached the staircase, two touchers were on the steps and another had just gotten to the ground floor. I sprayed the closest one and Blaine squirted the toucher in the middle of the stairs. They both died immediately. But before we could kill the creature near the top of the steps, it spread its wings and flew to the ceiling, hovering and staring at us.

"Can we kill it?" I asked.

"I don't know, but it's worth a try." Blaine squirted, but the toucher flew to the other side of the ceiling, avoiding the poison.

"Let me do it." Aiming my sprayer, I hit the flying thing just as it hurled itself at Blaine. He ducked and I jumped out of the way as the toucher crashed loudly in front of us.

"Thanks for savin' my life," Blaine said, smiling at me.

"Glad to help," I said. "But it came so close to touching us. What if it touched you or me when it was falling and dying?"

"An interestin' question."

"I don't want to be the guinea pig to find out the answer."

———

There were no more touchers in that house or in the other homes on the block. But there were lots more dead bodies. Although Blaine tried to keep me from seeing them, I did see one.

It was on the kitchen floor, another skeleton lady. She must have been holding a cup of coffee because a brown goop stain was still on the white tiled floor.

And there was a second body in the hallway of that house—a dead dog. Since touchers didn't kill animals, the little black dog must have died from something else. I hope the poor thing didn't starve.

I thought of my dog, Muffles, at home with Danny and Mom, and hoped they were all still okay. Then I tried to clear my head of bad thoughts about my family, dead people, and starving dogs as Blaine and I headed back to the car.

"One down, two to go," Blaine said.

"Yeah."

"What's wrong, Erin? We did good. We just killed eight of them."

"That's not nearly enough. There are so many more." I shook my head, trying to shake out the terrible thoughts.

"But these are the touchers closest to the base. If we can get rid of all of them, maybe we'll be free to walk around."

I shook my head again. "Not until we can get the flying ones."

Blaine didn't say anything because he knew I was right.

———

It was raining even harder as we drove to the second location. Although the roads were clear of moving traffic, there were so many crashed and abandoned cars and trucks that we couldn't even enter one street. As Blaine made a detour, I marked the blocked road on the map.

It was a creepy drive because I didn't see any people. I didn't even see packs of skinny dogs or cats. I hoped it was just the heavy rain that kept them away, not that they were all dead like the poor little black dog. And what about other survivors? We'd seen moving cars before, but now it was just Blaine and me. I shivered.

Blaine must have noticed. "Are you cold?" he asked.

"A little." That was true. I was wet and uncomfortable. But it wasn't the reason I had shivered.

"Why aren't people out in this rain?" I asked. "Anyone still alive would know it's safe to be outside now. Do you think they're all dead?"

"No. Your mom and Danny and other people on your block are still alive."

"Are you sure?"

Blaine glanced at me. "Is that what this is all about? You want to check on your family?"

"Can we?"

"Sure," he said, smiling. "After we kill this next group of touchers."

———

The place marked on the map wasn't a residential street; it was a shopping center—not one of those big enclosed malls, just a row of connected stores. After Blaine parked, we walked to the buildings, holding our sprayers.

The first store on the left corner was a CVS with totally smashed front windows. "Easy enough to get in," Blaine said.

"Yeah—for us and for the touchers."

We stepped into one of the windows, trying to avoid pieces of glass. Although it was daytime, the inside of the store was dark and smelled awful, like rotting stuff. Then I remembered CVS sold some fresh food, including milk and juice.

Blaine reached into his jeans pocket and pulled out a flashlight. But I put my hand on his and shook my head. If touchers were sleeping in here, they might notice the beam of light. We could see enough to move around without tripping over things on the floor.

And the floor was full of obstacles. Some of them were products that had been knocked from the shelves. Then there were the bodies—the aisles were loaded with skeletons. Maybe the dead people had been shopping when the bubbles fell or maybe they came into the store afterwards, looking for food and supplies like my family when we went to the supermarket. It was probably a combination of both.

I heard little scurrying sounds in a nearby aisle. *Rats.* I stared at my feet, not wanting any rodent surprises again.

Blaine touched my arm and I jumped, but didn't scream. When I looked up, he pointed to a corner in the back of the pharmacy area. Four touchers lay huddled together on the floor, surrounded by bottles of pills.

———

Blaine and I tiptoed towards the sleeping touchers, trying not to make noise, which was almost impossible with so much crap on the floor. We were about five feet from the nearest toucher when my shoe hit a pill bottle. Although the bottle rattled just a bit, the sound was enough to wake one of the creatures.

"Now!" I shouted as I zapped the toucher and it collapsed into a yellow heap.

After Blaine squirted the second toucher, the third tried to escape, but it was trapped in the corner and I sprayed it like it was a large yellow bug.

"Where's the fourth one?" I yelled.

"It must have flown away," Blaine said. "Watch your head."

I looked up and there it was—high on the ceiling light frame, staring down at me. I lifted the sprayer and squirted, but I missed and the toucher flew away.

"It's still flying," I said.

Blaine yanked my arm. "Let's get out of here now," he said. "We don't know where that thing is. This store is such a mess, it could jump us from anywhere."

"But our orders are to kill them all."

"I don't like our chances. It's dark and we can't see clearly so forget this one. Major Figueroa will understand."

"No. Turn on the flashlight so we can find it and kill it."

"Erin, the monster can be hidin' anywhere here and all it has to do is swoop down and touch us."

"We'll see it coming first."

"So stubborn..."

"Stop talking and start checking." I walked carefully towards the front of the store, my eyes darting in every direction, including up.

We didn't have to worry about making noise anymore. But with all the stuff on the floor, it was easy to trip and fall so I had to look down too. When I heard wings flapping, I ducked as the creature dive-bombed at my head.

Then I sprayed again. "I keep missing!" I shouted when the toucher escaped.

"It was your idea to stay here!" Blaine called back.

I heard more sounds of flapping wings and when I looked up, three touchers stood on the light fixtures. "Blaine!" I yelled. "There are more of them up on the lights!"

Grabbing my hand, he pushed me towards one of the smashed windows. "We're gettin' out of here now!" he ordered.

"No!" I yanked his hands off as I studied the creatures near the ceiling. They were still up there, watching us. But they weren't making any move to attack. *Maybe...*

"I have another idea," I said.

"Great."

I kept talking anyway. "Let's wet our heads with this spray."

"It's a poison, Erin."

"So was the other formula and that stuff didn't hurt us. This one won't kill us either—and it should keep us alive if the touchers dive at our heads. Just make sure it doesn't get in your eyes."

I took a spare bottle from my backpack and poured a little liquid on my hands and then rubbed it into my hair. The spray stuff didn't burn or itch so I hoped I was right and nothing bad would happen. Curtis hadn't mentioned anything about his formula being dangerous to people. But he didn't know we'd be using it on our heads.

"See?" I said, turning to Blaine. "The stuff's okay. Put some on your head."

As Blaine wet his hair, two of the touchers flew towards us and I sprayed them. This time, I hit one in the arm and it fell in the aisle with a loud thump.

The other toucher flew at Blaine's head. "Watch out!" I shouted.

He squirted the yellow creature and it landed on a box of diapers about three feet away from us.

When I looked up again, the third toucher was flying just above my head. As I sprayed it, I stepped out of the way. But the falling thing's yellow hand grazed my ponytail. "It touched me and I'm still alive!" I yelled. "My plan worked!"

Blaine hurried to my side and stared at the fallen toucher. "It could've already been dead," he said. "It touched you just when you sprayed it—at the exact same time."

"Maybe. But then we know we can touch them when they're dying and nothing can happen to us."

"We don't know that for sure because it touched your hair that you wet with the poison."

I stared at Blaine, puzzled. "One of those things has to be true. Either I didn't die when it touched me because I protected my hair or because the toucher was dying or already dead."

"Yeah, but which one?"

CHAPTER 21 – Home, Sweet Home

Blaine kept his promise. After we killed the last three touchers in CVS and before we searched for the next group to complete our mission, we headed to Walnut Lane.

My house wasn't far from the CVS shopping center so I knew the way and since it was still raining steadily, the trip wasn't real dangerous. But it wasn't part of Major Figueroa's orders. "Should we tell the major about this?" I asked Blaine as he again drove along the obstacle-filled streets.

"Not unless we find somethin' he should know."

"Okay." I felt a little guilty—but not guilty enough to turn back.

We reached Barker Street and turned into Walnut Lane. Although it was raining, no one was outside—not a good sign. At least the houses on the block looked the same: Most downstairs windows were boarded up, but not broken.

Blaine parked in front of my house and turned to me. "Ready?" he asked.

Nodding, I opened the car door. I was home.

————

I ran to my porch and banged on the door. "Mom! Danny! It's me! Open up!"

When nothing happened, I put my ear against the door and listened. No footsteps, no barking—nothing. "They're not inside," I whispered to Blaine. "And they're not in the street—so where are they?"

"I could try to break the door and go in..." His voice faded as he realized what he was suggesting.

"To make sure they're not dead, you mean."

"No. I don't think your mom and Danny are in there. I stopped talkin' because it would be dumb to bust the door. Then, when they come back, they couldn't live in the house."

I didn't believe his explanation. He was just trying to make me less scared, but it wasn't working. Backing away from the door, I stared at the other houses on the street. "What should we do now?"

"Knock on your neighbors' doors. We know the houses where people are alive."

We knew who was alive the last time we checked. *Were they alive now?*

"Maybe they're all together in one of the other houses," Blaine continued.

"They would've heard the car."

"Not if they were all together, especially with the little kids."

I hoped he was right.

———

Blaine and I crossed the street and walked to the Douglas' front door. Although we pounded hard and I called their names, nobody answered.

"I don't like this at all," I said, rubbing my arms, which had developed goose bumps.

"It doesn't have to mean what you're thinkin'."

"You're thinking the same thing."

"Not true. I still think all your neighbors are together in one of the houses."

We crossed back to my side of the street and went to Mrs. Perez's front door. "Kyle would be out, playing in the rain or at least waving from a window," I said, looking up for the spunky little kid who now lived with my next-door neighbor.

"If they're all in one house, Kyle would be there too."

No one answered our knocks on Mrs. Perez's door. It was completely quiet inside that house too.

"This is really bad," I muttered as we reached Mr. Ortega's house. After Cyndy Louise touched him, the Santangelos moved into his house. They had a little boy—I'm not sure how old he was now—but he was still a baby.

No one opened the door at that house either.

I didn't say anything as we continued next door to Connie Chou's house, forcing myself not to think about what might have happened to Connie and her two-year-old daughter, Emily. Unlike the Santangelo's son, I knew Emmy really well, having babysat her many times.

I wasn't surprised when nobody answered our knocks there.

"Don't give up, Erin," Blaine said, squeezing my hand as we crossed the street. "There are still two houses left."

We reached Rhonda Weiss' house. Her little boy, Jake, was about the same age as Emmy. After I knocked on her door and yelled their names, Blaine and I waited, although I didn't expect a response.

"Listen!" Blaine said. "I hear somethin' in there."

I put my ear against the door. "Footsteps?" I whispered.

"Yeah."

"But no voices."

Without saying another word, we both lifted our sprayers. The footsteps came closer and then someone—or something—opened the door.

We sprayed immediately because if we didn't, we knew we'd be dead. But we also knew this poison wouldn't kill a human. It didn't matter though: The door opener had bright yellow fingers. As Blaine and I watched, the toucher's hand and body collapsed onto the floor and turned a lighter shade of yellow.

Blaine motioned me to follow him inside so, stepping around the toucher, I entered Rhonda Weiss' house. It was a mess—upside-down couches, tables, chairs, lamps, and busted toys everywhere. At least there was no broken glass, thanks to boards that still covered all the downstairs windows.

But the boards hadn't kept the touchers out. And if one toucher had gotten in, that meant others were probably here too. *Rhonda Weiss and Jake*? I shuddered at the thought of finding their bodies.

Blaine and I tiptoed through the downstairs rooms, finding more overturned furniture, scattered pots, pans, and toys, but no dead people or live touchers. We circled back to the staircase and Blaine pointed to the steps. Very quietly we walked upstairs, our sprayers aimed and ready.

———

All the upstairs doors were closed. Blaine pantomimed that he would open the first door and I should be ready to spray immediately. Nodding, I got into position.

Without making any noise, Blaine turned the knob, opened the door, and I sprayed and hit—nothing. Like downstairs, this room— a girl's bedroom—was a wreck with clothes and toys tossed everywhere. But no touchers were hiding inside. *Rhonda Weiss had a daughter before the bubbles*. I tried not to think about that as Blaine and I tiptoed to the next room.

Again Blaine flung open the door and I sprayed—and this time hit something—a broken bookshelf jutting up in the middle of the room, books spilling onto the floor. This was a den. In the rear, I saw a desk, chair, and computer—all trashed—but no touchers.

Backing into the hall, we entered the bathroom. No touchers were sleeping or hiding in the tub.

There were two more rooms. I pointed to the door at the end of the hallway, figuring it was probably the master bedroom. If touchers were upstairs, that seemed where they'd be—in the biggest room. This time, I opened the door and Blaine sprayed. Bingo! A large toucher thudded to the ground. Another flew to the ceiling and I squirted its face.

"Look down!" I shouted to Blaine as a third toucher crawled from under the bed.

Blaine sprayed it just before the creature's fingers touched his foot. "Any more in here?" he asked.

"The closet?" I indicated the closed door to my right.

"Get ready," Blaine said, reaching for the knob.

I sprayed and hit clothes, but no touchers.

Hearing a noise behind me, I turned and aimed my sprayer at the doorway. But before I could shoot, the bedroom door swung shut.

"What the...?" Blaine started to say.

"Shh." I grabbed his arm to silence him because it sounded like furniture was being shoved against the door.

———

The noises outside finally stopped. "It's okay," I said.

Inching away from the dead touchers, Blaine leaned against the door, but it didn't budge. Then, looking really mad, he moved to the bed, avoiding the bodies and still holding his sprayer. "No," he finally said. "It's not okay."

"You know what I meant," I continued. "It's okay to talk now." I stood between two of the dead yellow things. Although I knew I wouldn't die if I touched them, I still didn't want to so, carefully, I walked to the other side of the king-size bed.

"What am I supposed to say now that you've given me permission to talk?"

Trapped in a room with three dead touchers and he was being sarcastic? I forced myself to be civil. "I thought maybe you'd have some ideas for getting out of here."

Instead of answering, Blaine looked at the dead creatures. "I hope they don't start to stink."

"We won't be stuck here long enough to find out."

"Really? You've got a way for us to get out? The door's blocked—and we're high up on the second floor. That was a tall staircase."

The room had two windows. But unfortunately, dead touchers were sprawled in front of each of them. "We could check the windows," I suggested, hoping Blaine would do it.

"Go ahead," he said, smiling at me.

Damn! "You're closer." I smiled back at him.

"You're closer to that window." Still smiling, he pointed to the window on my side of the bed.

"Okay," I said, dropping the smile. "You check that window and I'll check this one so we can find out which window is better."

"Better for what?"

"Jumping."

"You're nuts!" Blaine glared at me. "I'm not jumpin' out the window!"

I glared right back. "Well, I'm not staying in a room with three dead touchers!"

"You don't know what's out there. It must've been touchers that barricaded the door. They could be in the street waitin' for us."

"Not if it's still raining."

Blaine looked at me for a long moment. "All right. We'll both check the windows."

———

My window faced the house next door. New neighbors had lived there, people I never got to know and never would. Past them, just before the woods, was Danny's friend Bobby's house. If Bobby and his mom were still alive, maybe that's where everyone on the block was hiding. I crossed my fingers. "I don't see anything or anyone," I reported.

"Nothin' on the road either," Blaine said. "But I don't want to jump. It's a long way down and if we break or even sprain somethin', we're dead meat."

"There's a lawn with high grass underneath this window," I argued. "It'll give us a soft landing."

"Not soft enough for me."

"Scaredy cat!" Moving the latch, I opened the window and poked my head outside. "Nice and wet." It was raining even harder now. I left the window open as I pulled my body back into the room.

"So...?"

This time, Blaine shut me up with a forefinger to his mouth. Then I heard the sounds too—footsteps coming up the stairs and continuing to the door. Someone or something was right outside the room. Grabbing my spray gun from the bed, I aimed it at the door while Blaine did the same.

———

"Who are you?" The man's voice sounded familiar.

"It's Erin and Blaine," I called back.

"Erin?" The man sounded surprised. "Just give me a minute to move this stuff."

I put down my sprayer as I heard the furniture being shoved away. Then the door opened and Harold Douglas, my neighbor across the street, walked in.

"Erin!" he said, beaming. "Sorry to trap you in here, but we weren't sure what was going on." Walking around the dead touchers, Mr. Douglas hugged my shoulders and shook Blaine's hand. "It's so good to see both of you."

"Why the barricade?" Blaine asked.

"As I said, we didn't know who was in this house with the touchers. We saw the red car and figured it had to be people, but unfortunately, not all survivors are people we can trust."

"My mom and Danny? Are they all right?"

"They're fine, Erin."

"Where is everyone?" I continued. "Blaine and I went up and down on the block, banging on all the doors, but no one answered."

"We're in Norma Perez's house," Mr. Douglas said. "Those of us who are left."

I didn't follow up on Mr. Douglas' scary last sentence. Mom and Danny were okay, but some neighbors weren't. While I kept quiet, Blaine asked the obvious question.

"Why didn't you let us in when we knocked on Mrs. Perez's door?"

"We were down in the basement. All we heard were muffled voices and didn't know it was you."

"But it was raining so why were you hiding?" I asked. Before he could answer, I voiced the scary question. "And what did you mean by 'those who are left'?"

"It's been hard since the touchers moved into Rhonda's house," Mr. Douglas said. "Very hard." He glanced at the dead creature near him. "Can we talk in another room—one without all these bodies?"

The three of us wriggled through the doorway, past the bookshelf pieces, chairs, and books that had blocked our exit. Then we followed Mr. Douglas into the girl's bedroom, pushed aside the toys and clothes, and sat on the bed.

"What do you want to know first?" Mr. Douglas asked us.

"Who besides you, my mom, and Danny is alive?" I whispered.

Mr. Douglas sighed. "I was being overdramatic," he said. "Most everyone is still alive."

"Who isn't?" I prodded.

"Rhonda Weiss is gone...and so is Frank Santangelo."

That was awful news, but those two weren't neighbors I knew well. At least Connie and all the kids were still okay. *The kids*..."What about Mrs. Weiss' little boy, Jake?" I asked.

"He's fine, thanks to Frank."

"What happened?" Blaine asked.

"We were outside in the rain and then it suddenly stopped raining. Those monsters— the ones that you killed..." Mr. Douglas nodded towards the other room. "They appeared from nowhere and while Rhonda was trying to get Jake inside, one of them touched her. Frank swooped Jake in his arms and started running with him across the street. That's when another toucher got him."

"How did Jake survive?" I asked.

"When Frank fell, Jake jumped out of his arms and rushed to Connie. She's been caring for him ever since."

"When did all this happen?" I asked.

"About two weeks ago."

Blaine stared at Mr. Douglas. "That's horrible," he said. "But it doesn't explain why y'all were hidin' today durin' the rain."

Mr. Douglas sighed again. "That's another story."

———

Before Mr. Douglas began, he reached into his pocket and pulled out a gun—not a water pistol—a real gun. "I had this pointed at the door before I knew it was you, just in case," he said.

"In case of what?" I asked.

"In case you were planning to rob us...like the ones who came here last week."

"How many?" Blaine asked.

"Three young men," Mr. Douglas said. "But let me start at the beginning. We were still dealing with losing Rhonda and Frank. In fact, it was the first rain since their deaths and we'd buried them that morning. When the men showed up, Connie was watching the little ones and everyone else was huddled together in the street trying to figure out how to get the touchers out of Rhonda's house. The robbers drove into Walnut Lane in a banged-up van, jumped out of the car, and pointed two guns at us.

"Oh, God," I said.

"Yes," Mr. Douglas agreed. "We could have used some divine help. I'm the only man left and we've got children to protect."

"What did you do?" Blaine asked.

"After we all put our hands up, the leader—a tall skinny fellow— told us to give them our food. When I said we had lots of kids to feed, he punched me in the stomach and ordered me to shut up. Then he sent Jennifer and your mom to collect the food.

"'If you don't fill up a garbage bag, we'll kill everyone here,' the tall guy said."

"They managed to find enough food?" I whispered.

"Barely," Mr. Douglas said. "Thanks to you, the army's been giving us supplies. After the men checked the bag to make sure it was filled with food, they got into their van and drove away without another word."

"So they didn't hurt anyone?" I asked.

"Except for the hard punch to my gut, no."

"What have y'all been eatin' since then?" Blaine asked.

Mr. Douglas shrugged his shoulders. "Mostly cereal," he said. "Not much else."

———

It was great seeing Mom, Danny, and all my neighbors too. Although Jake seemed okay, I gave him an extra hug. I also told Mrs. Santangelo how sorry I was about her husband. She just nodded.

After everyone left Mrs. Perez's basement to enjoy time outside in the rain, Mom, Danny, Blaine, and I went into my house, along with Muffles, who jumped onto my legs and licked my face. "I missed you too, boy," I said, petting the dog's soft fur.

Before doing anything else, I cornered Blaine in the dining room. "We can't leave them here," I whispered. "They don't have food and the block's too dangerous."

"So what do you want to do?"

"Take them back to the base."

"Him too?" Blaine pointed to Muffles, who had attached himself to my side.

"Yes—everyone."

"What about our mission?"

"This is more important."

"You're givin' the orders now, General?"

"I think Major Figueroa will understand."

"Okay, say we take everyone on the block to the base. How do we get them there?"

"We go back first and bring cars for them."

"And what if they don't want to leave their homes? Except for the boarded windows, these houses are in pretty good shape."

I thought for a moment. "But they don't have electricity—and the weather's getting colder. What happens when it's winter?"

"It's not that cold yet."

"Blaine, what if this was your family and your neighbors?"

He nodded. "All right. Let's ask them."

Most everyone wanted to go to the army base.

"I'd stay, but after what's been happening here, I'm scared for Kyle," Norma Perez said. She had gotten real close with the cute little boy we'd rescued.

As Mrs. Perez talked, I watched Kyle run after Danny and Bobby, who were teasing him. The kid was faster than my brother and his friend, even though they were several years older.

Connie, now with two toddlers to care for, was anxious to leave. "Besides the danger here, I need electricity," she said. "Cold food, hand washing all the kids' clothes—it's been like living on the frontier." Emmy and Jake were kneeling on the porch, rolling little toy cars.

"True," Bobby's mom agreed. "Except the settlers out west didn't have to fight monsters. This is much worse."

Mrs. Santangelo stood quietly by herself, rocking sleeping baby Frankie in a stroller. "Too many bad memories for me here," she whispered. "I'm ready to move."

"You're already living on the base," my mom said, hugging me. "That's enough of a reason for Danny and me to be there."

That left just Harold and Lynne Douglas. "I can't leave," Mr. Douglas told everyone. "Lynne isn't well and she's comfortable here."

"But the army's got a doctor," I said. "She can help her."

Mr. Douglas shook his head. "No, she can't."

"Why not?" I asked.

"Cancer," he said. "Lynne can't be helped and she's happiest here, in her home, even with the danger and lack of power and hot food."

"I'm so sorry," Mom said. "I didn't know Lynne was terminal. If I can do anything..."

Mr. Douglas waved his hand. "You all go and I'll do my best to protect your houses."

"Thank you," I whispered. There was nothing else to say.

CHAPTER 22 – Moving Day

With the rain still falling heavily, Blaine and I returned to the base without a problem and again without seeing any people. Although it was late afternoon and I was starving, the first thing we did was check in with Major Figueroa.

And I was right; he did understand. "Saving survivors is crucial," he said, after I explained the reason for our side trip to Walnut Lane. "And when it's your own family..." His voice faded and I imagined him thinking about the ones he loved.

"Your mother and brother are great people," the major continued. "We'll make room for them and your neighbors." Then he turned to Blaine. "I'm getting the feeling you don't agree with Erin about this."

Blaine shrugged. "If we're gonna be stockin' the base with civilians instead of soldiers, how's the army ever goin' to defeat the touchers?"

"If we don't protect the remaining civilians, there won't be any people left to save," Major Figueroa said. "If it's still raining, we'll transport Erin's family and neighbors here tonight."

———

The rain continued to fall so after dinner, Blaine and I walked to the parking lot with two guards, who each carried a bag of food for the Douglasses—plus Manny, Rayna, Camille, and Darryl—who'd volunteered to help rescue the people on my street.

"There's not much room for everyone's stuff," I said as the guards handed us keys to three banged-up SUVs. We were bringing back eleven people—five women and six kids.

"That's right," Blaine agreed. "They'll just be able to take clothes and what they need for the kids."

Blaine drove out first, leading the way. Although I'd drawn maps for the others, the plan was for them to follow us. It was still light outside and we had about an hour before it got really dark. Like always, it was creepy on the rainy, traffic-free roads as Blaine maneuvered around the crashed cars.

"They're not even expecting us tonight," I said. "We told them we'd probably be back in a few days."

"If they're not ready, we'll help them pack."

————

Our three-car caravan reached Walnut Lane without any trouble. Like earlier, although it was raining, no one was on the street. But this time when I knocked on my front door, Danny opened it.

"We're ready to take everyone to the base," I told him.

"Cool! I'll tell Mom." As Danny ran up the stairs, his spot at the door was taken by Muffles, who jumped on my legs like he hadn't seen me in months.

"Easy, boy," I said, patting his head. "I was here a few hours ago and you're coming back with me." My explanation didn't work; Muffles kept two of his legs firmly planted on mine.

"Erin, you help your mom and brother pack and I'll give the Douglasses their food and help your neighbors," Blaine said.

"Okay." Prying Muffles' feet off my legs, I climbed up the steps.

————

It didn't take long for everyone to pack and it was just getting dark when our three loaded SUVs headed to the base with Blaine again leading the way. Danny, Mom, and Muffles rode with us.

"How long do we have to ride?" Danny asked. He held a bag of clothes on his lap.

"Only about fifteen minutes," I said. "It should be quick."

But it wasn't. Soon after I answered my brother, the rain became a drizzle and then stopped. Touchers started appearing in the street—lots of them.

"Shit," I mumbled.

"Watch your language," Mom said.

We could all be dead in two minutes and she's worried about my words? "Sorry."

A toucher tossed a rock at my window. It missed and clanged off the door. "Can we make it?" I whispered to Blaine.

"I don't know." He swerved out of the way of another toucher that bashed his side of the SUV with a huge branch. The road was filled with tons of smashed up cars. "I can't drive fast here so I'm gonna try side streets."

As Blaine turned right, touchers followed, but the other two SUVs were no longer behind us. "We lost the other cars," I said.

"Can't help it. Gotta get away from the touchers."

There was a big thump over our heads and the roof sagged.

"Was that a flying toucher?" Danny asked in a trembling voice.

"Yes," I said. I'd forgotten he was just a kid.

Muffles started barking very loudly. "Easy, boy," I said, turning to comfort the dog. "We'll be at the base real soon." I hoped I was telling the truth.

————

If Blaine hadn't needed headlights, maybe the touchers wouldn't have seen our SUV. But the roads were so bad that he had to use the lights.

In the backseat, Mom and Danny huddled together with Muffles, heads down, scared out of their minds. I was scared too, but I'd been fighting touchers so I was used to feeling that way. "Not much longer," I said as another rock smashed against the back of the car.

Blaine looped through side streets, going a little faster, but not fast enough to avoid every toucher. There was another thud on our roof followed by jabbing noises overhead.

"One's on top of the car," Danny whispered. "And it's trying to break through."

"But it can't," I said. Again, I hoped I was right.

The sounds on the roof stopped. "See?" I said, turning to Danny. "The toucher gave up."

Danny nodded, but his eyes were watery.

"It'll be okay," I said, trying to sound more confident than I felt.

"Yeah," Blaine added. Then he whispered in my ear, "I'm not sure where we are. I think I'm lost."

Mom caught Blaine's last word and bounced up. "You're not lost at all," she said. "I know exactly where we are. The army base is at Ridgeview Corporate Park, right?"

———

Thank goodness for Mom because I had no idea where we were either. Since these roads were clearer and Mom knew the way, Blaine was able to drive with his headlights off and touchers stopped attacking us. Finally, we turned into the driveway and pulled up in front of Headquarters.

"Do you see the other two cars?" I asked, opening the door.

Blaine shook his head. "They're not here."

"They probably had to take side streets like us," I said. "They should be here soon." But I didn't really believe my words.

"Sure." It didn't sound like Blaine believed me either.

The four of us, plus Muffles, walked to Headquarters, nobody saying anything, probably because we were all thinking very bad thoughts.

Even in the dark, I could see the tears in Danny's eyes. Maybe he was thinking about his friend, Bobby. My eyes were getting watery too. "Here we are," I said as we reached Building 1, trying to sound cheerful.

———

When Yvonne opened the door, Muffles gave one little bark. "What happened that it took so long?" Yvonne asked. "And where are the others?"

"We got attacked by touchers when the rain stopped," I explained. "Then we had to take back roads. Maybe the other two cars had the same problem."

Yvonne nodded. But I don't think she believed my story either. "Major Figueroa's been waiting for you," she said, leading us down the hall.

"It's so good to see lights again," my mother said, glancing at the ceiling.

"Do they have TV and computers?" Danny asked.

"No," I said. "But they've got DVDs so you can watch movies."

"Awesome." But Danny didn't sound excited. "Do you think Bobby and everybody's okay?" he whispered.

"I don't know." I didn't want to lie to him.

"We have to hope," Mom said, hugging Danny as we reached the major's office. "There's always hope."

———

After we all briefed Major Figueroa, Blaine and I walked Mom, Danny, and Muffles to their new home. They were staying on the second floor of Headquarters, in an insurance company's office. Desks and chairs had been shoved against the wall and the space was filled with two cots, two plastic storage bins, a cardboard box lined with a towel for Muffles, and the stuff from the SUV that soldiers had dumped in the middle of the room.

"It's not very fancy," I said.

Mom patted my shoulder. "Don't worry," she said. "It'll be fine for us."

"Can I see a movie?" Danny asked.

"I'm not even sure where the rec room is in this building," I said.

Danny headed for the door. "I'll find it. Can I go now?"

I looked at Blaine and he shrugged. "Mom?" I asked.

She nodded at Danny. "Just remember where we are. It says 'Sullivan Insurance Group' on the door and be back here at ten."

"Sure." My brother raced out the door.

"I'm surprised you let him go," I said to Mom.

"He needs to get his mind off all this. A movie could help."

I sat on her cot. "You don't think the others made it, do you?"

Sitting next to me, she took both my hands in hers. "No, sweetie. I don't."

After two guards escorted Blaine and me to Building 4, we headed for our rec room. But I wasn't in the mood for a movie or game of pool. "You think they're dead?" I asked.

Blaine shrugged. "Those monsters were all over the roads tonight and even though it took us a hell of a long time to get back, we're the only ones here."

"So far."

"Okay, we're the only ones here so far." Blaine tugged at my arm. "Let's at least sit." The room was empty except for four soldiers playing pool.

"How about readin' a magazine?" Blaine asked, lifting a ragged copy of *Time* from the nearby table.

I shook my head.

"Gin or poker?" He pointed to a deck of cards, also on the table.

"No."

"What do you want to do?"

"Let's just sit together like this," I said, leaning against Blaine's shoulder and closing my eyes.

"Sure." As Blaine stroked my hair, I tried not to think terrible thoughts. But I did anyway.

———

I must've fallen asleep because the next thing I remember is Blaine calling my name. "Erin," he repeated. "Somethin's happened. There's a soldier here from Headquarters."

When I opened my eyes, I saw a chubby young black guy smiling at me. "Sorry," he said. "But my orders are to take you both to Major Figueroa immediately."

We walked quickly to Building 1 and Yvonne waved us towards the major's office. "Thank God!" I shouted as soon as I saw the two people standing inside. "You're alive!"

"I sure hope so," Rayna said, laughing as I hugged her. "If not, I'm a ghost."

"I was so worried," I continued. "Who else made it back with you and Manny?"

"Your neighbor, Connie, the two little kids, and the other lady with the baby boy."

"Thank goodness," I said. *Emmy, Jake, Connie, and the Santangelos—all safe.*

"Do you know what happened to the third SUV?" Blaine asked.

Manny and Rayna glanced at each other, but neither immediately spoke. "We saw their car," Rayna finally said. "It was in the middle of the street with doors open."

"What about the people?" I asked. "Camille, Darryl, Mrs. Perez, Kyle, Bobby Mitchell, and his mother?"

Manny shook his head. "We couldn't stop and check. I'm sorry, but there was monsters everywhere so I just took off."

"Did you see anything inside?" I didn't want to say "bodies."

"No," Rayna said. "It all happened too fast."

"Where's the SUV?" Blaine asked. "Do you know which street?"

Major Figueroa, who'd been sitting behind his desk, spoke for the first time. "I have that information," he said. "We'll check it out first thing tomorrow morning."

"I want to go," I said.

"Me too," Blaine said, grabbing my hand.

"I figured you'd both volunteer," the major said. "A guard will pick you up at zero seven hundred hours."

———

I hardly slept, impatient to find the third car and the six missing people.

"Just don't get your hopes up," Blaine said as he drove a beat-up Jeep to the intersection where Manny and Rayna had seen the SUV.

It was a warm sunny day and besides getting ourselves wet, we were each armed with sprayers and water guns. We'd also hosed down the Jeep, but the sun had already dried it.

"There're touchers everywhere," I said as four ran towards us, heaving rocks and bottles.

Blaine quickly changed direction, heading into the nearest side street.

Even though the windows were closed, I still heard the flapping of wings and when I looked up, saw a squad of flying touchers overhead. "They're not attacking," I reported. "Just following us in the sky."

"Maybe they're waitin' till we get to the car."

"If you're right, that means there're survivors."

"Not necessarily. They might just want to get us outside in the street before attackin'."

"Or there were people in the SUV who escaped," I continued.

Blaine shrugged. "It doesn't pay to argue. We'll find out what happened soon enough—and I hope you're right."

––––––

The street was spookily quiet when we pulled up alongside the abandoned black SUV, which was still in the middle of the road, just like Manny and Rayna said. The driver's door and door behind the driver were both wide open. The front passenger window was partly open too.

I could see the front seat—and didn't like what I saw. A big body was slumped over the steering wheel. "It's Darryl," I said.

Blaine shook his head. "I figured he didn't make it. Do you see anyone else in there?"

"Yeah." Leaning against the window, I stared inside again. "In the front, on the floor. Damn! It's Camille."

Blaine sighed. "What about your neighbors? Is anyone in the back?"

All I saw in the rear were clothes thrown everywhere. "It's a mess—piles and piles of clothing—so there could be dead people underneath." I turned to Blaine. "I don't want to check. Can you do it, please?"

Leaving the Jeep running, Blaine grabbed his sprayer, and walked into the back of the SUV. As I watched, he tossed aside shirts and jeans until the seats and floor were exposed. "There's nothin' here," he said. "No more bodies."

I heard movement in the sky and so did Blaine. Both of us glanced up just as the flying touchers started landing. "Get in!" I shouted.

Blaine slid into the driver's seat and quickly locked the door. But touchers surrounded us, pelting the Jeep with rocks, sticks, and anything else they found in the street. At least two touchers landed on the roof, pounding it with something heavy.

"Can you drive fast enough to get them off?" I asked.

"Probably not."

"Should I spray them?"

"No!" Blaine shouted. "Stick your hand out there and you're dead! That's probably what got Darryl and Camille killed."

"Because the window was open?"

"Yeah. Touchers didn't do that."

The noise above our heads got louder. "They're denting the roof," I said, looking up. "They could break through."

"Hang on. I'm gonna try somethin'." Blaine pressed his foot harder on the accelerator. After speeding up, he slowed a little and then zigzagged across part of the street that wasn't blocked by car wrecks.

"I think it's working," I said. "It feels like at least one of them is off the roof."

"Good, because I can't drive like that anymore." The street ahead was full of broken cars with only a narrow lane open.

I heard pounding noises overhead again, much harder than before. "One is still up there and it's..." Pieces of metal fell onto my head followed by a yellow arm dangling through an open hole in the roof.

"Erin!" Blaine shrieked.

"I'm okay," I said, shaking off the debris as I squirted the yellow arm, which stopped groping down and started swaying with the motion of the car. "I think it's dead."

"Don't touch it!"

"I'm not. Just keep driving and I'll duck out of reach." But it was hard to do. The arm kept swinging back and forth like the pendulum on a big clock.

I heard more sounds on top of the Jeep and saw the wings of another toucher through the jagged hole. And this one was very much alive. As I squirted the roof opening, Blaine stopped the car and reached for his sprayer. "Why'd you stop?" I asked.

"Look at the road ahead."

I did—and then I understood. The street in front of us was blocked, not only by wrecked cars, but also by touchers. There was no way our car could get through. When I checked the back, I saw touchers everywhere. We were trapped.

"We have to get out of here," I whispered.

"Brilliant idea—and just how do we do that?"

"I'm thinking."

"You better think fast. They're gettin' closer."

Through the side window, I saw touchers forming circles around us—lots of circles. "How many touchers are out there?" I asked.

"You want me to count?" Blaine paused before speaking again. "Maybe a hundred."

"We can't wet ourselves and then get out and run, can we?"

"No, there's too many of them. They'd touch us first."

The closest touchers were just a couple feet from the Jeep. "Maybe run over them?" I suggested, staring at the dangling yellow arm that wasn't swaying anymore.

"Not enough room to drive through."

"There must be something..." I stopped when I heard the sound of water hitting the car. Somebody was hosing the Jeep.

———

Like magic, the touchers disappeared.

"I can't believe how fast those yellow things ran and flew away," Blaine said.

There was a knock on my window and when I turned, I saw Kyle's smiling face. "You?" Opening the door, I hugged the soaking wet boy. "You did this?"

"Me and him." Kyle motioned to Danny's pal, Bobby Mitchell, who stood a few feet behind him, still holding the dripping hose. "We got it from over there and turned the water on." He pointed to a house across the street.

Blaine reached over and squeezed Kyle's skinny shoulders. "Thanks for savin' us," he said. "How'd you guys manage to escape?"

"We hid under all the clothes," Bobby explained, dropping the squirting hose. "And when it got real quiet, we ran into that store." He pointed to a small building on the next block with broken windows and a sign that read, "Sally's Cards and Gifts."

"What about your mom and Mrs. Perez?" I asked.

Kyle shrugged and Bobby bit his lip.

"I didn't see anything," Bobby said. "But I heard stuff being moved around and when I got up, they weren't here. Just the ones in the front seat..."

"Them two was dead," Kyle continued.

"Yeah," Bobby said. "And my mom..."

I didn't let him finish the sentence. "Maybe somebody saved them like you saved us," I said, not believing my words. I just wanted to give Bobby some hope.

"You really think so?"

"I don't know."

"Miss Norma was a nice lady," Kyle said. "I'm gonna miss her."

Kyle had been through so much; he understood what'd happened.

CHAPTER 23 – New Weapons

We returned to the base without having to fight more touchers. In fact, we didn't see any of them. Maybe they stayed away because they thought we had the water hose with us. Of course we didn't, although we wet the truck and ourselves before taking the hose out of the road and turning off the water.

We searched nearby streets for Bobby's mom and Mrs. Perez, but didn't find them. It was like my dad—more people we loved who were gone and lost forever.

I cried during the funeral for Camille and Darryl and silently promised them we'd defeat the touchers. I just didn't know how.

Bobby and Kyle moved in with my mother, Danny, and Muffles. Their cots were in a small room the insurance company had used for storage. Adding two boys was good for Mom because it gave her more to do and less time to think about all the bad stuff.

She had continued school for Danny (I was excused—soldiers didn't have to go to class) and now had four students: the three boys and CeeCee. Major Figueroa let Mom use another empty second floor office for a classroom, which Blaine and I helped her and the kids set up.

"But we don't got no books," Kyle said as I arranged four chairs in a row facing a large office desk.

"We don't have any books," Mom corrected.

"That's what I said."

"No." Mom smiled at the boy. "You didn't say it properly."

"We still don't have books," Kyle insisted.

"You're right," Mom agreed. "We don't have schoolbooks, but we can find other things to read." She opened one of the drawers in the big desk, pulled out a magazine, and waved it at Kyle. "We can read this."

"'*Us*'? What's it mean?"

"I know that magazine," CeeCee said. "Camille used to read it..." The little girl's eyes started tearing.

"It's okay," I said, giving CeeCee a hug. But it wasn't okay. It wasn't okay at all.

———

The quiet time on the base didn't last long. During breakfast the next morning, we heard a siren and everyone in Unit 4 ran from the cafeteria to the front desk to listen to an update from Headquarters.

"...flying attack," we heard Major Figueroa say at the other end of the walkie-talkie.

"The enemy is landing on the base with real weapons—rifles and guns. We do have twenty gallons of formula and five sprayers, but counterattack at this time is too risky so all units are ordered to stay inside with doors and windows locked and covered."

"How many of the enemy are there, sir?" Lourdes asked.

"About a hundred."

"Are any marching on the ground?" I shouted.

"Not so far, Erin," the major replied.

I guess he recognized my voice.

"Everyone stay inside," Major Figueroa repeated. "I'll let you know when we're ready to fight."

Just after Lourdes turned off the walkie-talkie, I heard the sound of gunfire.

———

Although our orders were to keep windows covered, I ran to an unused office, opened the blinds a little, and saw exactly what Major Figueroa said: touchers filling the sky and instead of rocks or toasters, most carried rifles or guns. They were shooting their new weapons, but not at people, since nobody was outside.

"They're just wastin' ammo."

I jumped when I heard Blaine's voice behind me.

"Scared you, huh?"

"You just surprised me," I said. "I didn't know you followed me in here."

"Can't be without you," Blaine said, gently rubbing my shoulders.

Leaning against him, I sighed. "So what do we do now? Just wait for the touchers to break into the buildings and kill us?"

"The major said he'd let us know when we can fight."

I pulled away from Blaine and stared at him. "I'm ready to fight right now. How about you?"

He shook his head. "Erin, it was bad enough with the touchers before and now they've got guns."

"I don't like being trapped here."

"I know, but we don't even have a sprayer with formula."

"We can get one."

"They're all at Headquarters."

"So let's go to Headquarters," I said, grabbing Blaine's hand.

———

"This is nuts," Blaine said after showering, water dripping from his clothes.

"We can talk about it later," I said. "Standing here, we're getting the hallway wet." I headed to the rear door.

"But it's not warm outside. We'll freeze our asses."

"We'll be moving so fast, you won't have time to think about feeling cold."

"Because I'll be too busy thinkin' about dyin'...Erin, this is one dumb idea."

We reached the back door and I opened it slowly, checking the ground first and then the sky. "It's clear on the ground," I said. "No touchers have landed here."

"What about the sky?"

"They're still up there."

"And shootin'."

I heard gunfire, though not at our building. "They're mostly firing at Headquarters."

"That's because they haven't seen us."

"And they won't," I said. "We're dressed in green to hide ourselves in the grass and we'll move low on the ground."

"Crawlin' to Headquarters."

"Sounds like a song title."

"Hope it's not a song they'll be playin' at our funeral."

I pushed Blaine forward and the two of us stepped outside.

———

Blaine was right about the temperature. But I did what I'd told him—concentrated on crawling through the grass, trying not to think about being wet and cold, as we inched our way forward. Whenever I looked up, I saw flying touchers and heard their gunshots. But they weren't on the ground.

"Stop right here," Blaine ordered when we reached Building 3, holding out his hand like a crossing guard.

I saw why he'd stopped me. Just ahead, a bunch of touchers had landed on the lawn, blocking our way to Building 2. "Damn," I muttered.

"This is your great plan so what do we do now?" Blaine asked.

"Shh. Let me think."

"You better think fast before they see us."

"We can cut around the back of the building."

"How do you know touchers won't be there?"

"We'll look first."

"And if touchers are in the back too, then we'll be trapped."

"Okay, smart guy," I said. "What do you think we should do?"

"Run to Building Three, bang on the door, and pray they let us in before we're touched."

"We're still very wet."

"We're not that wet anymore. Are you willin' to risk your life to find out if you're wet enough?"

———

I didn't want to take Blaine's advice, but I also didn't want to die. And what if we stayed outside and a toucher got Blaine? His death would be my fault.

That's why the two of us rushed to Building 3 and pounded on the door. As we tried to get inside, a group of touchers ran towards us and Blaine and I squirted them. It was just regular water so they didn't die, but they did back off and I didn't see any rifles.

Nobody opened the door to Building 3. "Maybe no one's there," I said.

"Where the hell would they be?"

A clanging of a gong rang out from the direction of Headquarters. "The dinner bell in the morning?" I asked.

"It's gotta be a signal for somethin' else," Blaine said.

"A signal to fight. Look." I pointed to the grass. Lourdes and the rest of Unit 4 were heading our way.

———

The soldiers from our unit were wet like us as they squirted water at the band of touchers. Most flew away, but one creature turned and fired a rifle at the approaching people.

"Watch out!" I yelled as a soldier crumpled and fell to the ground. I heard another burst of gunfire, but this time the bullets missed hitting anyone.

By the time Blaine and I reached Lourdes, the flying touchers had regrouped and were shooting at us, forcing our unit to take cover under the bushes in front of Building 3. "We need to go to Headquarters and get formula," I told Lourdes.

"That's the plan," she said, eying Blaine and me strangely. "What were you two doing out here?"

I ignored her question. "Let me run to Headquarters," I pleaded instead.

"You'll never make it," Lourdes said. "They'll kill you first."

"I'll crawl through the high grass so they won't see me."

Lourdes shook her head. "They can still see you. We've already lost Mark." She pointed to a man's body lying in the grass.

Mark Fielder, another good guy.

"We can't just stay here and wait for them to shoot us all," I argued.

"Major Figueroa said he'd get weapons to us," Lourdes said.

"So where are they?" Blaine asked.

"I don't know," Lourdes admitted.

———

We crouched in the bushes for another few minutes, listening to riflefire from above. "Please let me go to Headquarters, Lourdes," I begged again. "I know I can make it."

"Not going to happen," she said, shaking her head. "We'll go inside this building and wait for the sprayer and poison."

"We already tried bangin' on the door and no one answered," Blaine said. "They must be out fightin'."

Lourdes stared at the two of us again. "You never answered my question," she said. "What were you doing over here?"

"Just getting a head start," I explained, smiling sweetly.

"Without orders?"

I shrugged.

"We'll deal with that later," Lourdes said. "Right now, we've got to figure a way out of here."

I still saw touchers overhead and heard gunfire, although the shooting was no longer near us. "I can get to Headquarters, Lourdes. Look." Dropping to the ground, I crawled a few feet into the open, hidden in the tall grass. "You don't see me at all."

"That's because I'm right next to you. They can see you from the air."

"Only if they're looking for me."

"That's a crazy chance to take."

I crawled back to the bush and sat next to Lourdes. "But I'm willing to take that chance."

Blaine put his arm around my shoulder. "I'll go with you." He pointed to his green clothes. "I'm already in camouflage too."

"No." I pushed him away. "I'm much smaller than you and it's easier for me to crawl real low. They can see two of us easier than just one so I should go alone."

Lourdes didn't say anything for at least a minute. But as touchers continued to fly above us, firing their newest weapons, our unit was trapped. She really had no choice.

"I don't like you doing this," she finally said, shaking her head. "If you die..."

"I won't die." Before she changed her mind, I dropped to the grass and started crawling towards Building 2.

I slithered like a snake, dragging my body through the tall grass so I was even lower to the ground than if I crawled. I didn't hurry, figuring I was safer doing my snake imitation, especially when the gunfire got louder. The touchers were definitely concentrating on Headquarters.

I made it to Building 2 without being seen and scrunched into a tall bush next to the front door. I don't know if Unit 2's soldiers were inside or outside, but I didn't see any people and couldn't risk standing at the entrance.

From my hiding spot, I saw two soldiers in front of Headquarters aiming sprayers at the flying touchers. But the touchers were too high. Then the monsters started shooting at the soldiers and they both rushed inside.

Now I was the only person outside Headquarters. Although I had a clear path, unfortunately, the grass here had been cut so I couldn't hide and touchers were flying directly overhead. If I crawled to the building, Lourdes would be right about me being killed.

I was trapped again, this time all by myself. Crouching low in the bush, I tried to think of a way out.

I don't know how long I remained inside the bush, but it seemed like hours. Then, finally, I heard a rumbling noise: A truck rigged with a huge slingshot was spraying formula high into the sky—and a bunch of touchers fell to the ground like ducks shot by hunters.

"It works!" a man's voice shouted from inside the truck. I recognized the speaker; it was Curtis.

The flying touchers didn't seem to know what happened at first because they stayed in formation, firing their weapons. But when Curtis launched the slingshot sprayer again and hit two more yellow creatures, the others got the message and quickly flew away. The sky was once again empty.

Rushing from my hiding place to the truck, now parked between Headquarters and Building 2, I yelled, "Curtis, you did it!"

He opened the door and jumped out. "Yeah, Erin, for now, anyway."

I ran into his arms and he hugged me, but didn't smile. *Of course not...* "Oh, Curtis," I whispered, mad at myself for not remembering right away. "I'm so sorry about Camille. She was a real hero."

"Maybe so, but she's still dead."

I stared up at his sad brown eyes and nodded.

CHAPTER 24 – Newcomers

When Lourdes told Major Figueroa that Blaine and I had disobeyed his orders, we were called into his office. "I'd like an explanation," the major began.

"It was all my idea," I said. "I forced Blaine to go outside with me."

"Is that true?" Major Figueroa asked Blaine.

"I didn't want her to go out there by herself."

"You couldn't talk her out of it?"

Blaine snickered. "Did you ever try to reason with Erin?"

"Okay," I said. "I already admitted it was my fault."

Major Figueroa glared at me. "You also told me you wanted to be a soldier, right?"

"Yes," I whispered.

"Soldiers have to obey orders."

Nodding, I lowered my head.

"If you do anything like that again, I'm kicking you out of the army and you'll live with your mother," the major said before turning to Blaine. "And if you know she's planning to do something crazy and let her, I'm throwing you out too."

———

"I'm never living here with my mother and Danny and the little kids like I'm a baby," I told Blaine after we were escorted back to

Building 4.

He laughed. "Major Figueroa didn't say where he'd put me. Maybe I could stay with your mom too. That wouldn't be so bad 'cause at least I'd be near you."

"It's not funny. I'm not living on the base with Mom and going back to her school."

"Then you'd better obey the major's orders."

I ran the last few feet to my room and flung open the door. "Don't tell me what to do!" I shouted, slamming the door in Blaine's face. Then I jumped on my cot, closed my eyes, and cried.

Blaine didn't follow me inside. Good move. I would have thrown something at him.

———

I fell asleep and when I woke up, I felt real bad about the way I'd treated Blaine. I'd gotten him in trouble with the army and he wasn't even mad at me for that. And when he said he wanted to be with me, was I grateful? *No.* I yelled at him.

There were cute girls here—including Lourdes and Rayna—who'd probably love to have Blaine for their boyfriend. And I'm sure they wouldn't have treated him like crap the way I did.

As I got out of bed, ready to apologize to Blaine, I realized I was starving. Leaving the dorm, I peeked through the blinds of an outside office window. The sun looked low so it had to be late afternoon. But the building was quiet. *Where was everyone?*

I ran to the entrance, but no one was at the desk. That was strange. *Touchers?* I looked out the window on the other side of the building and then checked the back. Nothing. No people. No touchers.

"Hello!" I shouted from the hallway. "Is anyone here?"

Nobody answered.

Suddenly, I felt very scared

———

I sat on the floor by the entrance, thinking. But I didn't come up with any ideas and was getting spooked so I decided to go outside and look around. Maybe I'd find something that would explain what was going on.

Rushing to the bathroom, I splashed water on my clothes, hair, and face, hoping that would be enough to keep touchers away. Then I filled two water guns and carefully opened the front door.

It was just as quiet outside the building. "Hello," I said, speaking in a normal voice, in case there were touchers around. But there weren't—not in the sky or on the ground.

I walked fast towards Headquarters, looking in all directions for anyone or anything. The sun was lower. I stopped when I realized why no one was around—at least, what I hoped was happening. Then I ran the rest of the way to Building 1 and pushed open the front door.

"Glad you could make it," Yvonne said, smiling at me from the desk. "Better hurry. Dinner's nearly over."

———

Three days later, early in the afternoon, the touchers returned. They carried appliances and guns and attacked us from the air and from the ground.

Soldiers sprayed the grass around Headquarters and that kept the walking touchers away. But they remained on the base, just further back. The poison couldn't protect everything.

Flying touchers were more trouble. We only had two planes and couldn't safely get to them. "It's hopeless," I said to Blaine as we watched through the blinds in what used to be a doctor's office. I'd been feeling mopey ever since Camille and Darryl had gotten touched and this new attack wasn't helping.

"Did you hear that?" Blaine asked.

I listened and heard it too. "It sounds like an airplane," I said.

"More than one."

We looked through the blinds again and I saw two planes—both heading straight for the flying touchers. I couldn't make out the words on the airplanes, but they didn't look familiar. "They're not ours," I said.

"Maybe not, but they've got to be humans flyin' them."

"Could be bad guys."

"Erin, right now, they're the good guys. They're sprayin' stuff on the touchers."

"But it's not killing them."

"It's stoppin' them. See? The touchers are flyin' away."

It was true: The sky was clear and the flying touchers were gone.

––––––

The planes dropped lower and squirted the touchers on the ground too. This time, the yellow things ran away until I could no longer see them. From an office on the other side of the hall, Blaine and I watched the planes land in the grass, not far from our "fleet."

I took a quick shower with my clothes on and then raced to the front door.

"No, Erin!" Blaine hollered.

"I'm going out to meet the pilots!" I shouted back.

"Remember what the major said!"

I stopped running and stood still, creating a water puddle on the floor.

"I'm guessin' you just remembered."

Instead of answering him, I sloshed to the office we'd just been in and peeked through the blinds. There was no one by the planes. Still dripping water, I squished back to my room to dry myself.

––––––

The two pilots—a man and a woman—sat next to Major Figueroa at dinner. But I had to wait until afterwards to find out who they were.

"I know you're all curious about the planes that helped us today," the major began. "The pilots are Marshall Foster and June Halwell. Now I'm going to let Captain Foster explain what he's told me." He nodded to the tall man with a mustache.

Captain Foster bounced up, smiling. "Greetings," he said in a voice that definitely wasn't American. "It's good to be here. As you probably can tell, I'm British, all the way from London."

The audience oohed.

"June is also from Great Britain," he added. The woman pilot waved to us.

"I don't know how much information you have about what happened in England," Captain Foster continued. "We never got any bubbles in May because it rained all the time during those two days." He chuckled. "Our wet weather saved us then, but that doesn't mean we're not in trouble now. When the yellow creatures started flying, they invaded our little island so we're fighting them just like you are."

I raised my hand. "Do you have a way to kill them?" I asked.

Captain Foster shook his head. "No. We just use water."

"I've given the pilots a brief rundown on Curtis' spray," Major Figueroa said. "And of course they'll be taking his formula back with them."

"We're very grateful," Captain Foster said. "So before we return home, we're going to kill as many of the yellow bastards as we can."

We all stood up and cheered. Finally, something good was happening.

CHAPTER 25 – Flying Partners

The next morning after breakfast, Lourdes came to our table. "Erin," she said. "Major Figueroa wants to see you and Blaine."

"What'd I do now?" I mumbled.

Lourdes shrugged. "I've got no idea. I just follow my orders."

I know, I thought, but kept my mouth shut.

"It doesn't have to mean somethin' bad," Blaine said, draping his arm on my shoulder.

And he was right; I hadn't done anything bad.

"How'd you two like to fly with our visitors?" Major Figueroa asked as soon as we entered his office.

"Huh?" was all I managed to say.

"They're not from around here so they need co-pilots, especially those who know the area."

"Oh," I mumbled.

"I'm not from here either," Blaine pointed out. "Are you sure you want me?"

"You're our best pilot—and you're familiar enough with this area to help them navigate."

Blaine nodded.

He's the best pilot?

"The mission's scheduled for this afternoon at thirteen hundred hours," Major Figueroa continued. "Be in my office right after lunch."

"Yes, sir," Blaine said.

"Sure," I muttered and we left.

———

I didn't talk much the rest of the morning and Blaine noticed. "What's the matter, Erin?" he asked when we reached the lunchroom.

"Just a little nervous, I guess."

"Really?" He grabbed my arms and stared into my eyes. "You're never nervous."

"Well, I am now."

Blaine kept staring, but when I didn't say anything else, he finally let go. "I don't believe you, but I don't want to start a fight."

"Me neither." That wasn't true. I would've loved a "best pilot" discussion.

Instead, I forced myself to eat a sandwich and smile at Manny and Rayna, who sat opposite. "It's so cool that you guys are flying with the English pilots," Rayna said.

"Yeah," I muttered.

"Is something wrong?" Rayna asked.

"She's been like this all mornin'," Blaine said. "Mad about somethin'."

"I'm fine," I insisted.

"Don't let anything mess you up in the sky," Manny warned, wagging a finger at me. "You guys gotta kill the touchers."

"I'm fine," I repeated, jumping up. "C'mon. It's time to go."

———

I was assigned to fly with June Halwell and Blaine got Captain Marshall Foster. Of course the "best pilot" was flying with the leader. As we headed to the planes, I tried to focus on the mission and not fume.

"Do you live in this area, Erin?" June asked. She was probably in her thirties—tall and skinny with a long face and big teeth—not pretty, but very nice.

"Yes, my house is about fifteen minutes away."

"How did you find the army?"

"Actually, the army found me." I told June how Major Figueroa killed Cyndy Louise and then asked me to become a soldier.

"What happened to your family?" she asked quietly.

"My dad didn't make it, but my mom and brother are safe. In fact, they're living on the base now."

"You're very fortunate," June whispered. "I lost everyone."

"I'm so sorry." I would have said more, but couldn't think of any words that would've made her feel better.

————

Major Figueroa had given us maps with places circled where groups of touchers had recently been seen. Each pilot had three targets and my job was to help June find the targets and then dump formula on them.

"We're coming to the first target," I told June. "See the church on the left? It's the red brick building on the next block." We were flying low so landmarks were easy to spot.

"I see the church," June said. "Prepare to release the poison."

As I got up, the plane lurched and I tumbled to the floor. "What happened?" I asked, clinging to the bottom of my chair.

"Damn yellow monsters! They flew in front of me and I had to maneuver around them. It happened so quickly that I didn't have time to warn you. Are you all right, Erin?"

"I'm fine." I crawled into my seat. "Where are they now?"

"Behind us, just following."

"Should I squirt them?"

"Certainly. Tell me when you're ready."

The seat in the back had a built-in gun meant for shooting bullets, but smart English fighters had turned it into a giant water pistol, which I now pointed at the lead toucher. "Ready!" I called.

June slowed the plane so I was just a few yards from the lead toucher. I squeezed the trigger, the liquid sprayed the yellow creature, and it dropped to the ground.

"Bull's-eye!" I shouted.

I aimed at the next group, but they scattered and disappeared before I could shoot. "They're gone," I said.

"They must have realized this was poison, not water. Damn monsters communicate with each other." June turned the plane.

"Prepare to fire," she said. "We'll drop poison on the target."

Unfortunately, before we reached the red brick church, a bunch of touchers ran out the front door, flapped their wings, and took off in the opposite direction.

I dumped formula on the building anyway. At least it would keep touchers from going back there.

———

"How did you become a pilot?" I asked June as I refilled the giant water gun.

"I'd taken lessons last year," she began. "And I volunteered to fly and fight after the yellow monsters killed my family."

"What happened?" I whispered.

"One of the yellow creatures landed next to my house. It was a beautiful sunny day so we were on the front lawn—my husband, my little girl in her pram, and..." June wiped away a tear. "We didn't realize they would attack us. We knew about America and what they were doing to other parts of the world, but we thought our island would be safe if we guarded the water." She shook her head. "We didn't know they could fly such distances."

"I'm so sorry," I said softly.

"Thank you. I can't bring my family back so I just want to kill them all."

———

"How far are we from the next target?" June asked.

After looking below, I checked the map. "We're getting close. It's a shopping center across the street from the park."

"Do you see any yellow monsters?" June asked when we reached the location.

"I don't." This time, the sky was empty and no touchers were on the ground. "It's all clear."

"Spray now!"

Moving to the seat behind the water gun, I squirted the entire shopping center. "I used all the formula," I said when the gun was empty. "But I don't see touchers so I don't know if it worked."

"It should have killed them instantly."

"Only if some windows were open or there were holes in the building. The spray has to actually hit them."

"Even if it didn't, the monsters can't go outside," June reasoned. "They're all trapped."

"Until it rains."

"Yes," June agreed. "The rain will dilute the poison."

"We can't even be sure any touchers are in there," I said as I reloaded the gun. "Maybe the ones from the church warned them to leave."

"The monsters can't read our thoughts," June said. "They didn't know where we were going next. I believe they're inside here, dead or trapped."

I wasn't sure June was right, but I didn't want to argue with her.

"Where's the next target?"

"Head east," I said, checking the map. "It's at the airport."

———

When we reached the airport, June didn't have to ask me if I saw touchers. They were everywhere—on the ground next to the planes and in the sky, where dozens were flying our way. "They're surrounding us," I said. "If we don't get out of here right now, we'll be trapped."

"Can't you spray some of them?"

"No time! Go!"

June turned the plane around, but not fast enough. I heard banging on the roof and the plane shook and then dipped. Unbuckling my seatbelt, I crawled to the back, hoping not to get smashed. "I'm going to try to squirt them!" I yelled.

"Hurry!" June urged. "They're pounding the wings! I'm having trouble keeping us steady."

I made it to the backseat and put my belt on as we swerved again. Without seeing what I was aiming at, I squeezed the trigger of the giant water gun. "I hope I hit touchers!" I shouted.

From the rear window, I saw something yellow drop straight down. "I got at least one!" I hollered.

"It's not enough!" June said as the plane flipped, almost knocking my head against the wall, and then dove towards the ground. "Hold on because we're about to land!"

———

June did a great job getting us on the ground without crashing. It wasn't the softest landing, but the plane—and the two of us—touched down without breaking apart.

"Being at the airport helped," June said when I congratulated her. "I had lots of open space." She didn't say "runways" because we hadn't used one. But we landed on the next best thing: the ground right beside the runway. It was deep grass, still soft.

I took off my seatbelt and checked the window. Touchers were everywhere. "Damn," I muttered.

"That doesn't sound good."

"There's got to be fifty touchers on the ground outside," I said. "So far, they're just standing and watching."

"I'm sure there are more monsters in the sky," June said, wincing as she spoke.

"What's wrong?"

"I hurt my leg in the bumpy landing." She smiled at me. "Evidently, I didn't do such a wonderful job."

"Can you stand on the leg?"

"I'll try." Gripping the seat with both hands, June pushed herself up, but then quickly collapsed. "I can't put any pressure on it."

———

I heard familiar hammering sounds against all sides of the plane. "They're attacking us," I said, without even bothering to look outside.

"This is a military plane," Jane pointed out. "It won't break easily."

"But the plane will break, won't it?"

"Eventually, yes."

Moving to the window, I watched touchers smash the plane. I saw one shovel, but most were using sticks and rocks. Then one yellow creature headed towards the plane and I ran to the giant sprayer.

"What are you doing?" June asked.

"A rifle," I said, sitting in the rear seat. "One of them's got a rifle."

June shook her head. "You don't know if our gun still works."

"It's our only chance," I said. "I have to try to squirt them." As the toucher lifted its gun, I squeezed my trigger, praying our rough landing hadn't damaged the sprayer.

"I didn't hear the rifle," June said. "What happened?"

"The sprayer worked. I killed three touchers and the rest backed away."

"But they're still here?"

"Yes."

———

At least I'd bought us a little time. "They won't go near that water," I said. "They know it'll kill them."

I hadn't bought us as much time as I thought because the roof started shaking and I again heard those awful pounding sounds.

"We can't spray the top of the plane," June pointed out.

"Not with the big gun." I grabbed a bottle of water, poured it on my head, then over my shoulders, and on the rest of my body.

"What are you doing now?" June asked.

"I'm going out there."

"That's insane. You're not even thoroughly wet."

"We don't have enough water for that," I said as I filled two water pistols with formula. "This will have to do."

Glancing at her left leg, June shook her head. "I wish I could help you, but I'm totally useless."

"Can you lock me out and then get to the spray gun?"

"Yes." Trying not to wince, June hopped on her right leg toward the door.

"Thanks," I said as I lifted the latch.

———

There was enough formula on the ground next to the plane's door to keep the touchers away. But since the other side wasn't wet, touchers there were working hard to destroy the plane. Luckily, with all the noise they were making, they didn't notice me.

Sloshing through the poisoned water, I tried to soak my feet so that if I had to, maybe I could kill them with a kick. Then I walked quietly around the plane where six touchers were beating the side with rocks and pieces of cement while another six stood on top of the roof, pounding it.

I aimed both guns at the touchers on the roof and four bounced off the plane and crashed to the ground. The two I didn't hit flew away immediately and the group hammering the plane's side backed off—and out of squirting range.

"That's right!" I shouted. "Run away, you cowards!" It was easy to be brave when touchers couldn't reach you. "I'd love to kick all of you in your yellow faceless faces!" I wasn't sure I could do that without dying first, but it sounded good.

Before returning inside, I squirted the ground next to the plane and then the roof with the rest of the poison.

————

"I couldn't see much, but I heard the monsters fall," June said when she opened the door. "So you must have hit some."

"Yes, but the others either flew away or ran off." I tumbled into my seat in the cockpit. "I gave us some protection, but it won't do any good unless we can get out of here. I couldn't spray poison everywhere so the touchers will be back."

June hobbled to the pilot's seat. "I'm sure this plane won't fly without repairs," she said.

"We are at an airport."

"But we don't know which planes, if any, are fueled and ready to fly."

"Then we have to find out."

June shook her head. "I can't go with you. I can barely walk."

"I'll help you and we'll walk together."

"No. That will make you too vulnerable and you won't be able to spray the yellow monsters."

"You'll have the guns—and we'll both be wet. We'll use some of the formu..."

I stopped talking when I heard a huge boom overhead and something really hard dented the roof. "We don't have a choice any

239

more," I said.

———

With June clutching two guns filled with poison, I gripped her waist with one arm, opened the door with my free hand, and we headed out. We were both very wet—especially our hair—since flying touchers were our biggest threat.

"Is this okay?" I asked as we walked toward the first plane.

"As long as I just drag my left leg, I'll be all right."

"Can you go any faster?"

June frowned and shook her head. "I'm sorry, Erin. This is as fast as I can walk."

Although I didn't see any touchers on the ground, I saw plenty of yellow in the sky—watching, but not coming closer. "They're following us, waiting to see what we do," I said, "and they can see we're wet."

"And we've got the poison on our heads," June pointed out.

"I'd rather not test that idea."

"What do you mean?"

"We don't know if touchers die as soon as they touch the poison or if they can kill us first."

June chuckled softly. "Well, I'm not fond of one of them landing on my hair anyway."

We reached the closest plane, a small one, and stopped. "Now what?" I asked.

"I have to see if it's got fuel and if it does, if it's in condition to fly."

"Can you do that quickly?"

"Why?"

"We have company." I nodded to the right where five touchers were running towards us.

———

Taking the guns from June, I squirted poison on the ground, which I hoped would keep the touchers from coming closer. Then I helped June to the plane's fuel tank, wetting the ground as we walked. "They've stopped," I said. But the monsters were only a few feet away.

Since the other side of the plane wasn't protected, I was uncomfortable with touchers so near. "Go away!" I hollered, squirting at two yellow monsters. Even though I hardly got water on them, they dropped dead immediately. Curtis' formula was awesome!

The other three backed off so they were out of spraying range, but didn't leave. "How're you doing?" I called to June.

"The plane has fuel!"

"Great! Is it good to fly?"

"I don't know yet. I'm still checking."

I refilled the guns with my spare bottle of poison water and checked the ground for touchers. It was clear, except for the three creatures that continued to watch us. Then I heard flapping wings overhead. "Hurry!" I shouted. "The flying touchers are back!"

———

I felt my hair and it was getting dry so I squirted my head as I rushed to June. "No more time out here," I said, spraying her hair. "We've got to get into this plane." The flying touchers were almost above us.

"I don't know if the door will open," June said.

"We have to try." Clutching June's waist, I helped her walk alongside the plane to the ramp leading to the door. The flying touchers hovered, watching us. "Shoo!" I yelled, raising my gun. But the yellow monsters were too high to spray.

June twisted the knob. "It's locked," she said.

"Let me try." I pulled on the knob and pushed against the door, but it didn't open.

A toucher landed a couple feet from us. I aimed the water gun, but the creature flew onto the roof of the plane before I could squirt.

Then I heard a clicking sound. "Gun!" I screamed as I shoved June to the ground. The bullet ricocheted off the top of the entrance, just where we'd been standing.

"They'll kill us for sure if we stay out here," I said as the toucher pointed a rifle at us again and I tried to squirt it. Although I didn't reach the shooting toucher, it lowered the gun and backed further away.

"I'm going to run at the door," I told June.

"If you break it, what good will that do?" she asked, crawling out of my path.

"Gotta try." I hurled myself at the door and it opened, knocking me into the plane. As I dragged June inside, I heard another bullet whiz above my head.

———

I'd busted the lock, but hadn't broken either the door or latch so touchers couldn't just walk into the plane. Feeling thankful, I secured the latch.

When I got to the cockpit, June was already in the pilot's seat, checking the controls. "Can it fly?" I asked as heavy pounding on the roof shook the plane.

"I don't know yet."

"What about your leg?"

"As long as I'm sitting, I can do this."

I heard shoving noises at the doorway. "Hurry!" I shouted as I raced to the entrance and threw my body against it. "I can't keep them out!"

With my back still against the bulging door, I reached into my pocket, opened the bottle of poisoned water, and poured some on the floor. The liquid trickled underneath and the pressure against the door stopped.

"What happened?" June asked, not looking up from the controls when I returned to the cockpit.

"I bought us some time again. But not that much so you have to move fast." Touchers still banged on the roof and sides and I already saw some dents above us.

"I've got to check everything."

"If you don't start moving, there'll be nothing left to check."

"All right." She steered with the tiller and we burst forward. "I'm not a hundred percent sure we won't crash, but I'll give it a try."

As we taxied to the runway, the pounding noises continued. We wouldn't be flying alone.

———

The runway was clear and June lifted off without any problems. When she reached a cruising altitude, she let out a long sigh and said, "I wasn't sure I could do it."

"We seem to be flying fine."

"For now. What about the yellow monsters? Are they still hanging on to the plane?"

I looked through my window and then walked into the cabin and checked the sky. "I don't see any touchers," I called. "And I don't hear any pounding."

"Can you guide me to the army base?"

"Sure."

We were just five minutes from the base when I heard a noise in the sky. "What's that?" I asked.

"It sounds like an engine."

Rushing into the cabin, I looked outside. "June!" I yelled. "It's Marshall's plane and it's being attacked by touchers!" *Blaine was inside.* "They must be out of poison! We've got to help them!"

"How?" June asked. "We don't have any poison either!"

"We do have a plane! Let's use it!"

———

There were at least twenty touchers around Marshall's plane, plus two touchers on top of it. One was banging on the roof; the other was spread in front of the pilot's window.

"How can we use the plane to help Marshall?" June asked.

"If we get closer, maybe they'll chase us."

"How will that help?"

"If they follow us to the base, the army's got more poison there."

"That's only if the yellow monsters don't destroy both planes first...All right. I'll try to lure them away." June flew towards the other plane and, when she got close, dipped underneath and made a quick turn.

"Is your idea working?" June asked. "Are they following us?"

I ran into the cabin to check. "Yes!" I called. "Marshall's plane and all the touchers are coming with us!"

———

I heard banging on the roof and sides of our plane as June headed to the base. But I didn't see rocks or other weapons so the touchers must have just been using their hands. But even their hands were real strong. "Can they break this plane with their fists?" I asked.

"I hope not. This isn't a military aircraft so it doesn't have extra reinforcement."

I checked the cabin and nothing was dented or broken. But I heard noises everywhere and saw lots of yellow blobs outside. "Touchers are all around our plane," I reported when I returned to the cockpit.

"Damn!" June shouted as a yellow body landed on her side of the window. Then a second one covered my side too.

"Can you see at all?" I asked.

"Not really."

"I've got a toucher in front of me, but I can still see a little on the bottom so I'll guide you. There's the park. We're almost at the base."

"I want to descend and prepare for landing. Are there any tall buildings?"

"I don't think so, but I'm not positive." The toucher was stretched across my window, banging hard on the glass.

"We have to try to land—so here we go." The plane dropped down, but when June tried to straighten it, the right side stayed tilted up.

"What happened?" I asked as I held onto the seat to keep from falling.

"The monsters must be doing something to the left wing—or just sitting on it."

"How can we land like this?"

"We can't." June tugged on the control wheel. "I can't turn the wings, and if I can't level the plane, we're going to crash."

The tilted plane was falling fast as I unbuckled my seatbelt, crawled to June, and grabbed the wheel.

"Turn!" she ordered.

With both of us pulling hard, the wheel moved just enough so June could straighten the wings. But we were flying really low.

"I hope there's nothing in our way," June said. A yellow blob still blocked her view.

But my side was now toucher-free. "The base is right ahead!" I shouted. "Keep going straight."

CHAPTER 26 – Army Mystery

We landed in the tall grass near the entrance. It wasn't the gentlest landing, but it wasn't a crash and the plane didn't break apart. "Are you okay?" I asked June.

"I'm fine except for my leg."

Her leg. I'd forgotten about that. I inspected the cabin again and everything looked good except for a storage bin that now lay on its side. "I don't see any touchers," I said as I straightened the box and shoved a towel back in.

"The monsters could still be here," June called.

"I know." There was plenty of unmowed grass for them to hide in. "I can't go out to check," I said when I returned to the cockpit. "There's not enough formula left to pour on or around the plane or even just on me."

"The soldiers on the base should have heard us land." June said. "If you recall, our plane made quite a lot of noise."

"What about the other plane?" I asked. "I don't see it on the ground."

"Marshall could have landed somewhere out of our vision—or maybe he wasn't able to land."

"Because he couldn't see?"

"It's certainly possible with the yellow monsters draped on the window."

Blaine, still up in the sky, trapped by touchers. I didn't like that idea at all. "So we have to sit and wait to be rescued?" I asked.

June nodded.

———

I was too antsy to sit so I returned to the cabin and looked outside again. I still didn't see touchers, but I noticed something in the tall grass. Scrunching, I tried to get a better angle, but couldn't figure out what it was.

"I need your help," I said, rushing back to June. "There's something in the grass—not touchers—and I need you to look at it."

As she stood, June frowned and bit her lip.

"I'm sorry. I know how much your leg hurts." She leaned on me, her arm wrapped around my shoulder, and together we walked to the left side of the cabin. "Over there." I pointed to the spot.

"It's part of Marshall's plane," she whispered. "A piece of a wing, I think."

"Just a piece—not the whole plane?"

"That's all I see."

I ran to the door.

"What are you doing?" June called.

"I have to go outside. Blaine was in that plane."

"Erin, you can't do that! You have no protection against those monsters."

"I don't see any touchers right now," I said, reaching for the door. "I need to go."

"Please! It would be suicide!"

I pressed my head against the door, crying. "But Blaine..."

"Come here," June said softly. "We'll wait for help together."

———

I walked back and forth in the cabin trying to come up with an idea.

"Stop pacing, please," June said from an aisle passenger seat, her leg propped up. "You're making me more nervous than I already am."

"Sorry." Moving to a window, I looked outside again.

"Do you see anything?"

I did. "Touchers," I said. "A bunch of them—and they're coming here." Pulling out my water gun, I rushed to the door.

"Erin!"

"Don't worry. I'm not going out."

'What are you doing then?"

I knelt and sprayed the sides and bottom of the doorway. "This should stop them from just walking in." I squirted again, but nothing came out. "Why isn't the army rescuing us?" I asked, returning to a window.

"Maybe the yellow monsters are blocking the buildings, trapping people inside."

"But the army has lots of formula."

There was a loud thud on the roof and pounding on the sides of the plane. When I looked out the window, a yellow face with no nose and blank blue eyes stared back at me. I ran to the rear of the plane.

"What are you doing now?" June asked, shouting her words over the banging noises.

"I can't sit patiently waiting for them to break the plane apart and kill us. There must be something in here I can use." I rummaged through the storage bin, pulling out a towel and blanket. "Aha!" I lifted a can of sunburn spray and squirted the smelly stuff on my head and arms.

"That's not water," June said.

"As long as it's wet, the touchers'll stay away."

"But that solution is meant to dry quickly. Erin, you won't survive out there."

"I'll take the spray with me. Do you have any water in your gun?"

June took out her pistol and shook it. "A little," she said. "Please don't do this."

"I have to." After making sure my clothes and shoes were wet, I headed to the door, holding the sunburn spray. "That was a full can," I said. "It'll give me enough protection to see what's going on outside." *And find the other plane—and Blaine.* But I didn't say that.

———

The water by the entrance kept the touchers away from the front of the plane and the loud banging again kept them from noticing me.

I crept near two touchers pounding the sides and quickly squirted one on its leg. "Shoo!" I yelled.

Although that toucher backed away, the second yellow creature continued hitting the plane with a rock. But when I zapped its eyes with sunburn spray, the toucher tumbled to the ground, rubbing its face.

The three pounding the roof were out of squirting range so I couldn't do anything to stop them. Instead, I ran to the left where that white thing jutted out of the grass. As I raced there, I heard footsteps behind me and flapping in the sky.

Like June said, the object was part of a plane's wing. Since the white metal piece wasn't that big, I tried to lift it with one hand, but it wouldn't budge. Then I walked behind the wing, hoping it would offer some protection.

"Stay away!" I ordered the four touchers that now surrounded me, raising the can of sunburn spray. "This stuff's wet!" I squirted one creature on the foot and it stepped back, but didn't leave.

Two touchers fluttered over my head, but they were too far away to reach so I squirted my hair to make sure they knew it was wet. "Scat!" I yelled, but none of the touchers moved.

I was trapped. Soon I'd run out of spray, dry off, and then the creatures would touch me and I'd be dead. "Help!" I shouted. "Somebody help me!"

———

"Erin?"

I couldn't believe the voice. "Blaine!" I yelled. "Where are you?"

"Right here."

I turned towards the sound of the words and there he was. He had a gash on his head and his clothes were a nightmare, but he was alive. And he held a water pistol, which he used to squirt the four touchers surrounding me. It must have been poison because the yellow things instantly dropped dead.

Then Blaine aimed his gun at the touchers in the sky. I don't think he could've reached them, but they must've seen what happened to their friends on the ground and flew away.

"You smell awful," Blaine said as he gave me a quick hug and ran his fingers through my wet hair. "What is that stuff?"

"Sunburn spray," I said, showing him the canister. "It's the only liquid I could find. What happened to your plane?"

"Touchers made us crash," he said. "Marshall's guardin' it while I went to get help."

"They forced us down too and June's leg is hurt. That's why I'm out here."

"With just the spray can?"

I shrugged.

"Where's everyone?" Blaine scanned the driveway. "They must've heard the crashes. The army should've come to rescue us."

"Unless they can't."

———

It was real quiet now—spooky quiet. The touchers were gone and there wasn't a sound anywhere. "It's like no one's here," Blaine said as if he'd read my mind.

A strong breeze rippled through me and I sensed a new danger. "Do you smell that?" I asked, pushing hair away from my eyes.

Blaine sniffed the air. "Somethin's burnin'," he said, pointing towards the buildings. "I think it's on the base. C'mon." Grabbing my hand, he pulled me forward and we ran through the grass.

Now I saw smoke and some flashes of fire. "Headquarters," I whispered.

Blaine nodded.

We ran faster, Blaine holding his water gun. "Do you still have formula?" I asked.

"A little, maybe two squirts."

We reached Headquarters and stood quietly in front of the burning building, watching the dying flames. "Do you see anything?" I asked.

"No people, but no touchers either," Blaine said.

"Any bodies?" I whispered.

He shook his head. "Not out here."

———

We sat together on what was left of the grass in front of Building 1, thinking our own thoughts. I don't know about Blaine's, but mine were pretty bad. *Mom, Danny, Kyle, CeeCee, the other kids and neighbors? Major Figueroa, Curtis, Kim? Everyone in Headquarters? Trapped? Burnt to death?*

Blaine jumped up and held out his hand. "We can't just sit here and wait for touchers," he said.

"Where do you want to go?" I asked as I took his hand.

"We haven't checked the other buildings yet."

"Do you think anyone's here?"

"No. They would've heard the planes and helped us."

I wasn't hopeful either. As we headed for Building 2, I touched my hair and it felt stiff, like cardboard. I must have looked awful, but that didn't bother me. Something else did. "Blaine, we need to get ourselves wet," I said.

"We have to get inside a buildin' first."

I started running and then Blaine did too. We reached Building 2 and like Headquarters, it'd been burned, but not as badly, and the fire was out. The front door was locked so we pounded on it and yelled our names, but no one answered. Then we tried the back door; it was locked too.

"It's no use," Blaine said, trying to glance inside. "Nobody's in here."

"Do you think they're all dead?" I whispered.

He shook his head. "We'd have seen some bodies so they must've left the base. Look at the parking lot."

I turned around and saw just two broken-down cars.

"That's good," Blaine said, nodding his head. "It means they used the trucks and cars to escape."

"But where'd they go?"

"I don't know."

"And what do we do now? We can't fly the planes and we don't have a car that works."

Blaine pointed to the tall grass. "We go back and report this to Marshall and June. Together, we'll figure out what to do next."

"Touchers," I said. "They could be hiding in the grass and we're not protected."

"We've got no choice," Blaine argued. "We can't stay out in the open like this and wait for them."

I heard a sound overhead and looked up. "Waiting time's over," I said. "They're here."

———

"To the car!" Blaine shouted.

"Which one?" I asked as I ran towards the two busted-looking autos—a gray sports car and a black car.

"The black one!"

I reached for the passenger door of the dented black car, tugged at the handle, and thankfully, the door opened. As Blaine slid into the driver's seat, two touchers jumped on the hood and stared at us through the front window.

"I can't believe the doors worked," I said.

Blaine didn't answer me. He had his penknife out and was fiddling with the keyhole.

"There's no key," I pointed out.

"I know that."

"Even if you get the car to start, they left it here so it probably doesn't run."

"I know that too."

The pair of touchers smashed the windshield with rocks. I heard pounding on the roof too.

"Oh, God," I mumbled.

"Shh."

"I don't want to die like this."

"Erin, shut up!"

"You shut up!" I glared at him. Then I heard a new sound. It was the car's engine and we were moving.

"Ha!" Blaine said, smirking at me.

———

One toucher still sat on the hood. But since the creature needed both arms to hold on to the moving car, it no longer smashed the glass.

"Don't you have somethin' to say?" Blaine asked.

"Like what?"

"Like, 'Thank you, Blaine, for savin' my life by gettin' the car to run.'"

"Thank you," I whispered.

"I'll accept the short version."

"Where are you going?" Although we were moving, we were still in the parking lot.

Blaine shrugged. "Right now, I'm not goin' anywhere, just drivin' fast in here. I want to go back to the planes for Marshall and June, but can't with this toucher hangin' on."

"Give me your gun and I'll squirt it."

Blaine gave me his water pistol. "Wet your hand first," he ordered. "And aim carefully because you're only gonna get one shot."

After wetting my hand, I opened the window and squirted the toucher's arm. The yellow thing tumbled off the car and onto the pavement. "Go!" I shouted as I closed the window.

Blaine drove from the parking lot to the long driveway. Just as he turned into the tall grass, I saw something strange on the left. "What's that?" I asked.

"The grass has been stomped on, but it looks like an arrow," Blaine said.

"If it's an arrow, then it's pointing this way. What direction is that?"

"North."

———

We reached June's plane first. Three touchers were still pounding the side I hadn't wet and making so much noise that they didn't notice our car.

I shook Blaine's water gun. "There's not enough left to spray them," I said. "So what should we do? We can't get out of the car."

"I'm gonna drive to Marshall's plane. Maybe it'll be free of touchers."

There were no touchers—at least none that I could see—around the second plane. "They could be hiding on the other side," I pointed out. "Or they could've gotten in. The plane's such a mess." Besides the missing wing piece, the whole body was squashed and dented.

"I'll drive around to make sure it's clear," Blaine said. "Then we'll see about goin' in." He circled the plane and the other side looked even more crushed.

"How'd you ever land this plane?" I asked.

"Marshall's a pro. He did it, not me."

"And he's okay?"

"He was when I left." Blaine stopped the car again.

"Then why isn't he signaling us—waving from the window or banging on the glass?"

"Good point." Leaving the car running, Blaine grabbed the door handle. "There's only one way to find out."

"I'm going with you," I said, reaching for my door. "No way I'm staying in this car alone."

Blaine shook his head. "If touchers come and we're both inside the plane, we'll be trapped again. We need this car to find the army so you have to stay here and wait."

Blaine's argument made sense. "Okay," I agreed. "But if you're not back in five minutes, I'm coming out."

"It's a deal," Blaine called as he ran to the plane.

———

Without a watch, I had no way of counting an exact five minutes. I'd decided time was up and was about to leave the car when Blaine ran out. Marshall wasn't with him.

"So?" I asked as he sat beside me and locked the door.

"So it's not good."

"Marshall?" I asked.

Blaine shook his head. "He's dead. No marks on him so it had to be touchers."

"I'm so sorry about Marshall," I said. "But what took you so long?"

"This." Blaine held up two water pistols. "I filled my gun and his so at least we'll have some protection."

"Plain water?"

"Yes. There's no poison left."

I shrugged. "It's better than nothing." Then I realized something scary. "Blaine," I began. "I left June alone in the plane—and she has a bad leg and can hardly walk."

"We're on our way."

———

Touchers still pounded on the sides and roof of June's plane. But they hadn't broken through and the door remained closed.

"Give me a water gun and I'll run inside," I said.

"I can go."

"No. This is my plane so it's my job."

"At least wet yourself. Touchers could be in there."

I shook my head. "If they were inside, the door wouldn't be shut and they wouldn't be out here smashing the plane."

"You're probably right, but be careful. You've got exactly five minutes."

Jumping out of the car, I ran to the plane. Blaine had a watch so I knew I had to be fast.

———

"June, open the door!" I shouted, banging my fists on the metal.

"Erin, is that you?" The voice behind the door was muffled.

"Yes! Hurry!"

I must've been too loud because the touchers, all five of them, came at me. I squirted the first two and they backed away, but the others flapped their wings and took off above my dry cardboard head.

"June!" I hollered. Then the door opened and I ran inside. "That was close," I said, quickly locking the door.

"I'm sorry. I can't move very well and I wasn't sitting near the entrance."

"You didn't hear the car?" I asked.

"You have a car?"

I nodded. "Blaine's driving it and waiting outside. We have to go right now."

"And Marshall is with Blaine?"

I hated that question. "I'm sorry. He didn't make it."

"The crash?"

"No. Touchers."

"Damn monsters." June shook her head, wincing as she stood. "I'm more than ready to leave. It's been horrid waiting in here, not knowing if those yellow creatures were going to break the plane and get inside."

"Hold on to me," I said. "I've still got a little water left in this gun."

June tucked her hand around my waist as I flung open the door—and immediately closed it. Touchers had surrounded our car.

———

Again I sat in the broken plane with June. "We've got to find a way to get to the car," I muttered.

"I'm sorry I'm such a burden. You might make it there without me."

"No. Too many touchers. I wish we still had some poison."

"And I wish this plane could still fly. Wishing won't help us, Erin. We need a practical plan."

I walked to the window and looked outside. "The car's gone," I said.

June nodded. "That's a good thing. I'm sure Blaine's trying to lead them away from us."

"But we're still trapped in here."

"Only till we find a way to escape."

"I can't think of anything that'll work," I said, sitting next to June, who took my hand and patted it.

"Keep thinking," she said, "and I will too. We need to come up with a solution before Blaine returns."

———

I closed my eyes tightly, hoping to force an idea into my brain. But all it did was make my head hurt. "Maybe there's something else here we could use," I said, walking to the back of the plane.

The storage bin was empty because I'd tossed the towel and blanket on the floor when I found the sunburn spray. Now I picked up the blanket, intending to put it back into the box, and a plastic bottle, hidden in the folds, fell on my foot. "June, look at this!" I shouted, running to her.

"Well, it is a liquid," she said, examining the eight-ounce container of hydrogen peroxide. "But rubbing this on your skin full strength might sting."

"I'll take the chance," I said, quickly wetting my hair, arms, and legs. "It burns a little, but smells even worse." I handed June the bottle. "Here. Put some on you."

June took the bottle, but closed the cap. "We should wait until Blaine gets here. Hydrogen peroxide will dry faster than water."

I touched my arm and it was nearly dry. "Damn!" I said. "I wasted all that liquid."

June shook the bottle. "Don't worry. There's enough left."

"Blaine better come back," I whispered. As I gazed out the window, I felt sticky, smelly, and most of all, stupid.

––––––

When I heard the honk of a car's horn, I jumped up and rushed to the window. "It's Blaine!" I shouted.

"What about the yellow monsters?"

"They've surrounded the car again—but Blaine's squirting them and they're backing off."

I ran to June, who was already wetting herself with hydrogen peroxide. "When you're done, I'll put more on myself," I said.

Blaine honked again. "We're coming!" I yelled, rubbing the stinky liquid on my arms. But I don't think Blaine heard me because he kept honking the horn.

After June and I used up the bottle, I took her arm and we walked outside together. Blaine still had his water gun aimed at the touchers, but they must've seen the liquid on us because they kept away.

"You two girls smell really bad," Blaine said as I helped June into the back seat and then slid into the front.

"That's some greeting," I said, smiling.

"Do I get a 'thank you' this time?" Blaine asked as he drove.

"Thanks so much," June said.

"And you?" He turned to me.

"Thanks, but what took you so long?"

"I needed to get more water and finally found some inside Building Three. It wasn't damaged and a back window was open."

"I guess that building was empty too."

"Yeah. No sign of anyone."

"Do you think all the people escaped?" June asked.

"We didn't see any bodies and most of the cars are gone," I said. "And it looked like someone made an arrow in the grass, pointing north, maybe a signal for us."

"It's too late to look for the army now because it'll be dark soon," Blaine said. "We need a place to sleep tonight so where do y'all want to go?"

"How about my street?" I suggested. "The Douglasses are still there."

"Let's hope so," Blaine whispered.

CHAPTER 27 – Road Trip North

It was nearly dark as Blaine drove through the streets, which were still full of crashed cars with dead people inside. But with the cooler weather, there were less bugs.

And we didn't see any touchers. "It's too quiet," I said.

"No touchers is good," Blaine said.

"Maybe. But no people, no other cars..." I shut my mouth as an SUV passed us, heading the opposite way.

"If you hadn't been talkin', we could've heard him comin' and honked," Blaine said. "Then maybe he would've stopped."

"It was a she," June pointed out. "And I don't think she would have stopped."

"Why not?" I asked.

"She seemed terrified."

———

Walnut Lane looked deserted, which wasn't surprising since only the Douglasses still lived there. "This is creepy," I whispered.

"That's because it's dark and quiet," Blaine said as he pulled into their driveway. "Nothin' here is different—no new busted windows or broken doors."

We'd all boarded up our bottom floor windows after the bubbles fell and the Santangelo's house at the other end of the street had burned to the ground so it's not like my block was in great shape.

I saw a flashlight beam and then Mr. Douglas' arm as he opened the front door a little. "It's me, Erin!" I yelled, rolling down my window. "I'm with Blaine and a friend. Can we come in?"

"Yes!" he called. "But hurry!"

With Blaine and me helping June, we ran into his house.

———

"Thank you," I said, leading June to the living room couch.

Mr. Douglas nodded. "I thought I recognized you, but it was dark and your hair..."

I'd forgotten about my suntan-spray head and smelly peroxided body. "I needed something wet and that's all we had." I glanced at the empty room. "How is your wife?"

Mr. Douglas fell into a living room chair and stared at the carpet. "Lynne passed away last week," he whispered.

"I'm so sorry," I said.

Mr. Douglas nodded again. I think he would have cried if he'd talked.

"So sorry," Blaine whispered.

"And I'm very sorry for your loss too," June added. "I appreciate you letting us come into your home at this most difficult time. I'm June Halwell, from England."

"From England?" Mr. Douglas repeated.

June told him about the planes and our mission. "...and that's how we came to your doorstep," she concluded.

Mr. Douglas seemed in better shape after listening to June's story. "Where are my manners?" he said, rising to his feet. "The three of you have had a difficult day. I'll make you something to eat."

That's when I realized I was starving. "Thanks," I said, following him into the kitchen. "I'll help you."

———

I felt much better after dinner. It was just tuna, crackers, and water because Mr. Douglas didn't have electricity, reminding me of the meals I ate in the dark with Mom and Danny before joining the army.

Mr. Douglas didn't talk much and when he did, it was to ask us questions. I think he'd been real lonely since his wife died. I know I'd hate to be by myself with no one to talk to.

After we answered all Mr. Douglas' questions, I asked him one: "Have you seen any touchers?"

"Several. The last time it rained, I'm pretty sure they were sleeping in one of the houses at the other end of the block."

"Have you seen any since then?" Blaine asked.

"No. But I haven't paid much attention to what's going on outside after Lynne..." His voice drifted off.

I yawned very loud on purpose. "I'm really tired," I said, stretching my arms and yawning again. "Could we sleep here tonight?"

"Of course," Mr. Douglas said. "I'm sorry if I didn't make it clear that you're all welcome to stay for as long as you want."

"Thank you," Blaine said. "But it'll just be tonight. Tomorrow we're searchin' for the army."

———

After going to bed soon after dinner—I really was tired—I got up early. It was like Mom's school days after the bubbles when we went to sleep as soon as it got dark and woke up at daybreak.

I needed a shower badly. "It'll be very cold," Mr. Douglas warned as he handed me a large towel.

I nodded, remembering those icy showers. "I'll be fast."

The water was freezing so I washed myself in record time and after putting on clean clothes, I felt a thousand times better. "Thank you for letting me wear these," I said to Mr. Douglas.

"Lynne would've wanted you to have them," he said, smiling. "You're about the same size."

His wife had been a little bigger than me, but the jeans and turtleneck—and even the bra and panties—fit well enough. Fashion wasn't exactly an important part of my life these days, although I wanted to look good for Blaine. But he'd seen me at my worst—like yesterday.

After Blaine showered and exchanged his torn clothes for Mr. Douglas' shirt and jeans (a little short and baggy), we ate more crackers for breakfast. When we finished, Blaine stood. "Thanks for lettin' us stay here and sharin' your food," he told my neighbor. "We're gonna be leavin' now." He stretched out his hand.

Rising, Mr. Douglas shook Blaine's hand. "I hope it's not presumptuous, but I packed a suitcase and I'd like to go with the three of you," he said. "Now that Lynne's gone, there's no reason to stay here."

I looked at Blaine who nodded. "Of course, Mr. Douglas. We'd love you to come with us."

———

We didn't know where the army had gone, except for the arrow impression in the grass that seemed to point north. "What's in the north?" Blaine asked.

"It's more rural," Mr. Douglas said. "Fewer houses and people."

"What should we look for?" Blaine continued.

"Maybe an obvious place," June said.

"Like what?" I asked her.

"A military base. Do you have one to the north?"

I didn't know the answer, but Mr. Douglas did. "There's an air force base in Glentree," he said. "But it's about fifty miles from here— a long and dangerous trip these days."

"And we don't know for sure that's where the army went," Blaine pointed out.

"Or where the yellow monsters are," June added. "I don't like that we haven't seen them since earlier yesterday."

"So do y'all want to go north?" Blaine asked.

"Let's take a vote," I said. "That's the fairest way."

"Okay," Blaine agreed. "Everyone who wants to drive to the base in Glentree, raise your hand."

I raised my hand and so did the other three.

———

Although I wasn't good on directions, I knew we had to take the interstate, which I hadn't been on since the bubbles. But Blaine had driven on that road before coming to Walnut Lane. "How was the highway when you were with Zach?" I asked.

"Loaded with busted cars, but we got through." He shrugged. "That was months ago—I don't know what the road's like now."

Mr. Douglas insisted Blaine drive his Subaru. "I've been starting the Outback so I know it works and it's got nearly a full tank of gas," he explained.

It felt good to be in a car that wasn't broken as we zigzagged around crashes until reaching the highway. No touchers stopped us.

"Where are the monsters?" June asked. "It's not raining, but they're not outside."

"Maybe it has something to do with the army leaving," Mr. Douglas suggested.

"You think the touchers are chasin' the army?" Blaine asked.

I had a better thought. "Touchers appeared suddenly with the bubbles so maybe they all just disappeared. Do you think that's possible?"

"No, Erin," June said. "I don't."

———

At first, the highway was okay. There were plenty of smashed cars, but enough lanes to get around them. Also, there wasn't any traffic.

"So far, so good," Mr. Douglas said, echoing my thoughts.

"I still don't like it," June said. "It's much too quiet. The yellow monsters must be up to something."

I didn't say a word. If I was right, there were no more touchers.

Blaine drove another few miles until we reached a part of the interstate that was completely blocked off, with at least ten cars and trucks covering all the lanes as well as the sides. There was no way we could squeeze through.

"Do you think this was a major accident or something the touchers did?" Mr. Douglas asked.

"I don't know, but we're not waitin' to see if it's a trap." Blaine quickly turned and drove the wrong way. "We passed an exit about a mile back. You guys watch with me to make sure we don't make our own crash."

It was scary driving the wrong direction on a highway, but

everything since the bubbles was scary. This was just a different kind of scariness.

"A car!" June yelled.

Blaine moved to the side of the road and waited while a gold van zoomed past us.

"They're going to have to turn around too," I said.

"Yeah," Blaine agreed. "They just don't know that yet."

———

Blaine drove the wrong way without anything else happening till he reached the exit and got off the highway. Then he took local streets for about ten miles before entering the interstate again—this time in the right direction.

We only saw one other car and no touchers. "Maybe the touchers really are gone," I repeated. "If they were still here, we'd have seen some by now."

"I hope you're right," June whispered. "But I'm sure you're not."

"I don't think they've magically disappeared either," Mr. Douglas said.

When nobody said anything else, I turned to the window and watched the scenery—a steady stream of wrecked cars, dead bodies, and busted houses.

"What's that sound?" June said.

I heard it too and scrunched lower so I could look up at the sky. It was filled with touchers—hundreds, maybe thousands. *So much for my great theory.* Leaning against the seat, I closed my eyes and cried.

"I'm sorry, Erin," June said, rubbing my shoulders. "It's not going to be as easy as you hoped. We can't just wish the yellow monsters away. We have to destroy them."

Even with the closed windows, I smelled something burning and saw a few wisps of smoke and flashes of fire.

"In the sky, where the touchers are circling," Mr. Douglas said. "I'm pretty sure that's above the air force base."

"Then we're headin' to the right place," Blaine said. "It can't be a coincidence that there's fire and so many touchers."

Mr. Douglas nodded. "Probably not. But that also means we

should expect them on the ground too."

I took the gun from my pocket and put it on my lap. "All we have is ordinary water, not the poison that kills them."

"The army could've brought poison," Blaine pointed out.

"We'll get some answers soon," Mr. Douglas said. "Here's the entrance."

Although the big blue sign was dented, like a car had hit it, you could still make out the words: "GLENTREE AIR FORCE BASE." Turning right, Blaine drove through the open gate.

CHAPTER 28 – Battle at the Base

I heard the crackling noise right after we entered the base. "What's that?" I asked.

"Some kind of electricity, I think," June said.

As we got closer, I saw flashes of yellow sparks in the sky, almost like lightning, and remembered the old electrical appliances the touchers had collected. "Are they using the busted stuff to set fires?" I asked.

"It looks that way," Blaine said.

Most of the flying touchers held toasters, light bulbs, irons and other small gadgets in their hands or between their legs—and all those machines beamed lightning-like flashes down to the building we were approaching.

"Those things shouldn't be working," I said. "The cords aren't plugged in and the bulbs aren't in lamps."

"We saw touchers makin' old broken machines work in the park and on the base," Blaine reminded me.

When we reached the large building, an airport hangar, part of the roof was on fire. "Mom and Danny," I whispered. "Rayna, Manny, Lourdes...They could all be in there."

"We don't even know if the army came to this base," Blaine said.

"But what if they are here and they're all trapped inside this burning building? We have to make sure."

"Erin, you can't go in there!" Blaine shot me an angry look.

"Why not? There're no touchers on the ground to stop me. They're all in the sky with those toasters and light bulbs. And right now, only a little of the roof is on fire. I can wet myself and check real fast that nobody's inside."

"Erin, Blaine's right," Mr. Douglas said. "Please don't go in there."

I didn't wait to hear anything else. Stepping out of the car, I squirted my hair and body, ran to the hangar, pushed in the double doors, and walked inside.

———

The place was full of smoke so I couldn't see much except that I was standing in a big open room. I heard crackling noises above and when I looked up, realized the whole roof was now on fire and chunks of the ceiling were about to fall. That's when I started coughing. "Is anyone here?" I managed to say before the cough got so bad that I couldn't stop.

"Yeah, me!"

I turned and Blaine was about six feet behind me. "There's no one else here, Erin. Come with me before the roof collapses." He held out his hand and, still coughing, I took a step towards him, but stopped when I heard a loud sizzle overhead and a piece of burning roof fell on the floor between us. Flames shot up high, creating a wall of fire.

"Erin!" Blaine yelled. "Are you okay?"

"Yes, but I can't move forward," I managed to say between coughs. It was smoky and my eyes were tearing.

"Stay where you are. I'm comin' around to get you."

"Be careful." I don't know why I said that. It was impossible for him to be careful with all the fire. Then I dropped to my knees and I don't remember anything else.

———

When I opened my eyes, I was buckled into the front seat of the Subaru and Blaine was driving. "What happened?" I asked, rubbing my eyes, which still stung from all the smoke.

"You passed out and I carried you to the car."

"I'm sorry about that, especially since nobody was inside the building."

"You don't always have to be so stubborn and reckless."

"I said I was sorry." Slumping into the seat, I closed my burning eyes again. "Where are we going?"

"We noticed some vehicles in the lot," June said. "So we're hopeful this base is still in operation."

"Cars without dead bodies inside?" I asked.

"Yes."

"What about our army? That would be a lot of cars and trucks."

"We didn't see many cars, Erin," Mr. Douglas said. "Just a few."

———

Blaine drove to another big building that could have been the headquarters of this base. But there was no sign and most of the windows and doors were busted. Blaine honked his horn. "Just in case someone alive's still in there," he explained.

As we waited, a hard object slammed the roof of the car, nearly knocking us all to the floor. "That's enough waitin'," Blaine said as he drove away. "They're throwin' stuff at us. Next they'll set fire to the car. I'm gettin' outta here now."

"But what if my mom and Danny and..."

"Erin, they're not here," Blaine said. "No one's here."

"You can't be sure. You saw cars—and why would the touchers set buildings on fire if no one's here?"

Mr. Douglas reached forward and patted my shoulder. "It doesn't pay to argue, Erin," he said. "Blaine's right. If we don't leave, the touchers will kill us because we have no weapons to fight them with."

I leaned against the seat and tried to stay awake as Blaine drove out of Glentree Air Force Base.

———

I must have fallen asleep because I don't remember anything after leaving the base. When I woke up, our car was parked under a tree and it was raining. "Where are we?" I asked, stretching my cramped legs and taking a drink of water.

"Further north," Blaine said. "I just kept goin' in that direction."

"At least there are fewer touchers here," Mr. Douglas said.

"Fewer of everything," June added. "Not many smashed cars or broken houses or dead people."

The rain was falling steadily—not pouring, but not drizzling either. "I'm going outside," I said, pulling the hood of Mrs. Douglas' navy jacket over my head. Then, opening the door, I stepped on the mushy grass.

I took a deep breath. The smoke was gone and the country air smelled wonderful—clean and flowery. Also, I didn't see any bugs, probably because there weren't rotting bodies for them to feast on. Best of all, with the rain, I knew I wouldn't see any touchers. Looking up at the sky, I closed my eyes and let the water pelt my face.

"Feels good, huh?"

I opened my eyes as Blaine joined me. "What are we going to do now?" I asked.

He shrugged. "June and Mr. Douglas want to try another base. Mr. Douglas thinks there's an army post about a hundred miles from here."

"Do you have enough gas?"

"Yes. This car's got a full tank."

Turning, I saw a blue van, not a white Subaru. "You switched cars while I was sleeping?"

"You didn't even wake up."

"How long was I asleep?"

"I don't know exactly." Blaine checked his wrist. "It's two o'clock now so I'd guess nearly three hours. How's your throat?"

"Better." I didn't feel like I had to cough.

———

According to Mr. Douglas, Fort Hallock was north and then west. "It's somewhere off Route Two," he said. "Hopefully, there'll be a sign."

It was creepy again driving on a road with no other cars except the occasional smashed one. The houses we passed mostly had broken windows and open doors or just looked deserted. I didn't see one live person. Except for the falling rain and the sound of our engine, it was totally quiet.

"How much longer till we get there?" I asked Mr. Douglas.

"We should see a sign soon. After that, it's another half-hour or so."

It was hardly raining and large patches of blue were breaking through the clouds. "What direction is this side?" I asked, tapping my window.

"West," June said. "Why?"

"It won't be raining when we reach the base. The weather's clearing up."

By the time we saw the first sign for Fort Hallock, the sun was shining.

––––

We were close to the base when I again heard those terrible flapping sounds in the sky. "The touchers are here," I said. "Do you think they followed us?"

"Maybe," Blaine said. "But there's nothin' we could've done about that."

Slumping into my seat, I tried not to listen to the touchers' wings, which always reminded me that we had no more birds. I loved drawing birds and I missed their grace and beauty. Flying touchers had no grace and they definitely were not beautiful.

As we entered Fort Hallock's broken gate, I heard sizzling noises. The touchers were using their broken electrical junk again—zapping buildings, trying to burn them down. "It's the same here as the air force base," I muttered.

"Not exactly," Blaine said. "There's a bunch of cars and trucks in the lot."

"Look over there!" June cried. "I see people!"

––––

People! What a wonderful word! Turning to where June was pointing, I saw a man and woman hosing down a burning building. The woman aimed her hose at the flying touchers, but the yellow things were too far away for the water to reach them.

Blaine parked the car and I jumped out. "Can I help?" I asked the big man holding the hose.

"Who're you?" He gave me a quick glance as he continued to spray the building.

"My name's Erin Fredericks. We drove here from outside the city."

"You did what?" His eyes widened and he almost dropped the hose.

"It's the truth, sir," Blaine said, joining me. "We're searchin' for our army unit and thought maybe they came here."

"We could sure use an army to help fight the yellow monsters." He shook his head, still squirting the flames. "But that hasn't happened."

Blaine held out his hand. "Let me take a turn," he said.

"Thanks, son."

The hefty guy gave Blaine his hose and stared at the building that still burned steadily. "It's not doing any good," he said, shaking his head. "Kleeber!"

The woman turned towards him, her brown ponytail flapping. "Yes, sir?"

"We can't put out the fire and we're just wasting water. Turn it off."

Nodding, she dropped her hose on the ground.

The man looked at me again. "You better get inside before those creatures touch you," he said. "You're not even wet."

"We've got other people in the car," Blaine said.

"Bring them too."

———

Blaine and I reached the van just as a flying toucher swooped down, aiming for our heads. I ducked and rushed inside while Blaine, wet from the hose, took out his gun and squirted the yellow thing.

"It flew away!" he hollered. "But y'all use the water in Erin's gun to wet your hair, face, and arms before comin' out. The touchers in the sky are still circlin' and shootin' off electricity."

When we were thoroughly wet, I opened my door. "Hurry," Blaine urged. "They're turnin' and comin' back." Reaching into the back of the van, he pulled out June while I helped Mr. Douglas.

"Follow me," the big man said.

Moving as fast as we could, the four of us walked behind him, with the woman, Kleeber, taking up the rear. I heard flapping again as the touchers flew nearer.

"Watch out!" the man shouted.

I put wet hands over my head as something hard and hot hit my left wrist before clanging to the ground. "Ow!" I screamed. When I looked down, I realized it was a toaster.

"Don't stop!" Kleeber ordered. "We're almost there."

We reached the entrance to a building, this one not on fire. Then someone opened the front door and we all rushed in.

––––––

"We should be safe here for now," the man said as he locked the door. We were standing in the hallway of what looked like an office building, with a small desk shoved against the back wall.

Blaine gently lifted my left hand. "What happened to you?" he asked.

Looking down, I saw a large red mark on my wrist. "A toaster hit me. I don't know how the touchers make those broken things work, but it must've been on." I felt my hand. "It's hot and it stings."

"I'll see if I can find something to make it feel better," Kleeber said, smiling.

"Let's go to the conference room," the man said. "I'm Colonel Bradley Peterson, acting commander of Fort Hallock, and that's Lieutenant Andrea Kleeber." He nodded in the woman's direction.

"How many soldiers do you have here?" I asked as we walked through the empty corridor.

"This is it—the two of us."

––––––

After we took seats around the conference table, Blaine and I recited the short version of why we were looking for the soldiers from our army base. "We think they came this way," I said, "because they left an arrow in the grass pointing north."

Colonel Peterson shrugged. "I'm sorry," he said. "No one else has been here."

"What happened to the rest of your soldiers?" Blaine asked.

The colonel shook his head. "The touchers—as you call them—have been attacking us since the bubbles fell. We managed to hold them off until last week when they began burning our buildings with their contraptions."

He sighed. "I sent the remaining twelve survivors away—and Lieutenant Kleeber and I stayed here fighting a losing battle." He nodded towards the dark-haired woman, who rubbed cream on my sore wrist.

"Where'd you send the soldiers?" Blaine continued.

"To Glentree—it's the nearest base."

I looked at Blaine and then at June and Mr. Douglas. None of us spoke for a few moments. "We just came from Glentree," I finally said. "The touchers burnt it down and no one's there."

Colonel Peterson lowered his head and didn't say anything.

"Our soldiers have a weapon," I said.

"Really?" Colonel Peterson looked up at me.

I explained Curtis' invention. "Even the smallest amount kills the touchers immediately," I said. "But we don't have any formula with us."

"That's too bad," Colonel Peterson said. "We could use..."

June interrupted him. "Do you smell smoke?" she asked.

"Yes," Mr. Douglas said.

I smelled it too.

"Quickly," the colonel ordered, rising to his feet. "We'll get out through the back."

———

We ran through the building, Blaine helping June, stopping only long enough for Colonel Peterson to reach into a hallway bin and grab a batch of loaded water guns, giving one to each of us. By the time we opened the rear door and stepped outside, the whole building was on fire.

"Hurry and wet yourselves," the colonel ordered. But we all knew the drill so even before he spoke, we'd squirted our heads, arms, and legs.

"Is there any other safe place here?" Blaine asked.

"I'm afraid not," Colonel Peterson said. "They've burned or destroyed everything. Our only chance is to get to the parking lot and drive away."

"Then let's go," I said. Looking up, I saw touchers continuing to torch the building we'd just been in so I ran as fast as I could to the parking area and stood beside a Jeep.

Gasping for breath, I waited for the others. When the colonel, lieutenant, and Mr. Douglas reached me, June and Blaine had just gotten to the entrance.

"We should all be able to fit into this Jeep," Colonel Peterson said, opening the door.

As I started to step inside, a flash of lightning lit up the sky and fire exploded everywhere. Dropping to the ground, I watched the Jeep and surrounding cars burst into flames.

———

"Blaine!" I shouted, backing away from the burning Jeep. "Where are you?"

"Over here!"

Crawling through the smoky haze towards the sound of his voice, I saw him kneeling on the ground just outside the parking lot. June lay next to him.

"Are you both okay?" I asked.

"I guess so," June said, wincing as she tried to sit up.

"Your leg?"

She shook her head. "Not so good. I think I fell on it."

"Do you see the colonel and the others?" I asked Blaine.

"I can't see a damn thing," he said, wiping his eyes. "Too much smoke."

"I'm going to take June and crawl out of here," I said.

"And go where?" Blaine asked.

"I don't know."

"Erin, there's no place to hide," Blaine argued.

"I don't care. We're not staying here and burning to death." I turned to Blaine. "If you won't help, I'm doing this myself." Clutching

June's hand, I tried to drag her with me while I crawled.

"You're not strong enough." Blaine took June's other hand. "We'll do this together."

———

When we'd crawled far enough away from the lot, Blaine and I lifted June and surveyed the base. "So where do we go now?" Blaine asked.

There wasn't much of a choice. All the buildings were either burned-out shells or on fire. "Maybe we can find some tall grass to hide in," I suggested.

"The yellow monsters will see us from the sky," June said.

Touchers were still flying overhead and I noticed flashes of other fires in the distance. The only good thing was the touchers were high and not directly above us.

"Do you still have water?" Blaine asked me.

"Just the gun the colonel gave us."

"I have mine too," June said.

"Let's get wet again before doin' anythin' else," Blaine said.

As we splashed water on our heads and bodies, I realized the fire had at least done one good thing: It warmed the air so I didn't feel cold. When we finished, June put her wet arms around Blaine's and my shoulder and the three of us walked away from the lot to look for a good hiding place.

"Do you think the colonel, lieutenant, and Mr. Douglas are still alive?" I asked, staring back at the burning cars.

"I hope so," Blaine said.

I shook my head. "We should have tried to get them out."

"You know we couldn't," Blaine said.

"Maybe they were able to escape the fire like you did," June suggested.

"Yeah, maybe." But I wasn't real hopeful.

As we walked, I saw only useless buildings and short grass—no place that would offer protection. Then I saw something else: a group of touchers on the ground, heading towards us.

———

We couldn't run away and even if we tried to run somewhere, it wouldn't have helped because the touchers were much faster. So we stopped walking and stood still.

"I hope we're wet enough," I murmured.

"They can just wait till we dry," Blaine said.

The eight touchers formed a circle around us. Although they carried broken toasters and other appliances, they didn't turn them on. I guess they figured it wasn't necessary to set us on fire; we'd be easy to kill.

I heard flapping noises overhead and when I looked up, at least twenty more touchers hovered directly above us. "This is the end," I said. "I have hardly any water left."

"Use it to wet your head," Blaine said, lowering his arm and lifting his water gun.

I let go of June's hand and squirted my hair with the rest of my water. June did the same.

The touchers all took a step closer and I shook my head, sprinkling a little water at them. They stopped walking forward, but didn't move back.

"They know we're finished," I whispered.

"Don't give up," June said, patting my arm. "There's always hope." Her words sounded just like my mother's, but I didn't believe them and I don't think June did either.

We stood silently until the touchers took another step towards us. Now they were no more than three feet away, nearly close enough for their yellow hands to make contact.

I tried to shake water from my head at them again, but this time nothing happened because my hair was almost dry. Standing still, I waited for the touch that would end my life.

———

I heard a familiar whooshing sound—water being sprayed from a hose. Someone was squirting the touchers—and I recognized the person holding the hose attached to a Jeep. "Manny!" I shouted.

He smiled at me as he continued to spray the touchers, who quickly backed away. Then he ran after the yellow monsters with his hose, spraying each of them lightly. But it wasn't Curtis' formula because the touchers didn't die. Instead, they stood nearby wiping off the liquid.

After squirting at the flying touchers and making them scatter, Manny dropped the hose and ran to Blaine, June, and me. "Just in time, huh?" he said as I gave him a huge hug.

"How'd you get here? Where's everyone? What's...?"

"Whoa." Manny stuck out his palm to stop my rush of questions. "Get inside and I'll explain everything when I drive," he said.

"We need to go to the parking lot first," I said, pointing to the smoke. "Three people are still in there."

———

Blaine helped June into the Jeep and Manny drove the short distance to the parking lot while I ran ahead of them, looking for the missing people. The fire was almost out, but the place was still smoky.

"Mr. Douglas! Colonel Peterson! Lieutenant Kleeber!" I yelled. "Where are you?" I didn't get an answer.

Manny came up to me, dragging the hose. "I'll wet you guys and the cars," he said. "Then you can go in and look."

Again I heard the whooshing sound as Manny squirted us and the remaining flames. Then Blaine and I entered the lot.

"Mr. Douglas! Lieutenant! Colonel!" I darted around the burned-out cars, looking for the three of them.

There was movement underneath one of the less damaged cars and Lieutenant Kleeber rolled towards me. "I'm so glad you're okay," I said, helping her up. "Did you see anyone else?"

"No," she said, flicking dirt from her shirt and jeans. "I dropped under the car as soon as the fire started."

"Erin!"

I turned when I heard Blaine calling from the back of the lot. "Come here!" he continued. When I reached him, he shook his head and whispered, "I'm so sorry."

A man lay on the ground face up. It was Mr. Douglas and he was dead.

I stared at Mr. Douglas' body for several moments. *Another neighbor gone...* "What killed him?" I finally asked.

Blaine shrugged. "Maybe the smoke or it could've been a toucher or even a heart attack. He's not badly burned."

I surveyed the lot. "Colonel Peterson must still be somewhere here too," I said. "He could be under a car like Lieut..."

"I found him!"

When I heard Lieutenant Kleeber's voice, I rushed to where she stood, next to a still smoking car. Like Mr. Douglas, the colonel was sprawled on the ground. But unlike my neighbor, the fire had burnt Colonel Peterson, especially his legs and feet. His eyes were closed and I couldn't tell if he was breathing.

"Is he still alive?" I whispered.

"Yes," the lieutenant said. "But I don't know how badly hurt he is."

We called Blaine and the three of us carried the colonel to Manny's Jeep, carefully placing him in the back. Then we returned to the lot for Mr. Douglas' body and Lieutenant Kleeber hopped into the rear. Finally, Blaine and I got into the Jeep, ready to hear Manny's story.

CHAPTER 29 – The Bait

"So you guys saw the fires when you got back to the base?" Manny asked as we sat in the Jeep, waiting for the rest of our army to arrive.

"Yes," I said.

"It all happened so fast." Manny shook his head. "We were real lucky to get out."

"Did everyone make it?" Blaine asked.

"Almost everyone," Manny said. "But we lost people in Headquarters."

"My mom and Danny?" I whispered.

"They're fine. It was two guards that didn't make it 'cause they ran out to warn us."

"Millie?" Blaine asked.

"Yeah. Her and Stan."

Millie who looked like Grandma Fay and helped us with the lions. I needed this to be over. "So how'd you manage to escape?" I asked.

"After we wet the ground and the parking lot, we loaded people in cars and Jeeps," Manny said. "And Kim got some soldiers in a plane. But we didn't have time to take food or nothing else."

"And no time to leave us a note," I added.

"Sorry about that...Rayna did make an arrow in the grass."

"That's why we headed north," Blaine said. "But you guys left hours earlier so why didn't we find you?"

"Because we had to get food," Manny explained. "We found a

school in good shape and stayed there overnight while me and a couple others went food hunting."

"Did you find stuff?" I asked.

Manny nodded. "It wasn't easy, but we got into a supermarket."

Yucch! I remembered the smells.

"Any touchers in there?" Blaine asked.

Manny shook his head. "But most of the food was rotten," he said. "We picked up canned fruits and vegetables and lots of boxes of cereal so that's what we've been eating."

"And then you went to the base at Glentree?" I asked.

"Nah. Major and them knew that place was empty."

"So the army came straight here?" I continued.

"Just in time," Manny said.

"Not for Mr. Douglas," I whispered.

"Look!" June pointed to the sky. "The monsters are back with their fire."

Manny let out a laugh. "Not for long," he said. "This time we're gonna get them."

"You have more of Curtis' formula that kills them instantly?" I asked.

"Even better. Curtis made new stuff."

What could be better than killing touchers immediately? But before I could ask Manny to explain, I heard the sound of a plane overhead.

"That's Kim," Manny said. "She's dropping new formula on the monsters in the sky and..." He motioned to his right. "The army's here."

———

Jumping out of the Jeep, I ran towards the approaching trucks and cars.

"Erin, wait!" Blaine called, waving Manny's hose at me. "You're not wet enough!"

I looked at the sky overhead, which was filled with touchers, and dashed back to the Jeep. "Sorry," I said. "I was in a hurry."

"Don't be so damn careless," Blaine warned, spraying me. "Okay, go."

The cars and trucks had stopped, but nobody got out so I ran down the line peeking into each auto. Near the end, I heard a familiar bark. "Mom!" I shouted as the back door of a green car opened, Muffles jumped on my legs, and I rushed into my mother's arms.

"I thought I'd never see you again," I mumbled, tears making my already wet face even wetter. "And you too." As I petted the dog, I gave my brother a kiss on the cheek and this time, he didn't stop me.

"Are you guys gonna do this forever?" someone in the front passenger's seat asked.

"Just a little while more," I said, reaching forward to hug Kyle.

———

I squeezed into the car that also held a driver, another soldier, and Bobby and sat on the backseat floor while we waited for Manny and Blaine, who were going down the line with the hose, wetting everyone.

"How bad was it getting out of the base?" I asked.

"We're here now," Mom said. "That's all that matters."

"Them yellow monsters sure know how to make fires," Kyle said.

"Yeah," Danny agreed.

"But we're gonna beat them this time," Bobby said.

"How?" I asked him. "Manny started to tell me."

Bobby shrugged. "I'm not sure exactly."

"We're gonna kill them dead!" Kyle shouted. "Boom!"

Danny shook his head. "It's not a special gun, Kyle. It's some kind of new poison."

"I know, but it's more fun this way." Kyle jumped up. "Pow!"

I heard the sound of water as the hose reached our car and we all stepped out. Blaine sprayed everyone except me since I was already soaked.

———

When everybody was wet, we all formed a circle. Maybe there were eighty people, a lot less than when I first joined the army. I saw Rayna and waved at her. She smiled and blew me a kiss.

It was scary being outside—even wet—because touchers were still flying above us with their electrical stuff. I saw Kim's plane as she sprayed the creatures with what Manny said was a powerful new formula. *But if it was so powerful, why wasn't it killing them?*

I glanced around Fort Hallock. There were no more buildings left to burn, but there were cars and trucks—and, of course, us. We were wet now, but that wouldn't last long. And when we dried, we had no place to go. I shivered, more at my thoughts than at the temperature, which wasn't too cold—maybe in the sixties—not bad for this time of year.

I knew my mother marked off each day on a calendar so I turned to her. "Mom, what's today's date?"

"October eleventh."

Just then, Major Figueroa walked into the center of our circle with Curtis next to him, holding a large sprayer. When the major saw me, he smiled. "Good to see you again, Erin and Blaine. So glad you found us."

I nodded, feeling my face flush.

"He's done it," Major Figueroa said, pointing to Curtis. "At the school, Curtis finished his latest formula for killing the touchers."

People in the circle clapped and whistled.

"And it's the last one we'll ever need," Curtis said.

"What does this formula do that makes it so special?" I asked, pointing to the sky. "The touchers are all still alive."

"That's true," Curtis said. "But not for long. Look at them closely, Erin."

I stared up into the sky and squinted. The touchers did look a little different. "They're not so yellow," I said.

Curtis nodded. "They're losing their color—and that's because they're losing their power."

"You mean they can't kill us?" I asked.

"No," Curtis said. "Right now, they can still kill us."

"Then I don't understand why we're all standing out in the open," I continued. "We've got no place to go if the touchers land and we dry off."

"Good point," Major Figueroa said. "But we need to lure them to us."

"Like a trap?" I asked.

"Yes," Curtis said. "Think of it as a big bug trap—and we're the bait."

———

Major Figueroa smiled at Blaine and me. "Everyone else already knows about this so I'll explain quickly. The new formula works as soon as the touchers get wet—and then, when they touch each other, they spread it."

"Like an infection?" Blaine asked.

"More like a plague," Curtis said, chuckling.

"But how do they die?" I asked.

"It takes a couple days," Curtis said. "Then their color fades completely and they're finished."

One thing didn't make sense to me. "The touchers communicate with each other," I said. "So why won't they warn the others to stay away?"

"Because they can't," Curtis said. "The formula also takes away their telepathic powers."

I heard a noise and turned around. "I hope you're right about all this," I said, pointing. "A bunch of touchers just landed and they're heading straight for us."

"We're wet so we should be safe," Major Figueroa said. "Even so, I want all the children in the cars."

"Damn! We never get to see any good stuff!"

I smiled at Kyle, who gave me a sad look just before Mom shoved him, Danny, and Bobby into the car. Then I focused on the seven touchers. They approached slowly, but when they saw how wet we were, stopped and backed away.

"Spray now!" the major ordered and Manny and another soldier turned on the hoses. But the touchers kept moving backwards so the water barely touched them.

"Are they wet enough?" I asked.

"It only takes a drop," Curtis said, smiling. "Soon this group won't be able to kill us and before they die, they'll infect others."

"It's kind of funny," Blaine said as he walked to Curtis and me. "They've been killin' us by touchin' and now we're doin' the same to them."

Curtis nodded his head. "There is a certain irony to it," he agreed.

Irony. We'd learned that word in our figurative language unit in English and it meant having the opposite effect than what you expected. I never expected we'd be able to kill the touchers by them touching each other so I guess that was irony.

I studied the group that Manny and the other soldier had just sprayed. I don't know if it was real or just wishful thinking, but they already seemed a little less yellow.

———

"We can't spray them all," I said to Curtis as we prepared to leave Fort Hallock to find a place to spend the night.

"True," he agreed. "But other people can make and use this formula. It's pretty quick and simple."

"How will they find out about it?"

"Once we get rid of the creatures here, we'll reestablish communication with the rest of the country and the world."

"Like phones, TV, and the Internet?"

Nodding, Curtis pointed to June, who was talking to Major Figueroa. "And very soon, she'll fly home to England with the formula." He smiled at me—suddenly he was doing a lot of smiling. "It'll all be good."

I looked up in the sky where a group of touchers still carried broken appliances and light bulbs. "What about them?" I asked.

"Kim's been spraying the flying ones and wetting the ground when they land. Remember, it only takes a tiny drop to infect them. Their fire-starting days are done."

Blaine came over to the two of us and took my hand. "Ready?" he asked.

"I sure am," I said, giving him a quick kiss on the cheek. "I'm ready to start the rest of my life."

EPILOGUE

So much has happened since Curtis figured out how to kill the touchers. And he was also right about how fast they would die. After Fort Hallock, we hardly saw any yellow touchers and a few days later, they were all either dead or dying. And as long as they were pale yellow, the touchers that were still alive couldn't kill us. If they touched you, nothing happened. I know this for a fact because I touched one of them—I had to make sure—and I'm still here.

In the first days after the touchers died, we found a group of apartment buildings and moved there while the army's tech people worked on getting the electricity, phones, and TVs working again.

Most of the rest of us were assigned cleanup duties—clearing the streets and stores and houses and burying the dead. I made sure to stay away from the bodies because I've seen enough dead people.

Like when we searched for pilots, soldiers drove around the streets with recordings that said it was safe to come out from hiding and about fifty people showed up, including two doctors and a nurse. The army fixed a hospital and brought Colonel Peterson there so the doctors could work on his legs. They don't look pretty, but the colonel is walking again.

We wanted to go back home so when the roads were clear enough, Mom drove me, Danny, Bobby, Kyle, and Muffles to our house. Connie, with Emmy and Jake, also returned to Walnut Lane and so did Mrs. Santangelo and little Frankie, although she doesn't want to stay.

Now I have three younger brothers: Bobby and Kyle, along with Danny. Bobby is sharing Danny's room and Mom fixed the dining room for Kyle. It's a pain with all those boys, but I'm glad to have a family. Though I miss Dad, I still have Danny and Mom. Bobby and Kyle lost everyone they loved.

The army is running the country until we have elections again, but that won't be until April. Meanwhile, we returned to school last week. Everyone's together in Grover Cleveland—Danny's school—because there aren't enough kids or teachers to fill even one building.

It's kind of weird being back in middle school, but it actually feels good to be taking classes again. There are just five kids in my grade—and the only person I know is Jeff Bannister, who wasn't a friend. But at least it's more like the real world.

We've got electricity now and TV, radio, and regular phones so we can communicate with other people again. TV is just news and reruns of old shows, which I don't watch because they remind me of all the things we lost.

We don't have cellphones or computers because something with the falling bubbles messed up the satellites. Mom says it's like living in the 1980s, before the Internet.

But it's not really like the 1980s or any other time because so many things are different. For instance, we don't use money to buy stuff. There are no supermarkets so the army gives us food. We have to listen to the radio or TV to find out when it's our street's turn and then we all have to stand in line. The food is mostly canned and boxed stuff. It's okay, but I really miss fresh fruits like bananas and apples.

From watching TV, we learned what the bubbles did to other parts of the world. The bubbles fell everywhere it didn't rain so as June said, places like England didn't get touchers till later when they grew wings and started flying. In the U.S., some states in the south—Louisiana, Alabama, and Mississippi—did better than us because it rained. But even so, people died everywhere and there aren't many humans left.

When we returned home, lots of my army friends did too, including Rayna. She searched for her family and although she didn't find her parents and brother, she connected with an aunt and cousin and now lives with them about twenty miles away. We talk on the phone nearly every day and when gas for cars becomes available, her aunt and my mom have promised we'll visit each other.

Manny doesn't live far from me either. He found his older sister and the two of them live near Fern Crest Park, the place where we saw all the touchers.

I miss Blaine. When the highways were cleared, he drove to Atlanta to look for his family. Although that's in the south, it wasn't raining there when the bubbles fell and so far he hasn't found his mother or sister. He's still looking though.

Even if he finds them, Blaine promised me he's coming back here to live. But I'm not sure I believe him. When we first got phones, he called every day. This week, he's only called twice and when I phoned him, he didn't have time to talk. I know he must be busy, but still...

Maybe Blaine doesn't like me anymore. I hope that's not true, but if he wants to break up, he'll have to do it in person. And if he won't come here, I'm going down to Atlanta.

Meanwhile, I spend a lot of time sitting in front of my window and drawing. It's great to have time again to draw. Yesterday, I finished a sketch of a dying toucher. I don't know if I'll ever be able to go to college and study art, but maybe I can find an artist or art teacher to help me.

I haven't been smiling much lately, but right now I feel a lot better about this strange new world: I'm watching two birds fly over Walnut Lane.

www.ingramcontent.com/pod-product-compliance
Lightning Source LLC
Chambersburg PA
CBHW070835280626
47161CB00015B/656